WITHDRAWN

THE ENCYCLOPEDIA OF ME

Karen Rivers

ARTHUR A. LEVINE BOOKS
AN IMPRINT OF SCHOLASTIC INC.

Text copyright © 2012 by Karen Rivers

Published simultaneously in Canada by Scholastic Canada Ltd.

Library of Congress Cataloging-in-Publication Data

Rivers, Karen, 1970-
The encyclopedia of me / Karen Rivers. — 1st ed.
p. cm.
Summary: As Tink Aaron-Martin writes an encyclopedia of her life, she also
tells the story of the summer leading into her eighth-grade year.
ISBN 978-0-545-31028-4 (hardcover : alk. paper) [1. Interpersonal relations —
Fiction. 2. Racially mixed people — Fiction.] I. Title.
PZ7.R5224En 2012
[Fic] — dc23
2011046292

p. 16: Grizzly Bear Growling © Dennis Donohue/Shutterstock
p. 55: Guy Jumping High on Sofa © Zurijeta/Shutterstock
p. 77: A Piranha © Stephen Aaron Rees/Shutterstock
p. 87: Hairless Oriental Cat © Vasiliy Koval/Shutterstock
p. 157: Young Polar Bear © Dennis Donohue/Shutterstock
p. 166: Pugapoo © rachelegreen / Wikimedia Commons / CC-BY-SA 3.0
p. 186: Bowl of Pasta © iStockphoto
p. 203: Man Playing Ukulele © iStockphoto
p. 241: Zebra © Michal Ninger/Shutterstock

10 9 8 7 6 5 4 3 2 1   12 13 14 15 16
Printed in the U.S.A.   23
First edition, September 2012

The author gratefully acknowledges the support of the British Columbia Arts Council.

To Mum and Dad

A

Aa

Some kind of lava.

Almost always the first entry in any encyclopedia.

And, more important, the very first entry in the Encyclopedia of Me, Tink Aaron-Martin. Exclamation point! Ta-daaaaa! Dance for joy! Etc.!

The fact that "aa" is a word at all is the most terrific thing I learned from reading the entire set of encyclopedias.[1] I'm sorry, but it's true. Things that are not true include the sentence, "I read the entire set of encyclopedias." But I did look at ~~most~~ some of them. They are quite attractive. The edges of all the pages are dipped in gold dust that shimmers like a pop star's eye makeup.

In my defense, it's too hot to read.

Likewise, it is also too hot to write. But that won't stop me! I am an unstoppable force of encyclopedia-writing brilliance! I am . . .

Grounded. Which means that I have a lot more spare time than the average almost-thirteen-year-old.

I expect this book will take a long time to write — a week, if Hortense, our hairless catlike animal, stops bothering me; ten

---

1. This was inspired by my dad, who took it upon himself to read the entire set of encyclopedias last year, which he began by buying a set of ancient books at a garage sale for $7. He did not get past A, although he lies and says he got to C. I know he is lying because if you ask him, for example, about Burundi, he just stares at you blankly and then says, "Is that a spider in your hair?" which is Classic Avoidance. I tried valiantly to outdo him — after all, imagine the accolades I would get for READING THE ENCYCLOPEDIAS! But after the first hundred or so entries I slipped into a deep and nearly irreversible coma triggered by severe boredom. I am just lucky I survived! And now know more than most people about Achill Island and the acoustic nerve.

years, if she continues to claw at my legs and head in a desperate attempt to get attention and/or love, which is hard to come by when you look like a shriveled handbag. I don't mind how long it takes, as I happen to love writing almost as much as I enjoy reading.

There is a chance that this book will become a bestseller and I'll become rich and famous! Of course, there is also a chance that Prince X will land in my backyard in his own private helicopter and whisk me away to his palace, which is to say, there is no chance at all. Sadness.

So, back to "aa," which was what I was doing before I had to stop to explain to you about the encyclopedia. "AA" (all caps) is also a battery type and a bra (of no) size and what you shout after a volcano erupts and you are running for your life from the river of jaggedy lava, as in "AAAAH! THE AA!"

That's not something you'd read in a regular encyclopedia, trust me.

This is *not* a regular encyclopedia.

It's better.

Aardvark

Apart from beginning with two *A*s, and thus being as fantabulicious as "aa" and "Aaron-Martin," the most noteworthy thing about aardvarks is that an aardvark is the mascot of my sad, crumply little school, Cortez Junior High.

I wish I was making a joke, but I'm not. Not about the relative crumpliness of the school itself, and certainly not about the pure, unadulterated sadosity of having an aardvark in your cheering section. It's very hard to get enthused about a sport when the thing that is cheering you on is a giant, slow-moving, piglike mammal that in real life drags itself on stubby legs through hot sandy deserts, snuffling ants, and hoping to die.[2]

Inexplicably, it was decided that this creature should also be purple. As you might have guessed, my school places last in most sporting events. In comparison, the mascot of our chief rival, the Prescott School for the Unnaturally Athletic, winners of every sporting event they have ever taken part in, is a large and ferocious, normal-colored lion.

You *never* want to get a detention on game days. Because then you have to wear the Aardie suit and spend hours running for your life from the (not) hilarious antics of the Prescott Lion. It is like being mauled by a vicious carnivore with paws the size of tennis rackets while entombed in a cocoon of stale sweaty socks and old spitballs as your so-called friends die too young from fits of laughter while occasionally shouting your name and whistling.

Aaron, Baxter (Dad)

My dad, Bax Aaron, is a plumber. Nobody calls Dad "Baxter." He says that "Baxter" sounds like the name of either a fat orange cat or a manservant on a British comedy, and he is nei-ther, although he'd not-so-secretly have liked to be on a British (or any) comedy. Dad spent his whole life wanting to be an actor on TV. But he's a plumber because his dad was a plumber and so plumbing was his thing to fall back on. The moral of this semi-tragic story is that you should probably make your "thing to fall back on" a lot more fun than plumbing. (Unless you enjoy plumbing, in which case, you should go for it.)

Dad is completely movie-star good-looking, so why he is not a famous actor is a mystery to most. Everywhere we go,

---

2. I assume all aardvarks are suicidal. Because, really, what do they have to live for?

women eyeball Dad like they wish they could capture him and keep him forever, like a piece of art or a hunk of cheese. Dad is generally oblivious and/or is very good at acting oblivious, more evidence of his incredible and overlooked talents.

Dad likes salads featuring tiny cobs of corn, Rollerblading, motorcycles, and reggae. He says reggae is his people's music, but I am one of his people and I don't like reggae at all. Frequently, he can be found dancing to the reggae that plays in his head, making him resemble a deranged person with an uncontrollable twitch disorder. He knows how to play a banjo, a guitar, a ukulele, and a strange stringed thing that is called a lute. He is quite brilliant musically, another gift I did not receive in the gene lottery.

Dad is British, and yes, he has an accent. He is African-American,[3] except not American. In Britain, they say "African-Caribbean." Dad would never say "African-Caribbean-American-Jamaican" or whatever. "Black" is an OK thing to say, at least in our family. Other families feel differently, or so I hear. The worst word is "colored." Don't ever say that unless you want to get punched directly in the stomach by me. I'd punch your nose, but I likely can't reach it, especially if you're tall, unless I stand on a chair, and you'd probably escape before I got properly positioned.

And NEVER say the *n* word. Not even jokingly. If you've ever said it, shut this book right now and get out of here. OUT.

---

3. Dad's dad is Jamaican. His mom is from St. Lucia, but actually she was born in England. It's complicated, except I guess it really isn't, as that's all there is to it. If they were white people from Poland and South Dakota, no one would be ooohing and aaahing at the exoticness of Dad's heritage, and Mom and Dad would just be a regular white couple who no one stared at in restaurants.

Aaron-Martin, Isadora (Tink)

That's me.

Tink Aaron-Martin.[4]

I am an exotic mystery of mixed heritage, half Dad's and half Mom's. Obvi. (My mom is a white redhead. She'll come up later, as Jenna Martin under the *Ms*. Sorry. I cannot help it if my family is alphabetically inconvenient. If you are dying to know all her details, you can skip ahead. I don't mind.)

When people ask me what I am, I usually say, "I'm a human being." Then when they say, "I mean, what RACE are you?" I say that I am *African* while fixing them with a patented look that I like to call my Are You a Racist? Face. Then I point out condescendingly that we are all African. I mean, think about it! Cradle of civilization? Look it up if you don't know what I'm talking about! Use the Internet. I'm sure you have access to it[5] and are free to use it with reckless abandon.

More about me: I used to think I was funny. At school whenever you are forced at teacher's gunpoint to describe yourself in five words, I would always pick easy things like "nice," "biracial," "smart," and "ambidextrous." And "funny." Because I thought I was.

But, then, I found out that I wasn't.

See, I had one joke I liked to tell all the time that usually made people laugh themselves senseless.[6] Then I got this note from Freddie Blue Anderson on the magnet board in my locker.

---

4. Aaron-hyphen-Martin because Mom didn't want to take Dad's last name when they got married and thought it would be perfectly nice to have her kids going through life sounding like they were named after a British sports car. Neither realized that it should have been "Martin-Aaron" because tradition says the dad's last name goes last, besides which Mom says it "sounds better" this way.

5. UNLIKE ME. There is only one computer in our house that has Internet access, and that is Mom's. In her office. Which she keeps locked. Unless it is truly an Internet "emergency" and/or Seb wants to use it. Seb is allowed. The rest of us? Not so much.

6. The joke was this: "What does a ghost say when he sees a bee?" "Boo, bee." You have to say it out loud in order for it to get a laugh, which it usually did, back when I used to tell it.

The note said: "That joke is embarrassing. I'm sorry. It's too babyish. I love you. And I'm only telling you this because you are my BFF, so don't get mad. AND DON'T CRY."

Freddie Blue is too nice to come right out and say that I'm just not funny at all, but I can read between the lines. I am an expert at reading between the lines. For example, when Mom says, "You have such an unusual face. If you were taller, you could be a model!" What I know she means is, "You are not pretty enough to be a model." Not that I'd want to be a model. I wouldn't! I can't imagine anything more boring or depressing, if you want to know the truth. But I'd like for it to be an option, and it isn't.

This is at least partly because of the Freckles. The Freckles are so dark, they look like a constellation of black holes. I realize it's hard not to stare, but staring is rude and you should know better.

My eyes are blue like Mom's. Just regular blue. Not anything anyone will ever compare to a lake or the sky or even a pair of jeans, unless the jeans are faded and drab.

And I'm short. Really short. So short that sometimes, depending on the chair, my legs dangle. The leg dangling is one of the major banes of my existence.

I just asked my dad what else he would tell people about me, if he had to describe me, and he said, "You're as sharp as a bag of tacks!"

"Dad," I said. "Be serious."

He scrunched up his face and scratched his head as though he was about to say something terribly wise. Instead, he said, "I'd tell them that you want a pony."

"DAD," I said. "I wanted a pony when I was FOUR."

"How old are you now?" he said.

"Dad," I said. "I'm almost thirteen."

"Oh," he said. "Do you still want a pony?"

"No," I sighed. "Forget it."

"I'm sorry, bunny," he said. "I would tell them that you don't want a pony."

"DAD," I shouted. "YOU AREN'T HELPING."

"Don't go off," he said. "I'd tell them that you are the Peacemaker." He hugged me. "And that you always smell like bubble gum."

I pushed him away. "Great," I said. "Very helpful. Thanks bunches."

There is a lot of fighting in the Aaron-Martin household, and I can end it by holding my hands up in the middle of the room and screaming, "STOP IT!"[7] over and over again while holding my breath. Sometimes this causes me to fall over as my brain struggles desperately for air. Usually, when I fall, they stop. Which is what Dad means when he says I'm the Peacemaker.

"It's the Peacemaker," he says. "We better stop before she dies!"

I hate that my dad calls me this. I do not want to be "the Peacemaker." I especially don't want them to think it's funny. Or cute.[8]

But mysteriously, sometimes (not always), they stop.

The fights are almost always about Seb. Seb — my brother — is the sun around which this whole family revolves. I'm one

---

7. I am sure that actual peacemakers in Afghanistan or Africa do not use this technique. At least, I hope they don't. If they do, it probably explains a lot about why there is no peace in the Middle East, or anywhere else for that matter.

8. When you are very, very short, there is grave danger in people viewing everything you do as adorable, in the way that everything that toddlers do is adorable. Also, some people — like your parents — forget that "short" does not mean "young" and treat you accordingly. Not good.

of the far distant planets that no one can see, like Uranus or Neptune — I forget which is farther away.

The thing that would probably surprise you most about me is that I love a tree. One specific tree, next door. The people there are away most of the time, so it's as good as mine. Freddie Blue says that it's cool to love a tree but that maybe I shouldn't tell too many people. I don't know what it is about that tree. I don't even know what kind it is; it's an unknown species. A mystery. Sort of like me.

I have twenty-six life goals. I keep them on a list that I have taped to the back of my closet door, so if I ever die horribly by being run over by a bus, you can take a gander at them. I will tell you that number seven on my list has to do with the tree next door.

Number two is "Don't be weird, dorky, or geeky. At least when anyone is looking. BE NORMAL."

The most embarrassing one is thirteen: "Get a boyfriend before FB. The Boyfriend Race is on!" Not only is it embarrassing, but Freddie Blue is my BFF! I should be happy if she has a boyfriend first. I shouldn't even care! But I do. Maybe I'm a kind of terrible person. I seem nice enough on the outside, but it's possible that deep down inside, I'm all shriveled up like a raisin, dark and chewy.

I hope not.

I'm not going to tell you the rest of the twenty-six. They're private and I'm already so embarrassed that my face is likely to melt and slide right off my skull, leaving me as blank-headed and terrifying as a horror movie ghoul. And that would be no way to end this entry, would it?

Aaron-Martin, Sasha Alexei (Lex)

Lex Aaron-Martin is my oldest brother, aged fifteen and three-quarters. Mom wanted to give him a Russian name because it reminded her of ballet. We do not call Lex "Sasha" for pretty obvious reasons, i.e., he won't let us. He was born a full seven minutes before my other brother, Seb, who was stuck.[9] Do not start thinking about what this means if you do not want to throw up repeatedly into the back of your own mouth.

There is very little that is interesting to say about Lex, except that he is good-looking according to all sources, if you consider Freddie Blue Anderson and the casting directors of last Christmas's Gap commercial to be "all sources." Like most teenage boys, Lex enjoys armpit farts and panting pointlessly after girls too pretty to care about him. He is on most sports teams and has an entire shrine of trophies devoted to his greatness. Needless to say, Lex goes to Prescott.

Lex is a big fan of everything in the world and is often shouting, "OH, MAN, THAT IS SO _____!" Or "Dude, that's seriously _____!" He doesn't feel it necessary to fill in the blanks. That is Lex. He has blanks and doesn't care. Actually, his blanks are kind of his defining characteristic.

If you ever tell him I said this, I will hire a hit man to rid the world of you and your big mouth, but Lex can be awesome. He takes care of Seb when Seb can't be taken care of. Not that Seb needs to be taken care of, it's just that Lex does it anyway. He may be dumb as a bucket of beach rocks, but he's got a heart of gold.

---

9. Mom LOVES to tell the Stuck Story, complete with Unwanted Details. The Stuck Story is why she went back to medical school and became a doctor who unsticks the stuck babies of the world. As a result of having listened to her tell the tale, I now hope to never have children, or maybe just adopt them from foreign countries like Australia or Brazil.

Lex often smells of something bad, such as Axe Body Spray or boy sweat. I cannot decide which is more disgusting.

What else can I say about Lex?

Exactly nothing, that's what.

Aaron-Martin, Sebastian (Seb)

Seb is Lex's twin, also aged fifteen and three-quarters, also ostensibly "good-looking," although much messier than Lex due to his refusal to cut his hair and his tendency to wear his explosive 'fro in a bun, making him look like a telephone pole sporting a large bird's nest. (It's a big bun.)

Seb does not have a middle name. (Neither do I, for that matter.) He is not good at sports, and he is autistic. Yes, Seb is autistic.

Gasp!

Twins!

And one is autistic and one is not!

Let's discuss that, if by "that," I mean, let's not discuss it anymore because if I have to hear about it again, I may just be reduced to stabbing myself violently in the eye.

Being around Seb is like being in a soundproof booth, except the opposite of that. You may be under the mistaken impression that people with autism are quiet, but you would be wrong.[10] Seb talks so loudly that I sometimes admit that I've wished I could slap a muzzle on him, just to make it STOP. I'm sorry if that sounds awful. It's just that I'm not always in the

---

10. We were in the mall one time and Seb starting freaking out about a video game that he wanted and Mom explained to the clerk that Seb was autistic and the clerk said — and this really is the worst thing ever — "Oh, I thought they were mute. You wish, right?" I am still in complete and utter shock that he said that. I was only nine at the time and I walked right over and stamped very hard on his foot. Then Mom said, "She's not autistic, she just knows an idiot when she sees one." I still can't believe I didn't get in trouble.

mood and sometimes I have a headache. It's not his fault, but it's as if he can't hear himself, so he just gets louder and louder in lieu of saying something that people actually want to listen to, meaning he does not stay on topic, ever.

Seb dislikes cameras with a violent tidal wave of "dislike" that borders on "scary rage." After he and Lex were in the Gap commercial, he suddenly decided that cameras of all kinds were soul-stealing monsters and never again could one be pointed in his direction! (It was very convenient that this change of heart happened AFTER he became semi-famous, and not before.) And so now, if he sees a camera, he releases a meltdown of epic proportions, the likes of which the world has never seen.

When Seb is talking to you, his eyes ping-pong around the room like those tiny rubber balls that will continue to ricochet off walls for ten minutes after you throw them really hard at the ceiling. *Ping, ping, ping, ping, ping.* If Seb had a sound track, it would have a lot of pings. He's like an orchestra of pings. He pings in ways you can't even imagine! He is a conflagration of unique PINGS! *Ping!* He does art! *Ping!* He remembers everything! *Ping!* He is unpredictable! *Ping!* He's awesome! *Ping!* He sucks! *Ping!* He's my brother! *Ping! Ping! Ping!*

Seb is really hard to explain to people, and I get tired of trying.[11] He is just my brother and as much of a pain in my side as Lex, who is not autistic, something I don't think about much either. I wouldn't think about autism at all if Mom and Dad were ever able to stop arguing about Seb's "treatments." Which is not actually Seb's fault, if you think about it.

Seb frequently smells as bad as Lex, but different. This is mostly because he staunchly refuses to shower more than three

---

11. Luckily, Mom just loves explaining Seb. In fact, she can talk for hours about autism and its many fascinating components! So I hardly ever have to say anything, which is handy as I have nothing to say.

times in a week. If you are ever not sure which twin you are dealing with, breathe deeply. If your senses are kickboxed into an eye-watering stupor by the stinging stench of cheap cologne, it's Lex. If they curl up and die due to the overwhelmingly hideous moldy pong of sweat, combined with the antiseptic, lemony zing of hand sanitizer, it's Seb. Easy, see?

See also Aaron-Martin, Sasha Alexei (Lex).

Adventure

As an alternative to peppering your life with terrifying things you must force yourself to do, you can have a small boring life in which nothing happens and you end up sitting on a park bench, shouting bitter insults at passing kids.

Yawn.

I, Tink Aaron-Martin, choose ADVENTURE! This is at least partly because I want to be a writer and I read somewhere that if you never do anything, you'll never have anything to write about, and your book will bore people to sleep.

In the interest of research, I just called Freddie Blue and asked what she thought of when she heard the word "adventure."

"Hmmm," she said. "I don't know," she said. "Adventure. Adventureadventureadventure. Ad. Ven. Churrrrrrrr."

"Freddie Blue," I said. "Please. Just answer."

"OK," she said. "Why are you asking me this? It feels like homework. And I'm pretty sure we're on summer break?"

"I'm doing research," I say. "For a book. I'm writing an encyclopedia."

"Tink," she said. "Tink. Don't get weird on me again, kiddo." She calls me "kiddo" as though she is my elderly maiden aunt from Ohio. It's bothersome, but I let it go because she's my BFF. Sometimes you make allowances.

"You are not my elderly maiden aunt from Ohio," I said.

"Oh, you're so funny," she said. "I didn't say I was! Don't be ridic."

"It was implied," I said.

"Was not," she said.

"Just answer the question," I said. "Like the first two things that come into your head when I say 'adventure.'"

"OK, fine." There was a long pause. I could hear her chewing. It was quite nauseating.[12] "So," she said. "I consider it adventurous to either go to see a horror movie at the Cineplex after paying to see an animated thing about robots and then being so scared we have to stay up all night watching YouTube videos about pranks that go wrong so we can try to forget the awfulness of the movie. We should do that tonight, by the way. Can you sneak out? Or . . ." There was another pause and more slimy-sounding chewing. I gagged and pretended I was just coughing. "Climbing Mount Everest!" she said dramatically. "IN HIGH HEELS."

"Thank you," I said. "I'll let you get back to your eating and vigorous chewing now."

Freddie Blue is a very adventurous person. She is the Queen Bee of All Things Adventurous. Like last week. It's not Freddie Blue's fault that my mom overreacted so massively to the fact that Freddie Blue's mom called the police to report us missing. We weren't missing! We were merely innocently playing on the trampoline in her neighbor's yard!

We had been in the tent, it's true, but the ground was wet, which made sleeping impossible and cold. We were shivering!

---

12. I have a number of phobias and one of them is saliva. I know that's weird, but I can't help it. I am ENTIRELY WIGGED OUT by the idea of ever properly kissing anyone because, think about it. SPIT EXCHANGE. Now, excuse me while I go and vomit.

We needed to move around to ward off hypothermia! The trampoline was springy and dry and completely free for us to use.[13] We didn't know that when FB's mom looked outside, she saw the open flap of the tent with no one inside and panicked. We didn't hear her shouting our names. How could we have? We were listening to iPods at top volume while competing to see who could jump the highest with our legs awkwardly (and painfully) bent and stuffed up into our pants!

I don't really see why this was a grounding-level offense. The swelling in my knees has almost gone away completely, and dancing is on a hiatus for summer break, so it's not like my knees were in hot demand for ballet, which I hate anyway. And, more important, we weren't kidnapped. Our parents should be having a party in celebration of our safety! They should not be sighing and then forgetting it happened altogether (like FB's mom) or grounding me for life in a fury (like mine). (Of the two options, I definitely got the worse one.)

The happy ending is that I will possibly become wealthy from the proceeds of this encyclopedia that I write about my lonely life spent unjustifiably indoors without friends or sunlight, so it all works out for the best at the end. Then I shall win a Nobel Prize. And an Oscar.[14] And happiness will abound!

As if.

Or, more likely, I may have destroyed my knee permanently and will spend a few years limping around on crutches, unable to pirouette or even plié. Which, come to think of it, wouldn't be the worst thing in the world at all.

---

13. FB's neighbors, the Beadles, were on vacation in Mason, Ohio, fulfilling part of their life dream of riding all of the World's Tallest Wooden Roller Coasters.

14. It is impossible to believe that once the book comes out, movie rights won't be snapped up immediately. I wonder who will play the part of me? Goodness, I can hardly wait! Exciting!

Afro

A hairstyle in which instead of growing like NORMAL HAIR in a NORMAL WAY, hair grows up and out such that your head resembles a dandelion clock, or worse, a wool pom-pom that has accidentally been put into the dryer.

When spotting an Afro in the wild, people will stare and then coo, "I loooove your hair! You are sooooo lucky!" What they mean is "Thank goodness that ball of unruly corkscrews is on your head and not mine."

Freddie Blue once straightened my hair, which we totally thought would make me look celeb. She used olive oil as a "smoother," which she claims (i.e., lied) that she read about in *Seventeen* magazine. But actually what happened was that the flat iron burned the olive oil, so everyone had to stand a hundred feet from me so that the stench did not cause their lungs to fail and result in their instant and painful deaths. Worse, my head looked tiny and sad, like a mostly sucked lollipop on a weird-shaped stick, leading me to the upsetting conclusion that an Afro actually suits me. Freddie Blue says I should embrace it and let it grow to be huge and glamorous, but that is because Freddie Blue does not have the option of doing that herself. Also, it would probably look good on her. Everything does.

I do not have the panache to pull it off. Believe me.

Alaska

I include the mighty state of Alaska because all encyclopedias need to contain geographical references to look legit. I do not know anything about Alaska, except where it is, which is guaranteed to be north of wherever you are right now.[15] Many types

---

15. Unless you are actually IN Alaska, in which case you already know all there is to know about it and can go ahead and skip this entry.

This bear is saying, "Welcome to Alaska!" What he likely means is, "Welcome to my stomach, tourist!" (I don't speak bear, so I don't know for sure.)

of bears live in Alaska, most of whom would eat you as soon as look at you. Killer whales go there in the summer to eat herring during herring blooms.[16]

There are also a lot of men in Alaska, and almost no women, making it a hot spot for old people who are single and can't believe they forgot to get married and need to find someone ASAP or else risk never being photographed in an unflattering white gown.

I've forgotten where I read that about the glut of single men. It's possible I made it up. If you are using this encyclopedia as a reference to write your school report about Alaska, congratulations! You just got an F.

Anderson, Freddie Blue

My best friend, age thirteen (OK, almost thirteen). Her birthday is the day before mine, which fits because she is also smarter and prettier and funnier, as though she grabbed up all the "smart,"

---

16. I do watch the Discovery Channel, so I'm not a total imbecile when it come to actual facts.

"pretty," and "funny" that was available during that particular batch of baby births. I don't mind, though. She deserves it all. We are both Virgos, which matters if you believe in astrology, which I do when it is favorable but disregard when it sounds like bad news.

Freddie Blue is short for Frederique Blue. Frederique is not a Swedish name, although FB is "of Swedish descent."[17] She is tall and willowy, with smooth hair that has expensive gold streaks in it. She used to say these were "natural," but then I went with her to her hairdresser one day, where I was shocked to find out that they were as "natural" as "hair dye painted on individual strands of hair and layered in a million pieces of tinfoil and stuck under a heat lamp for three hours" can be. Still, her hair is shiny and as long as her waist and moves like seaweed underwater, if seaweed were unbelievably gorgo[18] and the consistency of hair. She is the prettiest girl in school, in town, and possibly on planet Earth.

Freddie has a lot of other noteworthy qualities, beginning with "she wears a bra." If you guessed that I am jealous about this, you would be mostly wrong but with a tiny dollop of right. She is also very fashionable and is trying to teach me to appreciate clothes in the same way that she does, but without copying her because copying makes her as "mad as monkeys." She says that her mother is "in fashion," so she comes by her styliciousness naturally. (Her mom owns a shop that sells used vintage clothes designs.)

Freddie Blue has a crush on Lex, even though he's fifteen and calls her "Frank" because he says "Freddie" is too hard to remember. She says he has gorgo eyes.[19]

---

17. Yes, that is how she talks.

18. Short for "gorgeous" and one of many words that Freddie Blue and I have created together to help improve the English language, which I'm sure you know could stand some jazzing up.

19. I don't have a crush on anyone. If only the boys I know weren't such total drips, it would help. If I'm going to grow up to become a famous writer and celebrity personality, I'll need to experience a lot of heartbreak. And soon.

Sometimes when Freddie Blue laughs really hard, she accidentally pees her pants. She doesn't get upset about it; it just makes her laugh harder. I admire that kind of bravado. If that happened to me with any sort of regularity, I'd move to Switzerland, change my name to Priscilla Von Spats, and devote my entire life to the avoidance of all things funny.

We are slightly competitive, but not really, because in any and all competitions, Freddie Blue wins. She's just that kind of person. A winner. A funny, nice, hilariously crazy winner. Which makes me only a bit jealous, but I pretend it doesn't. Because I would suck if I was jealous of my BFF. And I don't want to suck.

Freddie Blue would never in a million years be secretly competing with me to get a boyfriend first. She would never in a billion years think something bad about me.

Freddie Blue is my favorite person on the entire planet, with the exception of one specific European prince. I can't really explain her except to say that FB is the sparkly rainbow decoration in my white box of a life. We will probably be BFFs forever, unless she grows up and marries my brother, in which case I will lose all respect for her and start referring to her as Mrs. Armpit Fart and making jokes at her expense.

See also Adventure.

Apple

A round fruit that grows on trees. Crunchy. Good with cheese.

It is impossible to think of the letter *A* without thinking of apples. It must be a very dark time in a kid's life when they realize that *A* is also the first letter in, say, "ambulance" or "asphalt." It is obviously SO confusing and painful that no one remembers it.

My grandma once built me a tree house in an apple tree. I loved it, but in the spring it would be all full of these little green inchworms that crawled out of my hair at inopportune times, such as during class, causing classmates to scream, "TINK HAS WORMS IN HER 'FRO!" I hated that apple tree at those times, and the word "Afro," but mostly I loved the tree and my grandma, who is now dead. My love for the apple tree probably explains a lot about why I'm happiest when I'm in the Tree of Unknown Species.

Apple seeds contain arsenic, which is poison. Don't eat the seeds.

That's some useful advice for you. This isn't just entertainment, you know.

See also Afro.

Arms

Useful limbs that attach at the shoulders and act as levers for the hands, which can then be used for good.

For example, earlier this summer, I used my arms to dognap Mrs. O'Malley's[20] miniature pugapoo, Mr. Bigglesworth, out of her big gnarly plastic purse, as commanded by Lieutenant Commander In-Charge-of-Me, Freddie Blue Anderson. The handbag also contained a rumpled romance novel with a shirtless, long-haired man on the cover, four chocolate bars that

---

20. Mrs. O'Malley — although she has the name of a queen-sized, happy, Irish lady — is actually a thin, nasty local woman who sits on a bench exactly halfway between my house and Freddie Blue's house and says things to us that are blatantly rude. For example, she might say "You girls are trouble!" or, my favorite, "Better seen, not heard!" — you know, the kind of witty gems that elderly people like to embroider onto throw cushions. Mrs. O'Malley could stand to do a bit more embroidery and a bit less shouting.

looked so old I didn't even recognize the wrappers, a stuffed bird (!), and a fat wallet. If you're going to carry a dog in a purse, at least dedicate a purse to the animal, don't just cruelly throw it in your regular bag with all your junk. If Mr. B. hadn't ferociously bitten my finger and caused me to scream, he would now be free of his vinyl prison and in no danger of accidentally eating chocolate and going into liver failure. I'm surprised he was so ungrateful. Obviously, he has Stockholm syndrome[21] and will need more encouragement before he is ready to be truly free. (Coincidentally, number twelve on my life-goal list is to free all wrongfully imprisoned animals.)

Yes, I just wanted to tell you about the Mr. Bigglesworth Incident, and not actually about my arms. I didn't want to make you wait for the Bs. Also, this is the first encyclopedia I've ever written, and it's harder than it looks.

See also Adventure.

Autism

Autism is not a disease, but rather a syndrome. Do not confuse them for fear of having everyone in your family screech at you simultaneously like a parliament of angry owls.[22]

Dad says that Seb's autism just makes Seb more human than most humans, but Dad often says things that make no sense in such a way as to suggest they are nothing but 100 percent pure, fresh-squeezed, not-from-concentrate fact.

The definition of autism is elusive, which means that no one

---

21. Weird phenomenon wherein you fall in love with your evil kidnapper and forget that she is keeping you prisoner in an ugly purse, and instead believe that she is your BFF and doing you a favor by carrying you around all day to the point where your legs probably don't work anymore anyway.

22. That is really what a group of owls is called — look it up if you don't believe me. I almost used "murder of crows" because that is also cool, but they really do sound more like owls.

can say exactly what it is in one sentence, but they are more than happy to write a book about it and sell millions of copies by writing very long paragraphs about how autism is different for everyone who has it, which is a nice way of saying, "We have no idea either!" and which is why we have two thousand books about autism on our bookshelf. My mom is working on writing one of these dreaded books in her spare time. The fact she has no spare time makes me hope we will never have to read it.

I think that everyone is overthinking it. It's just a way that some people are. People are all different: People with autism are all different, and so are people without it. So, seriously, what is the big deal about that?

Autism has made my mom famous-ish. Being the head of Autism Abounds! she's on the radio a lot, and also she blogs about it, which Dad hates because he says it's too personal. They fight about the blog all the time, which is why I didn't bring it up before. I just don't want to get pulled in the whirl-pool of crazy that I feel when Mom and Dad start bickering, shouting, and then storming out of the house.[23]

The storming gives me a headache.

Much like Seb gives me a headache.

And Lex gives me a headache.

When people find out that I have an autistic brother, they sometimes look at me differently, apparently waiting for me to do something inexplicable so they can nudge each other and stage-whisper, "She's got it too."

Autism is not contagious. These people are idiots.

Talking about autism makes me feel as though I'm being forced to listen to someone slowly dragging their nails along

23. The storming is definitely a Peacekeeper Fail.

a chalkboard while chewing Styrofoam and tinfoil simultane- ously. It's like I'm so bored of autism-talk, I can't stand it, but I have to care about it because I love Seb in the way you are forced by biology to love your siblings, even when they tend to spit in your hair when you aren't looking.

A lot of people have autism.

It's really not that big of an issue. Except when it is.

See also Aaron-Martin, Sebastian (Seb).

B

Ballet

The art of tippy-toeing painfully around a room in a tight pink dress with a ridiculous froufy skirt in pretty slippers to boring classical music while someone shouts at you to stand up straighter.

My mom is a former ~~ballerina~~ ballet teacher, the result of which is that since the very second I was able to toddle across the room in an effort to escape from my brothers, *BAM*, I was put into ribbony slippers and forced to plié and arabesque my way through my days. Some people are designed to bend and twirl and stand very straight while their hair is compressed into a bun so tight that their eyes can't blink, and some people are not.

I am *not*.

As a result of all that dancing, I now walk with my toes out, like a duck. Thanks, fifth position!

I am currently seeking a new activity that my mom never did and so she can't endlessly make remarks about "hard work" and "sweat and sacrifice" that make me want to scrape out my brain with a plastic fork and throw it out the window at high velocity.

I will likely never mention the ballet again in this encyclopedia as it is a part of my life that gives me a tiny, throbbing pain inside of my head, just above my left eye.

Barbie Dolls

Oddly curvaceous blond dolls with bent feet and vacant expressions, usually dressed in something that sparkles or is so blindingly bright it can be used as a flashlight when the power goes out.

Obviously, at my age, I think Barbies are pointless, but I never liked them. As a child, I would rather have eaten four pounds of liver[24] than been subjected to hours of Barbie games. I think you're either a person who loved Barbies, or you are a person who used to cut off their hair, encouraged them to choose a life that didn't involve wearing glittery bikinis for a living, and painted their creepy white plastic skin a more flattering warm, brownish shade. I'm more of the second type.

Freddie Blue is the first.

Sometimes I think our friendship is doomed.

See also Anderson, Freddie Blue.

BFF

Best Friends Forever.

See also Anderson, Freddie Blue.

Boarding, Skate

The sport of standing on a rolling board and doing impressive things at high speed without accidentally mortally wounding yourself, all the while maintaining an expression of genuine aloofness. People who skateboard are automatically cool by default, due to I'm-not-sure-what. Automatic coolness is rare and is making me consider skateboarding as a hobby. That, and the fact that I think I'd be good at it. Certainly better than I am at ballet.

"Freddie Blue," I said. "Have you ever skateboarded? Do you think skateboarding is (a) totally hip or (b) only cool for boys?"

---

24. Did you know that the liver is just basically a giant filter that animals use to separate gross waste from useful stuff? IT'S A GARBAGE FILTER. You would eat a garbage filter? THINK ABOUT IT.

"I don't think that 'skateboarding' is a word," said Freddie Blue from her position on the floor, where she was systematically flipping through my dad's entire collection of *Everybody* mags, looking for a hairstyle to try. "It sounds better to just say 'boarding.' I'd probably be good at it," she said. "I was, like, really good at snowboarding, remember?" She sat up, looking all excited, awash in her happy memory.

I stared at her blankly. I was dumbfounded. (Yes, that is a word.) FB was terrible at snowboarding. Not even good enough to be terrible. She was abysmal, appalling, catastrophic, cataclysmic!

And she hated it!

But!

I was actually good at it. Really good at it. As soon as I strapped the board onto my feet, it felt right. I didn't want to stop, not to eat or anything. By the end of the day, I could swish like a pro. The snow swooped up with a definite *fwoooom* sound and showered down on my board in a crystal wave. Don't laugh, but I felt like I could fly.

I still have dreams about it sometimes. They are the best kind of dreams, a billion times better than the dreams I have of being forced to perform *Swan Lake* with broken glass strapped to my feet.

But to be honest, I sort of pretended I wasn't as good at snowboarding as I was because of Freddie Blue. She couldn't even stand up! And when she did, she just teetered wildly in place until she finally tipped over and sank into the snow. She said it was hilair,[25] but I could tell she hated it, even though

---

25. As in "hilarious." Here is a fun tip from me to you: If you want to be cooler than you are, you should always abbreviate words, unless it sounds stupid when you do it. Like you'd never say "soop stoop" instead of "super stupid." But "hilair" is made of win and makes you seem super sophisto.

she giggled giddily through her blue, shivering lips. (There were a lot of boys around. Supercute boys. Obvi.)

Poor Freddie Blue, I thought now. Her beauty and smartness make it all the more mysterious why she sometimes steals my scenarios and makes them her own. I looked at her, worried. She might steal this encyclopedia too. Then what?

"Um," I said. "Never mind."

"Are you still writing that book?" she said. "It's so boring. Are you writing about boarding? You don't know anything about boarding! That's so ridic, Tink."

"I'm not writing about skateboarding," I lied. "I mean 'boarding.'"

I flopped back on the Itchy Couch and scratched my bare legs while picturing myself swooping gracefully up a ramp and then flying off the other side. *Bam!* I was sure the wheel-sounds-on-pavement would be just as good, if not better, than the crunching-snow-sounds of the snowboard.

I sighed. If only I wasn't *grounded.*

Mom and Dad were both at work, putting me in charge of meting out my own punishment, which made me feel kind of like I was raising myself, much like an orphan but not nearly as glam.

"Do you think a movie star would adopt me if both my parents were gone?" I asked Freddie.

"No," said Freddie Blue. "You are too old. They only adopt really adorable big-eyed babies from exotic nations."

"Oh," I said. "Not fair."

"Life isn't fair," she said wisely.

"Right," I said.

"Oh, sigh," she said. "I'm so bored. We've got to do something."

"I know," I said. "I wish I could." I closed my eyes and imagined a skateboard under my feet.

"Hey!" she said, reading my mind. "I've got it! We're going to go boarding! I am so psyched. This could be our way of being super ultraglam this year at school. We'll be the only girls who board. I bet by Christmas, everyone will be doing it. Then we'll stop and do something else that's less . . . malg."[26]

I squinted at her. "Ruth Quayle boards," I said. I felt stupid saying "boards," like I was pretending to speak a language I didn't know.

"Ruth!" FB barked with laughter. "So?"

"So," I said. "I mean, maybe it won't make us popular. Ruth isn't."

"She would be if she wasn't so . . . Ruth," said FB. "It's not the boarding that's the trouble. It's just her general Ruthiness."

"I like Ruth," I said. I actually think of her as Ruth! with an exclamation point. (This is because Ruth is always exclaiming! About everything! All the time!) Not that I would tell Freddie Blue that, because Freddie Blue is not the most tactful person in the world and she might let it slip and hurt Ruth!'s feelings. The way Ruth ~~skate~~boarded was cool because she was the only girl who was ever out there, jumping around and whatnot in baggy pants and amusing T-shirts.

"Whatever," Freddie Blue said. "Ruth is a dork. Her whole thing with Jedgar Johnston is weird."

Sometimes FB's scorn is so sharp, it's like a glittery paring knife peeling the skin off an apple in one smooth, long curl. You do not want to be the apple.

"What's weird about it?" I said. "They're best friends. So what?"

---

26. A made-up word, just an example of the many words we have created.

"SO she doesn't have any girls who are friends," said FB. "That's weird."

"I don't think so," I said. "It's just what it is."

"You aren't going to help us be pops[27] if you like people like Ruth," said FB. "Sorry, but you know I'm right. I'm just trying to help you, Tink. To help *us*. We're in this together, right? Cause you're totally my BFF."

"FB," I said. "Go back to your magazine. I am trying to write."

"Don't be snappish," she said. "I love your crazy idea! About being boarders! It's the best idea you've ever had! Let's go right now. Don't look at me like that. I know you're grounded. But you can sneak out! Besides, you've been good, you get time off for good behavior. And this is important. AND a sport! You know how your parents love sports! They would actually WANT you to do this."

Hortense leaped onto my chest, whumping the air out of my lungs. It was so hot in the room, I felt like I was drowning. I gulped a big breath of air and tried to pry her off me. Going outside actually did sound sort of good, but only if I could guarantee I would not be caught. Being caught would mean . . . well, I had no idea what, but I knew it would be capital-B Bad. Hortense struggled and scratched my arm. "OUCH," I yelled. She scratched me again in a frenzy of claws and skin. "Ouch, ouch, ouch!" I said. "Dumb cat."

FB laughed. "That cat is so ugly," she said. "You're maimed! You're maimed!"

"It isn't funny!" I said, pushing Hortense off. My arms stung. I looked out the window. The leaves of the Tree of

---

27. Pops = popular. As in, "All Freddie Blue Anderson wanted out of life was to be totes pops."

Unknown Species were rising and falling in the breeze, like they were whispering, "Come outside, come outside . . ."

"You are such a goody-goody, it gives me a pain in my heart." FB rolled around dramatically, clutching her chest.

I tried to think of the right Tink Aaron-Martin Patented Stare to give her,[28] but I couldn't come up with one. Besides, outside sounded good. And it was a sport! My parents DID like sports! So . . . maybe . . . I . . .

"OK," I said. "Let's do it."

The minute we stepped outside, the heat hit us like the kind of massive tidal wave that will one day crush all of humanity and even New York City if you believe what you watch on movies. It felt tolerable until we got to the end of the driveway, by which time we were sweating like pigs, although I've never seen a pig sweat as much as we were.

Freddie Blue kept staring at my maimed left arm and wrinkling her nose. "That's going to leave a scar," she said.

I shrugged. I was about to say something witty about how the scars would look like dot-to-dot drawings on the freckles when she suddenly shouted, "OK, cover me. I'm going in."

"What?" I said.

Before I could stop her or even figure out what she was doing, she scampered up the long, steep driveway of the house next door. A house where I have never been. A house that I purposely *avoided*! Because whether they knew it or not, the people who owned that house ALSO owned the Tree of Unknown Species. *My* tree. (Which was technically theirs, even though it was closer to my house than theirs.)

---

28. There are three: Disapproval, Disdain, and Disgust. They are pretty similar but slightly different, especially around the eyebrows.

Ringing their doorbell was tantamount to saying, "HELLO, WE WOULD LIKE TO DRAW ATTENTION TO THE FACT THAT WE EXIST! AND WE LIKE TO TRESPASS IN YOUR TREE!" I would never do that!

"Don't ring the bell!" I shouted.

She didn't answer. But in about thirty seconds, she ran back to me with two skateboards under her arms, like a bad guy making a getaway, except she was laughing her head off.[29]

"Let's go!" she said. "It's an adventure. Adventure Number 308 in the Famous Adventures of Freddie Blue and You!"

"Um," I said. "Whose boards are those?"

"Some blue-haired kid's," she said. "Borrowed them. Don't worry about it."

"Freddie Blue," I said. "I am worried about it. Did you ask? You didn't have time! Did you even ring the bell? You don't just borrow someone's skateboard. That's like borrowing their . . . socks. And really is it 'borrowing' if you don't ask?"

"How is it like borrowing their socks?" she said. "It's totally different. You don't wear a skateboard on your feet. Borrowing socks would be like borrowing underwear. Hey, socks are the underwear of your feet! You can put that in your encyclopedia if you want, but give me cred, OK?"

"It's not that kind of book," I said. "It's . . . deep."

She snorted. "Oh, sorry. Anyway," she said, "don't worry about it, OK? Just do it. You steal their tree all the time, this is the same thing."

"You can't steal a TREE," I said. "It's attached to the ground. I just . . . borrow it."

---

29. Her laugh was weird. I shouldn't probably say this, but it made me think of the laugh that girls sometimes have that I call the OMG LOOK AT ME I'M SO PRETTY laugh. I'd never before heard FB do this laugh.

"So we are just BORROWING these!" she said triumphantly. "Now let's do it!"

"Freddie," I said. "Do what? What are we *doing*?"

"We're going there," she said, pointing down the hill.

I stared.

"Don't think like that," said Freddie. "You have to believe in, like, the power of positive thinking. You won't hurt yourself if you don't THINK you'll hurt yourself. It's all up here." She tapped her head knowingly.

"Freddie," I said. "You are being obnoxious. And ridiculous. I was thinking 'I've always wanted to try skateboarding, but maybe skateboarding down a steep hill on a stolen board is a dumb place to start.'"

"Borrowed," she hissed. "Don't be a coward."

Freddie Blue tossed her hair and dropped her board. It slid three feet and rolled onto a lawn. She put it back on the sidewalk and stared at it with grave determination. I hoped she didn't hurt herself too badly, but I really couldn't help her. I knew I was going to be OK, thanks to my talent at snowboarding, which was virtually the same thing. Probably. Or at least, it looked similar. I put my foot on my board and waited for it to feel right.

Then I lifted my other foot of the ground to push off.

But something was wrong.

And that something was that I was on a hill.

And I was facing the wrong way.

But luckily I have excellent balance!

Unluckily, this meant I stayed on all the way to the bottom of the hill!

Where I shot out into traffic! And was almost killed! By a bus!

And then I hit the railroad track and was catapulted sky-ward at great speed, landing jarringly on the sidewalk! On my head!

My *head*!

"OMG," said Freddie Blue, jogging to a stop beside me. I noticed she was not using her skateboard. Typical. "You're bleeding! That's so gross! Call the paramedics! 911! 911! Why didn't you put on this helmet?" She thrust an olive green hel-met on my head. I took it off. "Pretend you were wearing it, OK? It might be illegal not to! You'll go to jail!"

"Holy cow, are you OK? Did you, like, steal my boards and stuff?" said a boy. I was dizzy. I couldn't really see his face, but his hair was blue. "Like, you've got brutal road rash on your arms." I hate people who start their sentences with the word "like."

I said, "I'm perfectly fine, thank you. Those happen to be the scratches of a hairless cat." I added, "And we just borrowed them."

Then I stood up and immediately fainted dead away. Faint-ing is kind of my thing, so I'm pretty good at it.[30] But this was a real, big, and different sort of faint: a grayed out, nauseating one. It was the mother of all faints! The Big Kahuna!

It was an embarrassingly awful wet-your-pants one.

It was a seriously catastrophic may-the-world-open-up-right-now-and-swallow-me-whole one.

When I came to, I immediately wished I hadn't. I felt like one of those vacuum-sealed bags that had just had all the air sucked out of it in a violent rush. I closed my eyes and prayed

---

30. This is due to the breath holding I do in my unwanted role of Peacekeeper.

for instant death, in the form of a sewer alligator suddenly appearing and dragging me under the road for lunch.

"You swooned!" cried Freddie Blue, quickly shielding my wet parts with the helmet that I was still holding. At least it was good for something.

"I fainted," I said. "It's different." My head felt funny and my heart felt like it was tripping on stairs. I tried to breathe slowly.

"Is not," said FB, hauling me to my feet. She began steering me up the hill, which was whooshing around and bucking under my feet. It was like trying to ride a pony[31] by standing on the saddle.

I stumbled. The blue-haired boy grabbed my arm. His hand felt cold and strange, like a dead fish landing on my skin.

"Hey," I said. "Don't touch me." I wasn't very friendly, I'll admit, but I wasn't feeling friendly. I was feeling angry. With him. With FB. With everyone. Especially with the alligator, for not showing up on cue.

The walk home took about seven hours or twenty minutes, I have no idea. FB half dragged, half carried me all the way up the gravelly driveway to my house, still holding on to the helmet over my crotch.

In that moment, I truly loved her.

I did not invite the blue-haired boy to come inside. He must have waited outside on the porch, because when FB left, I could hear them talking. At first I thought, *Oh, that was sort of sweet of that boy to make sure I was OK.* But then I heard FB doing that fake laugh again and then the lower, more rumbly sound

31. Not that I've ever ridden a pony, due to Dad's allergies, Mom's busyness, and Lex's and Seb's hatred of horses, ergo, my unfulfilled dreams, but I could *imagine*.

of his voice. He had a very low voice. And then enough fake laughing to make me feel like crawling out of my own skin and into the nearest swamp.

Giggle rumble giggle rumble.

Was FB getting a boyfriend? Without telling me? What was she doing?

Now I probably had a brain injury AND she was going to beat me in the Boyfriend Race she didn't even know she was running.

"Unfair," I moaned.

"It isn't unfair," said Mom. She was still in her hospital scrubs, having rushed home to be with me. I was confused about how that went down, really. Did FB call her? I wish she hadn't. It would be more peaceful to be alone. "It was a silly thing to do and now you're injured because you made a dumb mistake. 'Fair' has nothing to do with it."

"That's not what I was talking about," I mumbled.

"You could have been seriously hurt!" she said. "I'm so . . ." She stopped. "Disappointed."

"Fine," I said. "I know. OK?"

She frowned.

"Maybe you could yell at me some more when my head stops hurting," I said helpfully.

"Tink," she said. "Don't be rude." But she went out of the room and closed the door gently behind her.

I spent the rest of the day alternating between lying on my bed and lying on the Itchy Couch with ice packs on my head while my mom shone beams of Angry and Disappointed out of her eyes and in my direction. I hoped Freddie Blue and the blue-haired boy had a nice afternoon! If by "nice afternoon," I mean "I hope a wild orca leaped out of the ocean and dragged them both to a watery grave."

Books

You know what a book is, right? Pages? With writing on them? Between covers? So why is this entry here?

Because *B* is for "Book." That is why. You know, like *A* is for "Apple."

I like books. If I was going to make a top-ten list of everything good in my life, I'm almost sure that "Books" would feature, but if not, I'll give them an honorable mention[32] because books are mostly awesome, except the ones that are stupid and don't bear mentioning or even reading for that matter, and why yes, I am talking about *The Hobbit*.

One day, I will write a book that will be as brilliant and amazing as my favorite book of all time, which is called *I Capture the Castle*, by Dodie Smith. If you have not read it, drop this book right now and go find a copy. Your mom probably has one. It's an old book.

Boy, Blue-Haired, Who Just Moved in Next Door

I do not know anything about the Blue-Haired Boy Who Just Moved in Next Door, except that he is a boy. And he lives next door. And he owns MY tree. And his hair is blue. And he has skateboards that he leaves on his front porch, completely unsecured.

---

32. Instead of ever winning anything, I am always getting "honorable mentions," which are really a nice way of saying, "You didn't win, but you didn't come last either! So, way to not totally lose." I do not like honorable mentions. I really prefer to win. Or at least, I'm sure I would, if I ever won anything.

His hair is bigger than mine, the biggest hair I have ever seen. It has big fat curls, like you'd see on a kid competing in a beauty pageant whose mother has labored over that hair for six hours with a curling iron. It is long and thick, like a shiny, loose, soft, white-kid Afro. It is mostly dark brown but then has blobs of blue in it, such that it looks like a flock of angry birds who have been dining exclusively on blueberries have recently flown over his head.

If you guessed that this boy is the boy from the entry *Boarding, Skate*, you would be 100 percent correct, and you have won a beach towel and a year's supply of charcoal briquettes! Congratulations!

Freddie Blue told me that his name is Kai. When I say "Kai" out loud, it sounds like the barking sound that harbor seals make while they beg for fish down at the wharf. "Kai, Kai, Kai," she said. "Kai this and Kai that and Kai this and blah blah blah."

She said Kai is as "cute as a cracker" and will also be going to Cortez next year, even though he does not look very "gifted"[33] from a distance or even up close. Not that I have seen him up close, except that one time when I was only half-conscious on the road.

I do not know if Kai is cute or not cute. He may be as cute as toast or even a Pop-Tart, for all I know.

I thought ~~skate~~boarding kids were supposed to be cool and aloof and inaccessible to the likes of me, but whenever this "Kai" sees me, he waves in a way that reminds me of a small dog who wants to climb up your leg while slobbering on your

---

33. Although it is true that Cortez has a pretty elastic definition of "gifted," which can mean you are good at art or music OR that you are smart. I think it should just mean "smart," which would weed out most of the annoying people in our school. I actually think Cortez uses the word "gifted" to mean, "gifted with parents who make enough money to afford to send their kids to Cortez."

shoes. I do the only thing that I can do when this happens, which is to hide, usually in *his* tree. This is probably ironic.

Freddie Blue says that Kai is probably going to be my first real boyfriend because in after-school TV shows, boys who live next door are always sweet and kind and give people their first kisses. They are never bad boys at all, and while she herself prefers "bad boys," she thinks that I should have a "sweet and kind" boyfriend because I am not "streetwise." Freddie Blue apparently equates "streetwisery" with "talking to her BFF like she is idio."[34]

Kai will not be my boyfriend. My first boyfriend is required by law to have lovely, smooth, straight, blond hair; blackish eyes; to be from a small European nation; and also to be a prince. Freddie Blue finds my crush on Prince X "hilarious to the max." She won't be laughing when he takes me to the Zetroc Prom, will she?

No, she will not.

See also Afro; Boarding, Skate.

Boyfriend Race, The

A race between me and Freddie Blue Anderson, which she does not know she is running, to be the first to possess true boyfriend-dom.

She would die and/or kill me if she knew. AND then she'd win because when you have long legs like she does, you can run pretty fast. Really, my only chance of winning comes from her not knowing that she's playing.

Whose dumb idea was this anyway?

Oh, right.

---

34. Can be short for "idiot" or "idiotic," depending on the rest of the sentence.

Boys We Wouldn't Touch with a Ten-Foot Pole List

Freddie Blue and I have agreed that any boy who is not actively on our Crush Lists is automatically on our Boys We Wouldn't Touch with a Ten-Foot Pole List, which is not actually written down, it just exists in our heads.

If there was a prize for most disgusting boy ever, all the boys in our class would be winning. One of these days, one of them will fart their way to the top. His farts will be used to propel him in a giant weather balloon into outer space, and no one will miss him even slightly, except maybe his parents.

Bra

An undergarment used to support breasts if you have them, or to invite bullying if you don't.

Freddie Blue gets her bra strap pulled constantly, which is so far beyond rude, I can't even classify it. What's worse is having the bullies reach for your bra strap and finding nothing there.

I may just buy a bra and stuff it with Play-Doh. I've heard that this works into fooling people that you have breasts. The Play-Doh sort of sticks, so you don't accidentally drop your (fake) boob out of the bottom of your shirt at an inopportune moment.[35] I'm not sure that the smell wouldn't give it away, though.

Sometimes I write things that are so embarrassing that even my fingers blush and wish they could run away to a forest to

---

35. Which is really at any moment, because there is probably not ever an opportune moment for this to happen. If you can think of one, please write to me immediately and you will win a prize, the prize being the satisfaction of knowing you are the only person who could come up with a good time for your boob to fall off.

hide without the rest of my embarrassing self. I don't blame them. I'm about ready to do the same.

See also Aa; Anderson, Freddie Blue.

Bullies

People who derive pleasure out of being jerks and saying horrible things to other people. They are probably deeply insecure themselves, but I can't say that I care too much about a bully's feelings.

I have been bullied since the very second I set foot in the schoolyard in kindergarten and Wex Stromson-Funk came running up behind me, lifted me off the ground, and hurled me across the grass like I was a shot put. It knocked the wind out of me and I thought I was going to die right there, with a face full of dirt. He has bullied me relentlessly ever since, like it is my fault that he nearly drowned me in soil.[36] Luckily, he no longer throws me around, but instead makes idiotic comments in a kind of spasmodic reflex whenever I walk by.

Worse than Wex is Stella Wilson-Rawley,[37] who regularly writes mean things about me on the wall of the basement bathroom with a Sharpie, next to crudely drawn stick figures with large Afros.

Freddie Blue says I don't get picked on much anymore because now I'm pretty, but I believe it's actually because I'm BFFs with Freddie Blue and SHE is pretty. All the boys want to stay on her good side in case she bestows upon them a smile or

---

36. And/or he is just angry that I survived, after all.
37. Both the people who bully me the most have hyphenated last names. But! SO DO I! Are people with hyphenated last names meaner than regular people? (Am I meaner than regular people without even knowing it?) Is it a thing? Like how serial killers always have triple names? Or is it just coincidence? Feel free to use that question as the basis for your next essay assignment. Good luck!

a handwritten note. She always used to say that Wex like-likes me, which is so funny that I forgot to laugh. Now she admits that he clearly loathes me for unknown reasons, likely to do with his unhappy childhood.

Stella Wilson-Rawley doesn't care about being on Freddie Blue's good side and so is free to stare condescendingly at my hair with reckless abandon, uttering such brilliant wisecracks as "OMG, you could, like, rent space to birds in there for nesting!" Oh, she's so hilair. If by that, I mean "not even slightly funny and really pretty horrible."

C

Camping

The act of pitching a tent in the woods and sleeping in it, while outside a campfire crackles merrily and frightens away all man-eating wildlife.

When he was younger, Seb loved camping more than anything in the world. Until he was fourteen or so, every single weekend he would beg and beg until my dad took him and Lex camping. I guess Lex liked it too. Then! Suddenly! After an "incident" involving Lex accidentally dropping an Italian wall lizard into the fire, Seb decided that he would no longer be participating. That nicely put an end to that, as I'm sure you can imagine.

I want really, really badly to go camping. But Mom hates camping. And it's not like I'd go alone with Dad and Seb and Lex, even if they still went. Ew. And Freddie Blue says she'd rather set herself on fire and hurl her burning body into a pool filled with wood before she'd ever camp. Ergo,[38] I never have to (or get to) camp. So I guess I will never know if I'm a fun, outdoorsy girl who loves to commune with nature in the woods or a girly-girl who shrieks at the sight of a mosquito.

Sad, really.

See also Adventure; Autism.

Celebrities

People who other people idolize due to their appearance or otherwise questionable "accomplishments."

---

38. "Ergo" is a word that means the same as "so," basically, but it also makes you sound smart and intimidating. Try it!

My brothers, Seb and Lex, are celebrities! OR NOT.

They were in *one commercial* for Gap, not an Oscar-winning performance in the Most Loved Movie of Our Time! I should also add that there were 150 other kids in the ad and you could only see Lex and Seb if you really looked, which I did, and then instantly wished that I hadn't, as I've seen quite enough of Lex and Seb already, and seeing them grinning maniacally in snowflake-patterned sweaters did nothing to endear them to me at all.

Freddie Blue probably will be a celebrity one day. She's just that kind of a person, the kind of person who was made to be famous. She already *looks* famous. I would rather be famous for being smart than pretty, actually, so maybe there is hope for me still.

See also *Aaron-Martin, Sasha Alexei (Lex); Aaron-Martin, Sebastian (Seb); Anderson, Freddie Blue.*

Cell Phones

Technological wonders that allow you to make phone calls, send texts, watch YouTube videos, and play addictive video games from any location in the world!

Fact #1: I do not have a cell phone.

Fact #2: Lex has a cell phone.

Fact #3: Seb has a cell phone.[39]

Fact #4: Mom has a cell phone.

Fact #5: Dad has a cell phone.

Fact #6: They have a family plan.

---

39. Seb used his phone to call *National Geographic* magazine to correct something they'd written about pygmy tarantulas. It turned out that Seb was wrong, but he'd never admit that. He does not believe that it's possible for him to make mistakes. His phone did not have a long-distance plan, so the call cost $102.37. MISTAKE.

Fact #7: I am part of this family too.

Important Conclusion!: IT DOES NOT PAY TO BE THE YOUNGEST.

Coffee

Hot drink containing caffeine that smells much, much better than it tastes.

Public Service Announcement!: Coffee-flavored ice cream, which tastes like coffee smells, is delicious. Actual coffee, which smells like coffee-flavored ice cream tastes, is not. Do not try it, unless you enjoy the flavor of ashes and burned water searing the top layer of skin from your tongue.

"I'm exhausted," Mom groaned when she came home from work this morning.[40] "Tink, I'll give you ten dollars to make me a pot of coffee and some eggs. Where's your dad? What a crazy night. Seven babies! Why do I do this job? I'm so tired. What time is it?" She yawned so wide I could see her fillings and her tongue. Tongues are the weirdest parts of the body, I think. It's like having a pink slug dwelling permanently in your mouth.

"Um, OK," I said. "It's eleven thirty."

"Uh," she said, and staggered out of the room.

I set about making the coffee, which entailed pouring beans into the top of the machine and turning it on. My parents worship coffee, so the machine is actually plumbed (Dad's specialty!) directly into the water pipes and filtered and whatnot while the beans are programmed to be ground to some specifically perfect consistency. I could hear the shower going in the

---

40. When your work is delivering babies, your hours are not "normal." Most babies seem to present themselves in the middle of the night, hence we never know when Mom will or will not be home, arriving home, or just leaving.

other room and Mom singing, something she denies that she ever does, like we can't hear her all over the house.

"Nice singing, Mom!" I shouted. The singing stopped.

When it was ready, I poured her coffee into a half cup of steamed milk and dumped the eggs on a plate with some toast. If no other career choices work out for me, I've had good training to be a waitress in a coffee shop. Then I grabbed this laptop, which I finally found under the Itchy Couch, buried under six new layers of dirt,[41] so I could get back to work on my MASTERPIECE!

(Which I am still going to finish, even though — in a surprise move that I can't believe I didn't mention sooner — Mom has lifted my life sentence last night by ungrounding me.[42] Call the presses! Alert the media! TELL THE INTERNET! I am freeeeeee!

I could not have been more shocked if she'd announced that she was running for president or had recently developed a love for macramé. Even though the ungrounding was actually quite anticlimactic. It should have warranted at least a parade or confetti.

"I hope you learned something from this, Tink," was all she said.

"Well, I learned that 'aa' is lava," I said.

"Everyone knows that," said Seb.

"Do not," I said.

"If you start fighting, you're grounded AGAIN," said Mom.

---

41. No one uses the laptop except me, as the fact that it is not hooked up to the Internet renders it 92 percent useless. Which means they have no compunction about kicking it under the couch if it happens to be in their way.

42. Ironically, now that I'm allowed to go out, I really don't want to, although it is likely I will take the laptop up my fave tree and work up there until the battery runs out. I'm pretty excited about it, to be honest. When I get famous and people say, "Where were you when you wrote this book?" I can say, "I was up a tree." They'll be all, "Oooooh, brilliant. So unique! So creative!" Right?

Now that I was free, there was no way that I'd go back to my former life of imprisonment and hopelessness! But . . . "Eat dirt," I mumbled to Seb, under my breath.

"Ssssss," he hissed.

"Seriously," said Mom. So we stopped.)

Until now. Because when I got back to the kitchen — unbelievably! shockingly! — I found my two pig brothers *eating Mom's eggs.*

"Stop it!" I screamed. "WHAT ARE YOU DOING?"

"Mmmm," said Seb. "You're a good cook, Freckle Peckle."

Lex laughed uproariously, displaying grotesque egg bits lodged between all of his teeth. (I really should have taken a picture for FB because it would cure her for life from her horrible affliction of crushing on Lex.) "Really good," he said, licking his lips.

"MOM!" I yelled. "MOMMMM!"

"What?" she said, padding into the kitchen in bare feet. The sound she makes when she walks is just like Hortense — which is to say it's a sound that isn't quite a sound.

"The boys ate your eggs," I shrieked. They looked at each other and then took off out of the room, like they'd suddenly grown rockets on their feet. You could practically hear the whooshing noise.

"Oh," she sighed. "I was looking forward to those. Oh well, at least there's toast." She crunched into a piece.

"Do I still get my ten dollars?" I asked.

"Yes," she said. "Sure. We should get back at them for this, Tink. We should play a trick on them." She brightened up a bit.

"We could steal their Wii," I suggested.

"Not bad," she said. "Maybe not steal it, but just hide it so they can't find it."

We giggled. We could see the boys out on the lawn randomly rolling around on top of each other, like oversized and particularly ugly puppies. We snuck into their room and took the whole game console, then hid it in the bathroom cupboard. Then I stuck a note on their table where it had been. The note said, "Hope you loved those eggs!"

It was pretty awesome. Sometimes Mom can be a lot of fun. Mostly she isn't. But sometimes, it's almost like she's my friend.

See also Aa.

Computer

Technological wonder that allows you to search Google and know everything in the entire world instantly, without ever having to think about anything!

WHEN YOU HAVE YOUR OWN ACCESS TO THE INTERNET, THAT IS.

Without Internet access, a computer is like a paperless typewriter with a screen. Which I guess is better than just having a typewriter, so I shouldn't complain.

Freddie Blue says it's imperative that I get my own access to the Internet immediately so that I can connect with social media at all times, instead of just for thirty minutes on Sunday afternoon. Without texting (cell phone) or IM (computer), she says I will likely be "stranded in a desert of loneliness" as "everyone else" at Cortez communicates constantly online or on their phones.

I think I'd rather have instant access to Google and a UNIVERSE OF FREE AND INSTANT INFORMATION than to a list of status updates about what my "friends" ate for lunch, but I'm "quirky" like that. Not that it matters, as Mom says I will have unmonitored access to the Internet the day after the sky starts raining pugapoos. In other words, never, or around the same time as I get my own cell phone.

See also Cell Phones.

Copwell Beach

The beach at the bottom of the hilly road that leads to my house. Made up of sand and pebbles and rocks the size of eggs and stony outcroppings and logs and way more litter than should be allowed. There are usually too many people there, also. Copwell Beach is situated a block from the best ice cream shop in the universe. And a 7-Eleven.

Making it "the most obvious place to go when you suddenly find yourself with $10 and your BFF doesn't answer the phone and your laptop battery is too dead to type outside in a tree." So that's what I did.

Or what I planned to do.

But I was only barely out of my own driveway when Kai — yes, the Blue-Haired Boy from Next Door — leaped out of the hedge. It was very startling. My heart shrieked in fear, skittered away, and disappeared behind the fence.

"Hi, Tink," he said. "Got a rad new board, want to see it?"

"Mmmf," I said as aloofly as possible, which was hard as my heart was still missing all its beats. Being aloof seemed suddenly really important. Just looking at his bobbing blue head made me think of FB's fake girly-girl laugh, and my stomach dropped like it does on fast fair rides or express elevators. I tried to regain my composure. *Breathe*, I reminded myself. *In, out. Out, in.*

"That's not my name," I said finally.

"No?" he said. "What's your name, then?"

"Isadora," I said. "My name is Isadora."

"Huh," he said. He scratched his giant cotton-candy head. "OK, so hi, Isadora. Does anyone call you 'Is'? I like 'Is.' 'Is' is cute."

"Hello," I said frostily. I wish I hadn't told him my name was really Isadora. I hated the name Isadora.

I kept walking. I was super aware of every step, like I was walking strangely, but I wasn't. There was a huge awkward silence, as though a bubble of awkwardness was trapping us in. I'm not sure why he was walking with me, like we were out for a stroll together *on purpose*. Only he wasn't strolling, he was rolling. The skateboard was the biggest that I'd ever seen. It looked like a surfboard. It was almost ridic.

"Isn't this the most awesome board ever?" he said finally. "I designed it myself. And, like, built it."

"I can tell," I said. The board was bright Day-Glo orange. It was decorated with a purple skeleton that was holding on to a butterfly. It was both creepy and beautiful, like a piece of art that I didn't understand exactly but still wanted to look at. "It's OK, I guess. If you like that sort of thing. I do. I like it. I mean . . ." I trailed off. What did I mean? I had no idea. "Shut up, Tink," I said to myself. Not out loud, of course.

"So where are you going?" he said, doing a show-offy spin type thing.[43] The butterfly glowed in the sun. It must have been some kind of special paint. "Want to hang out? I'm new here. I mean, you knew that. But you're my neighbor so we should be, like, friends."

"Beach," I said. I'd decided that I'd participate in the

---

43. I do not know what any skateboarding or longboarding or whatever words are. Note to self: Learn the words! How can I be a cool boarder girl if I don't know what anything is called? Embarrassing.

conversation but only use one-word answers so he didn't think I *liked* him–liked him. Because I was suddenly afraid that I *might*. I don't know where it came from! It was just like a bolt from the blue! I've heard people say things like that before, but I always thought they were making it up! Craziness. I blushed.

Then I didn't want to confuse an already confusing situation by being friendly. Or friendlier. Or unfriendly. I wished FB were there. Don't laugh, but I had never been *alone* with a boy before, just having a conversation, like it was a normal thing for me to do.

"Can I come?" he said. "I like the beach."

"No!" I said. I didn't mean to be rude, it just kind of leaped out of my mouth. I had been struck by awkward-itis!

"Please?" he said. "I've got to get out of the house for a while. My parents, you know." He wheeled around, and the wooden deck of his board made a scraping sound on the pavement.

"No?" I said. I kind of wanted to ask what he meant but that would involve more than one word. Dilemma!

"My parents are *fighting*," he said. He rolled his eyes, like it didn't bother him, but I could tell it did. "Biff, pow." He threw a couple of air punches in the direction of a hedge. A bee flew out and landed on his hand, and super gently he blew on it and it flew off again. "If you do that, they don't sting you," he said. "They think you're the wind."

"Oh, cool," I said. I thought about his "Biff, pow." "Um, your parents don't really . . . punch, right?"

"No!" he said. "That was just like a . . . metaphor. I guess. They shout."

I looked at his face. His nose was interesting, like it had been broken a long time ago. It kind of lay slightly flattened on his face like a bird's wing, but in a good way. He looked like he'd been crying. I quickly went back to looking at sidewalk cracks.

"You know how it is. Sometimes you just gotta get out of sight for a bit," he added. "They need to be alone. To work out their . . . stuff."

"Oh," I said.

"Your parents fight?" he said.

"Um," I said. "Yes." I thought about it. My parents fought a lot, actually, when they were together, which was pretty rare because they were both so busy. Luckily. They always said they weren't fighting, but rather "disagreeing." They disagreed loudly and with lots of slammed doors about 90 percent of Seb-related stuff, like what therapy he should have or if he should have it or whether he should take medication or whether he shouldn't. I didn't want to talk about it. "I mean, no," I said quickly. I snuck another look at him. He was staring at me in a funny way, cocking his head to the side.

"You're lucky," he said, getting off his board.

No, I'm not! I wanted to correct him, but I couldn't explain it all. It was too much. He got off his board and shuffled on the sidewalk for a few steps, and then kicked a stone. We both watched it skitter down the hill. I felt funny, like there was a lump somewhere inside my chest.

Then I took a big breath and really quickly said, "My brother's autistic, so there's always lots of . . . stuff going on. It's complicated. It's not like they're mad at each other, it's more like they are mad at the situation. It's not my fault or anything. Or anyone's. Not even Seb's. He's the autistic one. Anyway, it's not a big deal." I blushed and right away wished I had a big rewind button so I could take it all back.

"Oh," he said. "I saw a thing about autism at my old school. There was a kid with that and he traveled around and talked about it. He was OK. He was a decent boarder."

"Cool," I said. "Seb doesn't. Travel, I mean. Or skateboard. He *has* one. He just doesn't like it."

"I mean, this kid was just . . ." he continued. "He was just sort of regular but then he had this whole movie he was in, a documentary or whatever, and in the movie it was all about how he freaked out in, like, train stations. Does your brother freak out in train stations?"

"I don't know," I said. "I don't think he's ever been in a train station." I started to laugh. "Where is there a train station? That's so random!"

He smiled. "This kid was from Chicago or something."

"Oh," I said. "Well, Seb freaks out about cameras. Maybe it's the same. I haven't seen that movie. I kind of get enough of autism at home. You know. Too much, really."

Suddenly, it was like the bubble of awkward that was holding us in burst open and all the fresh air rushed back in. I took a big breath. It felt good.

"I'm just going into 7-Eleven for a quick sec," I said. "Wait here."

"OK," he said. He got on his board again and started hopping on and off the sidewalk.

I bought an *Everybody* magazine and two Cokes. I couldn't very well sit and enjoy a Coke if he didn't have a drink. When I gave it to him, he sort of lit up, and when he did, I noticed that he has really interesting eyes. They were golden brown with a lighter ring around the middle.

"Hey, thanks," he said. "You're, like, awesome."

"Thanks," I said. "I'm not awesome!"

He shrugged. "I don't know you very well yet, but so far I think you are."

"You do?" I said.[44] My heart plinked in my chest like a rock falling into a bucket. Did he like-like me? I really needed to talk to FB, and fast. But I also wanted to hang with Kai. I wanted him to stay.

"The Coke's no big deal," I said. "My mom gave me ten dollars to make her coffee." I did not mention the eggs. It seemed too complex to bring up.

We found a good spot on the beach in a circle of logs, and we propped some logs up over the top like a shade. I'm terrible in the full sun. My freckles go crazy. Well, crazier. They're already crazy.

We sat and talked for a long time. I didn't get a chance to read *Everybody* at all.[45]

When we got to Kai's house, he waved and jumped up the stairs in one bound, then slid down the railing on his board and fell over. I don't think he hurt himself because he got up really quickly and ran inside before I could go and see if he was OK.

"See you," I called, even though he was already inside and the door was closed.

I was in such a good mood, I didn't even notice that to get back at me for the missing Wii, Seb and Lex had rearranged my bedroom so when I threw my bag on what is usually my desk, it spilled its sandy contents out all over my bed.

---

44. I was mostly just shocked that he said what he was thinking, not just that he was thinking I was awesome. I couldn't imagine just going up to someone and saying, "Hey, I like you. What's up?" But I bet he could. I bet he did it all the time. Actually, he probably had a whole herd of girls he thought were awesome. I was probably no one special to him. Just one of a lot. Or maybe he just had really low standards.

45. We talked about music, boarding, school, his old hometown, his parents, and just . . . everything. I felt like I was talking to myself, except not in a crazy way. I guess I mean I felt like he got my jokes. He laughed quite a lot. It was pretty amazing.

Oh, they're so funny. A brilliant future in comedy awaits them! But only if the entire world accidentally loses all its IQ points in a mysterious and top secret alien attack.

See also Autism; Boarding, Skate.

Cortez Junior

Cortez Junior is my school, named after the Spanish conquistador[46] Hernando Cortez, who apparently was the person responsible for ending the Aztec empire. I'm really not sure why he has so many things named after him, as ending an empire as amazing as the Aztecs' does not seem like something you should be rewarded for, especially when you think about the cool Aztec stuff they built before he marched in with his army and killed them all.

Cortez is a school like any other, I guess, but I have never been to any other school, so what do I know? It has classrooms and hallways and motivational posters on the wall that say things like "STRIVE" and "EXCEL," which are regularly vandalized by disenchanted students in ways that make no sense. For example, someone wrote "OW" over the "EL" at the end of "EXCEL," so now it says "EXCOW." Hilair! But not really.

The only difference between Cortez and other similarly depressing places is that, like I've mentioned, it is a school for "gifted" children. We have been "gifted" with the chance to attend Cortez Junior, which is the kind of gift you would like to return to the store to exchange for an iPod, only to find out that the gift is handmade and can't be returned.

We do not wear uniforms at Cortez, but we do have jackets that we have to wear to team events. The jackets are an

---

46. "Conquistador" may be the best word in the entire history of words ever spoken. Try saying it out loud! You won't regret it. Con-KEEEES-ta-dor!

unhealthy shade of purple and have the crest of the school on the back. Under the crest, it says CORTEZ SCHOOL, then under that it has FINDING EXCELLENCE: COGITO ERGO SUM.[47] However, due to a horrible design flaw, after a few washes the small letters fade away, leaving the wearer with a jacket that says — I couldn't make this up if I tried — CORTEZ SCHOOL, F E C E S.[48]

Cortez is a series of small, randomly colored buildings that, from the street, looks like a rainbow that has been stepped on by a giant. Last year, I was in the green building — Cortez Elementary (CE) — and this year I will be in the yellow building — Cortez Junior (CJ). Eventually, I guess I will be in the orange bulding, Cortez Senior (CS). Is that something to look forward to? I am undecided. The orange building IS the newest, so I suppose it will be the best.

It's going to be very strange to be the youngest kids in the building again, after being the oldest last year. Freddie Blue says this is a good thing because there will be older, more interesting, and much cuter boys there. I'm not the least bit intimidated by the hugeness of CJ because I know that me and FB will be going together, so everything will be an adventure. A super-awesome, fun adventure.

I just know it.

See also Anderson, Freddie Blue; BFF; Bullies.

---

47. This means "I think therefore I am." I would argue that even if you never think (see: Lex), you still ARE, but Lex did not go to Cortez.
48. Feces! Do you know what "feces" means? DO YOU? Well, everyone else does. Trust me.

Couch, Itchy

This is not my couch. Those are not my brother's feet. (But it is exactly what my brother WOULD have done if I'd tried to take a picture of the ACTUAL couch for your viewing pleasure: SHOW OFF.) Like the rest of the pictures in this book, I "borrowed" this one from the Internet, because REAL encyclopedias all have useful illustrations. If this picture was a scratch and sniff, it would smell exactly as awful as my brother's feet, and you would be forced to burn the book and endure a nasal cleansing ritual involving lemons and boiling water in order to survive.

Crush List

List of boys who we have crushes on, but unlike the Boys We Wouldn't Touch With a Ten-Foot Pole List, for some misguided reason this one *is* actually written down.

Freddie Blue currently has seven boys on her Crush List. *Seven.* However, her list is also full of crossings-out and arrows and add-ons, which does detract slightly from the prettiness of the page. It includes a bunch of older boys who don't know she exists, as well as the likes of Wex Stromson-Funk. ("What?" she said. "Why are you all mad and rolling your eyes? He's mean as a pit viper, but he's cute. That's all I mean by it.") At one point, Jedgar Johnston was even on her list, even though now she says that she was kidding when she wrote it and that his association with Ruth Quayle makes him the least pops boy in school.

Freddie Blue's list has recently been updated in capital letters at the top with the name "KAI." Not the worst, as in the worst choice. But the worst, as in the worst for me. When I saw his name there, my heart stuttered and then stopped entirely. She saw me looking and she said, "Whaaaaaaat, you don't like him, do you?"[49]

"No!" I said. "You have him! I thought you didn't like him, though, because he's too nice?"

"I changed my mind," she said, waving her hand in the air like she was brushing off a fly.

I felt sick. "OK," I said. And just like that, I decided to stop my crush clear in its tracks. I refused to compete with my BFF. And I couldn't win, even if I tried. Against FB? Never! I'd only HAD the crush for a few days! What a waste.

Ergo, my Crush List was blank. A VERY long time ago, I wrote Shane Dubois on my list, which has now been crossed out so thoroughly, there is a hole in the paper. He was OK looking and had great teeth. But when Shane found out,[50] he stuck a charming note on my locker that said, "I love you, I love you, I love you. NOT." Oh, that was so funny. I laughed so hard about that! What a jokester! Except the part where it wasn't the least bit funny and I did not laugh.

I also did not speak to Freddie Blue for five days afterward, and did not entirely forgive her until she got a baby picture of Shane Dubois from his mother, who happens to teach French

---

49. The way she said it said, "I know you like him but I don't care." Or that's what I thought it said. Reading between the lines.

50. Freddie Blue told him in the age-old way that disloyal best friends tell boys about their best friends' feelings. That is, she wrote him a note with check boxes: "Do you like Tink? Yes No." Guess what he said? That's right. Even writing this is making me die a little on the inside.

at our school, and blew it up to poster size and added a bubble above his head that said, "I wear diapers! I'm Shane Dubois!"

Before Shane, I also — and I hate admitting this but it's true, so I have to — had a small potential-crush on Wex Stromson-Funk. But! That was ONLY because Freddie Blue was working hard at the time to convince me that he was only mean to me because he was in love with me. It didn't take long to figure out that she was just being nice and that actually he hated me. Which was fine, because I hated him too. I only would have liked him if all the bullying had been a way of masking the pain he felt of having a terrible unrequited love for me. Then I *might* have made an exception.

Keep in mind, that happened when I was eight. I didn't understand much about love back then.

Under pressure, I just wrote Brendan Carstairs, because he's nice enough — kind of a smiling guy who is always in the background but never stands out, sort of like wallpaper with a not-too-ugly pattern — and would never laugh at me if he found out about the list, but he's so boring that I'm really mostly lying by putting him on the list at all.

See also Bullies.

D

Dark

The opposite of light. Well, obvi.

I hate the dark. I'm not scared of it, I just don't like it. (I blame Freddie Blue. Freddie Blue enjoys films that involve people in bikinis being killed brutally while at summer camp.)

When it is dark, because my house is farther up the hill than Kai's, I can look down and see into his family's TV room. Not that I'm spying on him. I am not. Don't even think that! I can usually see only the TV, not the people. When I watch, it sort of feels like we are watching TV together, even though I can't hear the sound or really even see what show he is watching. I haven't seen Kai since we went to the beach, but I know he is still alive because there is the TV — I can see it right now — showing either a sporting event or a movie, I can't really tell which.

I wonder if he is watching it, or if it's his dad or his mom, taking a break from their fighting, which I imagine goes on all the time.

I wonder if he is going to hang out with me again.

I wonder a lot of stuff. Most of it has nothing to do with the dark, so I now return you to your regularly scheduled program of alphabetical facts, currently in progress.

Devil-May-Care Attitude

An attitude that says, "I just don't care what you think about me and what I'm doing, and the devil doesn't care either."

Grandma used to say that I should always have a devil-may-care attitude. This means that I should never let anyone see when I'm upset. If I ever have a rock band[51] or a line of clothes[52] or even a record label or a small yacht, I will call it "Devil-May-Care."

The devil may care if Kai is cute. The devil may also not care.

Drop Mac Park

Drop Mac Park is the neighborhood skate park. It's also got a playground and grassy field, but it's mostly a big cement pit with slopes and walls. Graffiti artists go crazy on all that concrete. The kids at Drop Mac Park are mostly from the big public school or Prescott. I guess "gifted" kids aren't as into boarding as everyone else.

Except me, I guess.

I keep thinking about ~~skate~~boarding and having dreams at night that I'm really doing it, with the clatter of the wheels on the pavement and the feel of the board under my feet. Which makes no sense, because other than that one terrible awful erase-it-from-your-memory INCIDENT, I've never done it! Not properly, anyway. Still, it's like it's *calling* to me, like when you are super hot, all sticky with sweat and ick, and you go to the beach and you look at all that cold bluish-grayish water and it's all you can do to not dive in with your clothes on.

I wanted to dive into Drop Mac Park. (That's a metaphor! If I dove into concrete, I would break my neck.) I wanted to just swoop and glide. I wanted to . . . try. Just to see if it was as *awesomesauce*[53] as I thought it might be.

---

51. Unlikely.
52. Even more unlikely.
53. I promised FB I would stop saying "awesomesauce" because it reminded her of "applesauce" and she believes she is allergic to applesauce and claims — which I'm a tiny bit skeptical about — that if I say "awesomesauce" in her presence, she will break out in head-to-toe hives. But I doubt FB will read this book, so I'm not worried! Oh, hi, FB! SORRY ABOUT THOSE HIVES, MY BAD.

I stopped typing and came down from the Tree of Unknown Species.[54] I went to the basement where Seb's old skateboard was kept.[55] It was painted a faded dark green with a picture of a pirate flag. The wheels, however, were lit up and glowed orange. If I was hoping not to be noticed, I wouldn't have a chance.

"Go big or go home," I whispered to myself, by way of encouragement. I found a helmet and knee pads and put them on.

Doing something alone felt weird and wrong, like I had my shoes on the wrong feet. Could I have an adventure *without* FB? But she was at her dad's and I wasn't allowed to call her there! What could I do? I hoped she wouldn't be mad.

I didn't try anything on the way. Instead, I carried the board all the way to Drop Mac Park. To get there, I had to walk directly by Mrs. O'Malley, who was perched, as usual, on her bench. She was enshrouded in a large plaid blanket, which was odd, as it was ninety degrees. She glared at me. I glared back.

"You look like a juvenile delinquent!" she shouted.

"How's Mr. Bigglesworth?" I said.

On cue, poor Mr. Bigglesworth stuck his head out of the bag and barked. His bark was quite listless. It was clearly a call for help.

---

54. Oh, yeah, I should have mentioned that. I was in the tree. I've decided it's the best place in the world to write an encyclopedia, way up high, your legs dangling over the green lawn fifteen feet down, where no one bugs you, and by "no one," I mean "Hortense doesn't hurl her skin sack of a body against your keyboard, accidentally erasing your genius entry about 'dogma,' which you've now forgotten and can't re-create."

55. Before Seb was diagnosed, my parents thought he had a behavioral problem and tried to hook him into any hobby they could think of. As a result, we have a million pieces of sporting equipment and art supplies and stuff, none of which he ever touched again after the first time. BUT just because he doesn't want to use them, doesn't mean that anyone else is ever allowed to touch them. So I'm risking my life! Sort of! Or at least risking the wrath of Seb, which is pretty huge! And scary. I must really really want this.

"I'm calling animal control," I whispered to him reassuringly. He growled. I kept walking.

"Woof," said Mrs. O'Malley. I don't know if she was talking to me or to the dog.

I sighed. It was too hot to think of a witty comeback.

But underneath the hotness of the day, the air had that funny smell it has when fall comes, which made me think of back-to-school. Thinking about back-to-school made me feel off balance, so I ran. Running is a good way to stop your brain from turning. It works every time. I couldn't outrun back-to-school, but I could try.

When I got to the park, I had to rest in the shade until I could stop sweating and panting. Then I got up and self-consciously put the board in position. At first, I was really nervous. I couldn't get the feel of it. I scooted around a bit, keeping my pushing leg close to the ground so I didn't tip over. It felt way more wobbly than I'd thought it would. After a few passes just going back and forth on the flat, I tried lifting my foot a little higher. It didn't quite click. It was nothing like snowboarding either. I kept looking for the feeling inside me, the feeling of how to do it, and it just wasn't there. Inside, I was empty.

I thought about giving up. From across the park, I could hear music. A bunch of kids were sitting on the climbing thing, drinking huge Slurpees. They were laughing. I felt dumb.

But I didn't have anything else to do. And I just wanted to feel how it was supposed to feel. I wanted it to feel like the ground was like music I could hear through my legs, carrying me. I wiped the sweat that was dripping down my nose. I wished I'd brought a drink.

I picked the board up and looked at the wheels like I knew what I was doing, in case anyone was watching. Just so maybe they'd think it wasn't that I didn't know how to skate, but that something was wrong with my wheels.

Then I made myself try again. This time, I tried to relax the whole top part of my body. I pretended the ground was water and I was surfing. I breathed as deeply as I could. And I pushed off hard. Before I could even think about it, I swooped down one ramp. It was so fast, I crouched down automatically because it seemed like being closer to the ground was a better idea than being farther away.

And I did it! I was doing it! And it felt totally amazing! For about ten seconds!

And then I fell off. AGAIN. The board skidded out from under me, and my body twisted and hit the ground hard enough to knock the wind out of my lungs. I lay on the smooth, hot concrete, frying like an egg.

I looked up at the blinding sky and I felt . . . kind of giddy inside. Because I DID it. I knew I'd find it, and I found it: the feeling. Sort of like what I think love might feel like.

The same feeling I had when I climbed the tree for the first time.

Sort of the same feeling I had at the beach with Kai. NOT that I would tell anyone this, not even Freddie Blue. ESPECIALLY not Freddie Blue.

I was about to stand up and try the swoop again when someone blocked the sun. I squinted, but I could only see a silhouette.

"Hey!" said the person. "Whatcha doing?"

It was Ruth Quayle.

"Hi, Ruth," I said.

"Are you OK?" she said.

"I'm good," I said. "Really good."

"Cool," she said, plopping herself down next to me. I moved over a bit. I don't really like it when people are in my space too much. "I'm so psyched you're here! There are NO GIRLS at our school who have boards. SO LAME! Are you good? Let's see you do something!" Then she started listing these things, like ollies and wheelies and whateveries.

"I don't know the jargon," I said. Then I shrugged, like I'm too tough to care about jargon, so she wouldn't think I was a total loser.

Not that I care what Ruth Quayle thinks! Freddie Blue doesn't like her, so it's not like she and I will ever be friends.

"Who cares?" she said. "Let's just kick it!"

"Sure," I said. "I mean, I can try."

"I'll show you stuff," she said. "It's not hard! Really!"

I tried to do what she was doing without looking like I was trying to do what she was doing. She was AWESOMELY AMAZING! I don't know how she got so good. It was like the board was part of her. It looked easy and loose and not like she was trying or worrying.

Mostly I fell off over and over again, but with the pads on, it didn't hurt. I tried not to grin too much every time I did something where I didn't fall. After a couple of hours, I could swoop full speed down the big ramp and not fall off. I couldn't swoop back up the other side, but who cared? It felt amazing!

It may just have been my favorite new thing I've ever tried. Ever.

I mean, except for all the adventures I've had with Freddie Blue Anderson, of course. Those are still the best.

See also Adventure; Boarding, Skate.

E

Eels

The terrifying underwater equivalent of worms or snakes. Electric eels are the scariest, as they can send electric impulses out with their brains, killing their prey with their minds. Eels have poisonous blood — do NOT eat them raw. And why would you? Disgusting!

Seb is currently obsessed with eels. He collects them from the beach in empty margarine tubs and leaves them all over the porch. Then he forgets about them and they die and stink to high heaven. If *I* accidentally killed an eel, he would never forgive me and would likely have me arrested and thrown in jail with no hope of parole. Ever. Seb goes totally berserk if anyone kills a living thing for any reason.[56] However, the accidental murder of a creature by Seb does not seem to count as a crime at all. This is an excellent example of a paradox, and you can use it for your next English assignment if you want to impress your teacher and get bonus points for brilliance.

Sometimes the porch is just a writhing mass of disgusting eeliness. Other times, it is a stinking cesspool of decomposing flesh.

Which is the state it was in when I was interrupted from my work by a knock at the door.

"DAD, SOMEONE IS AT THE DOOR," I shouted pointlessly. Dad was in the basement, rebuilding his Harley-Davidson

---

56. Although he somehow also manages not to be a vegetarian, and I'm going to guess that he knows that "meat" is just a fancy word for "dead animal."

motorcycle.[57] I could hear the *clunk, whirr* of some kind of tools and the beat of the reggae he was blasting in the background. Seb and Lex were locked in mortal paddle-ball combat in their room. And Mom was, as usual, at work.

"I have to do everything around here," I grumbled, swinging open the door.

Then I gasped. And blushed. And nearly fell into a bucket of congealed eel corpses.

"What are you doing here?" I said stupidly.

"Um," said Kai. "Hi." He lifted his hand in kind of a half wave.

"Hi," I said, trying to get it together. I took a deep breath and then nearly gagged from the stench. "OMG, I am so sorry," I blurted.

"Why?" he said.

"Because of the smell!" I said.

"Oh," he said. He inhaled dramatically. "I can't smell anything," he lied. "It reminds me of what my mom's cooking smells like, actually. Aaaah."

"Liar!" I said, laughing. "It's totally grot, I mean, grotesque. Sometimes I shorten words because . . . well. Anyway, I know it! It's just . . . well, it's a long story. I guess." I scratched the scab on my arm that was just healing, and it started to bleed. Great. I didn't want him to see, so quickly I said, "Anyway, what can I help you with?" I sounded like a greeter at Walmart, all formal and underpaid.

He looked over my shoulder. I knew he could see into

---

57. The hilarious thing is that there is no basement exit. I don't know how he's going to get it out of there. Really, it's kind of funny when you think about it. Will he carry it up the stairs? How much do those things weigh? Will it be stuck in the basement forever? Only time will tell.

the house. I turned to see what he was looking at, which was just the living room, stacked with my dad's *Everybody* mags, encyclopedias, and general junk.

"It's a mess," I said. Then I nearly shrieked because I could see, on the top of the pile of *M* thru *Z*, a white piece of paper, covered in FB's handwriting, titled THE CRUSH LIST.

And on the top was Kai's name.

"You should go!" I said. "Thanks for coming by!"

"But I . . ." he said. "I wanted to . . ."

"OK THANKS SO I'LL SEE YOU AROUND," I shouted.

Which is why he left.

And why I cried. I just couldn't let him see the list! What if — once he knew that Freddie Blue liked him — he stopped liking me and started liking her instead? Because she was so much prettier than me and really better in every way! So why wouldn't he? ANY boy thinking that FB liked them would go crazy with happiness! And I wanted him to be happy. I did.

Sort of.

But I also . . . well.

I think I have a really big, really bad crush on him. Big, because I can't stop thinking about him. Bad, because I *can't* have a crush on him. Because of Freddie Blue. So don't tell anyone I said that EVER or I'll tell Seb that you kill mosquitoes for fun and sport.

Anyway, I think I speak for everyone in the neighborhood when I say that we will all be relieved when the eel phase is over.

***See also** Autism; Crush List.*

Elephants

Giant, soulless pachyderms who enjoy long walks in the woods, lifting logs, spraying water out of their trunks, and the taste of preschoolers.

I saw an elephant at a circus when I was four. Do you know how big an elephant is when you are four? Really big, I can tell you. And smelly. Also hairier than I would have expected. The eyes of this particular elephant were terrifying. I would have said elephants had kind and gentle eyes until I saw one. This one's eyes said, "I would like to eat you for lunch in spite of the fact that elephants don't eat meat."

I was forced to ride the kid-eating elephant, squashed between Seb and Lex, and sobbing my little four-year-old head off. We still have the photo on the fridge. Boy, that's a magic moment you really want to remember forever.

The thing about it that I do remember most is the way that Seb and Lex each held one of my hands and sang to me so that I'd stop crying. They were pretty OK when they were little. I don't know what went wrong.

Ellery, Charlotte

Charlotte Ellery is Seb's counselor. She comes to our house once a week to talk about how we all *feel*. She continually looks at me with an expression that I think she believes says, "I *care* about your feelings, Tink Aaron-Martin."

Mom loves Charlotte because Charlotte makes Seb "open up." Frankly, I feel like Seb could stand to be more closed. Seb is very, very good at talking about how he is feeling. His feelings, however, are the only ones that he is familiar with. For example, Charlotte asked him how he thought I felt when he called me Freckle Peckle, and he just stared at her. Like,

"What? Tink has a *thought*? Actual *feelings*? Well, I never." He couldn't come up with anything. Go figure.

One thing that Charlotte said early on, when we first met her last year, was that Seb was probably never going to change that much, so it was actually going to be us who would have to change. This is just one more example of how Seb really has it made. No chores, no expectations, no changing, no compromising.

No *fair*, is what I say.

See also Aaron-Martin, Sebastian (Seb); Autism.

Everybody Magazine

A half-celebrity, half-"normal person" magazine that both Dad and Freddie Blue are completely obsessed with, copies of which flop listlessly on every surface of this house.

I was, in fact, lying on the Itchy Couch watching the sweat run in little rivulets down my maimed forearm, engrossed in an article about a certain royal celeb's bedroom furnishings, when Mom burst in through the kitchen door like her hair was on fire and the fire extinguisher was somewhere under my seat.

"Tink!" she shouted. "What are you *reading*?" she said, emphasizing the word "reading" so hard, she practically spat.

"Nuh. Thing," I enunciated. The nothingness of what I was reading was practically visible, like an aura that is as blank as Lex's sentences. *Everybody* magazine wasn't READING material. It was SKIMMING material! Everyone knew that. I tossed the magazine on the floor, and she picked it up and cradled it for a minute in her arms before putting it down on the table.

I squinted. Something was definitely up.

"Where are the boys?" she said, hopping back and forth from foot to foot as though she desperately had to pee.

"Don't know," I singsonged.

"Tink," she said impatiently. "Tink, where is your dad?"

I pointed at the stairs to the basement. I can't believe she'd had to ask. If he was home and not on the couch, he was in the basement, whirring, clunking, and singing.

"I have the most exciting news!" she shouted, like she couldn't contain it.[58] "I want to tell everyone at once. Where did you say your brothers are?"

"MOM," I said. "I don't *know*. I *like* not knowing. Then I can pretend I'm an only child! A dream come true!"

Mom kept talking as though I hadn't said a thing. ". . . magazine is going to do a story about our family," she said.

"What?" I said. "What? WHAT?"

"*Everybody*," she repeated. "*Everybody* magazine. Isn't that great?"

"Erfhvbla?" I said. I looked at the copies stacked up on the coffee table in a messy heap and then I looked back at Mom. I picked up the top one and looked at Angelina Jolie and Brad Pitt and an assortment of orphans. Then I dropped it on the floor, where it landed with a sad-sounding smack.

AS *IF* WE WERE GOING TO BE IN *EVERYBODY* MAGAZINE.

She was obviously lying!

I wanted her to be lying!

But also I didn't! For a split second, I allowed myself to imagine that we suddenly became hugely famous and paparazzi followed me to Cortez Junior and photographed my every move. Then I went ahead and wondered what kind of TV shows

---

58. I dreaded hearing it. I get all weird when someone starts telling me something I know they want me to be all jump-up-and-down-OMG-wow! excited about. I just can't do it. I freeze up inside, like their words are liquid nitrogen, and my reactions are a giant wart.

I'd get to be on and who my boyfriend would be. Maybe my first boyfriend would be famous! Way better than Kai! Maybe even Prince X!

Then I felt sad. Prince X probably *wasn't* better than Kai. I didn't want to be famous. And I hate looking at pictures of myself. My mouth always looks like I'm chewing something huge, like a gobstopper or an entire tomato. And don't get me started about my hair. If paparazzi followed me to school, I'd have to have good hair at least!

"It is the greatest thing ever!" said Mom. "Your dad is going to die of excitement!"

"How did this happen?" I whispered.

"Well," she said, plopping herself next to me and wrapping me up in a hug like she used to when I was little. I wriggled away. "Because of me, of course. Someone at *Everybody* heard me on the radio, read the blog, and the rest is history! Of course, people are interested in our story and there are so many families like ours. And," she added, "I'm sure it doesn't hurt that the boys are so photogenic."

"Gak," I said, which is what you say apparently when you are choking to death on the tidal wave of acid that has just unexpectedly slammed into your mouth.

"Of course," she said, "you'll get to be in it too. I'm not sure they'll interview you, but you'll definitely be in the pictures."

"No thanks," I muttered. "I'd just wreck them."

She laughed, even though I didn't mean it in a funny way. "It's a story about autism and how *families* cope," she said. "And you are part of the family, Tink. Obviously. Boy, your dad will be thrilled, won't he? And Freddie Blue is going to be so jealous!" She elbowed me.

I elbowed her back. Hard. "What. Ev. Er," I said, for the sake of saying something. Inside my brain, there was a loud scream of staticky noise, like a ringing in the ears by a million different off-key bells. It sounded like *dread*.

"Dread," I mumbled.

Not that Mom was listening as she paced around the room, yelling, "BAX! BOYS!" every few seconds.

I tried to imagine how this was going to go. Badly, I could predict with 100 percent certainty. I would likely be edited out anyway. I shut my eyes and pictured someone at *Everybody* hard at work Photoshopping a potted plant over me, or perhaps an adorable photogenic puppy.

"More dread," I whispered. "Extra dread. Dreadsome." I patted Hortense, which I rarely do, and she meowed in a horrified sort of way and climbed down my leg, glowering at me from the floor.

"You aren't photogenic either," I said.

"Oh, Hortense is so exotic," Mom said. "I bet they put her in the picture for sure. We'll have to get you some great new clothes! Maybe get your makeup done professionally."

Mom flew out of the room like a fairy with a drinking problem, knocking over a teetering pile of mail that we keep conveniently balanced on the newel post. I heard her pounding down the stairs to tell Dad. I have no idea why she didn't tell him first. It's really HIS dream come true, not mine. My dreams don't feature Lex and Seb looking into the camera with fake serious looks. Ugh.

I picked up the phone, pressed Freddie Blue's number, and listened to it ring. Her voice mail came on, and I didn't leave a message. I called back again. And again. Finally, she answered.

"Oh, hey," she said.

"Why didn't you answer?" I said. "I have some news."

"Do you?" she said. "Can you hang on? I'm on the other line."

"No!" I said, but she'd already cut over. I listened to the silence for about ten seconds before I hung up. I lay back down on the Itchy Couch. It itched. I glared at Hortense and tapped her with my foot. She purred.

"I'm not being nice," I told her. "I'm in a terrible mood." I stared out the window. The sky was so blue, it was insulting to my grumpiness. I could see the roof of Kai's house. Kai. I sighed.

KAI.

Wait!

Freddie Blue NEVER puts me on hold. We have a deal! We wouldn't put each other on hold! UNLESS!

Unless we were talking to a boy!

I got up and ran to the window, as though I'd be able to see Kai talking on the phone (if he was). All I could see was reflections in the glass.

"Argh," I said, and kicked the wall. What if he saw the list? What if he had called her to confirm?[59]

Kai and Freddie Blue. What if they were RIGHT NOW talking about their mutual like for each other? What if they were Liking each other on Facebook? What if they were IN LOVE?

I mean, sure, she could have been talking to someone else. But I couldn't overcome the thought. It was like the thought was a hungry seagull and I was a tiny crab trapped on an

---

59. I know this sounds crazy, but sometimes I think something, and no matter how far-fetched my dumb thought is, it's like as soon as I THINK it, I instantly believe it. There is probably a name for that. If you find out what it is, let me know, but in the meantime, I call it "thoughtasthesia." Please note that "thoughtasthesia" is not a real word so if you use it in conversation, people will almost certainly point and laugh. AVOID.

expanse of sand. And just like that, my silly crush on Kai was swallowed by a noisy, annoying seabird.

I stomped up to my room and flung the door open, like there might be someone in there who cared. Of course there wasn't. AND my bed was in completely the wrong place.

"IDIOTS!" I shouted, in case my brothers Dumb and Dumber were somewhere where they might hear me. I lay down and waited for FB to call back. It wasn't until I really started to think about the photo shoot, though, that I realized something.

The problem with the whole *Everybody* thing wasn't going to be me. It was going to be *Seb.*

Because photo shoots involve cameras.

It was going to be a huge FAIL. Because when Seb says, "No more pictures," he isn't going to change his mind. At least, I doubt it. He once changed his mind about something. ONCE.[60]

Mom would be crushed! Dad would be destroyed! And I would never be famous! So the whole thing would be filed, once again, under *S,* for "Seb Didn't Want To So We Didn't."

I laughed out loud.

"DREAD," I shouted, not that anyone was listening. "DREAAAAAD."

See also Aaron-Martin, Sebastian (Seb); Autism; Celebrities.

---

60. This is going to sound crazy to you if you don't also have an autistic brother, but one day, out of the blue, he said, "I've changed my mind about flagellated worms. I think they're pretty interesting." Up until that point, he'd have a fit if he even saw a picture of a flagellated worm. He thought they were the most disgusting thing ever. So if he can change his mind about a flagellated worm, I guess he can change his mind about any old thing. Why not?

F

Fame

The lofty position celebrities enjoy, i.e., being stared at in Starbucks and photographed in unattractive sweatpants. People who are in *Everybody* magazine are either already famous or they gain fame just by being in the magazine.[61]

When Freddie Blue finally called me back, I told her about the photo shoot, and then I said, "So if I get famous, will you still be my friend?"

Then there was this long silence. I knew she was there because I could hear her breathing. I laughed. "Freddie Blue, seriously! Answer!"

She sighed. "I guess," she said.

And that was it. Just like that. "I guess."

My heart fell into my stomach. I could practically feel it disintegrating in the acid. My stomach gurgled.

"What?" I said. "I was kidding, FB. We aren't going to be famous, except maybe at school for five minutes, because people forget and don't care about stuff like that. Or else something dumb will happen and the whole thing will be totally embarrassing and no one will ever forget, but I'll have to move to the south of France and change my name to Alphonsine Le Noir to escape the humiliating shame of it all."

She didn't laugh. I could practically hear her shrugging. "Can I call you back?" she said.

"No!" I said.

---

61. Or they are dead. *Everybody* magazine always has some story in it about someone who was killed in a terrifying way. Frankly, I could live without that article. I find it very jarring to be reading about a star's close relationship with her hairstylist and then turning the page to find an article about a corpse found in someone's backyard while they were digging up their tomato plants.

"Oh," she said. "OK. It's just that I don't have much to say."

"Freddie Blue?" I said. "Are you OK? You're being totally weird."

"I'm fine," she said. "It's just that . . ."

"What?" I said. I thought she was going to say Kai, so I interrupted. "Look, if it's about Kai, you can have him. I don't even like him!"

She giggled. "Tink," she said. "I know I can have him. If I want him. I haven't just quite decided yet. It's hard to know what to do. We haven't been back to school yet. What if I say yes to Kai and then it turns out he isn't pops? I can't have an unpops BF!"

"Unpops?" I said. "Um, is that a word?"

"Oh," she said. "Yeah, I've been hearing it from some of my other friends."

Other friends?

"Like who?" I said.

She giggled again. "You sound jealous or something. Don't be idio, Tink. When I'm at Dad's, you know, I don't just sit and stare at the dead fish floating around in his fish tank."

"That's so grot," I said. "Why doesn't he flush them?"

"I don't know," she said. "They're falling apart now anyway. Fish corpses disintegrate really fast. The other fish have practically eaten the dead ones clean away."

It was only when I hung up that I realized we spent more time talking about fish than about *Everybody*. And isn't *Everybody* bigger news?

Doesn't fame count for more than dead fish?

And who are these other friends?

Everything that is happening to me lately feels like a dream, and it's not really a good one, more like one that isn't quite good but isn't bad enough to wake you up either. I keep hoping for some sort of reprieve that involves realizing that I have been in a coma since the Boarding Incident, and it will all go away when I finally wake up. (Except the good bits, of course.)

Feel free to pinch me. Not that a coma sufferer in the history of comas has ever been woken by a pinch before, but maybe that's just because no one's ever tried.

See also BFF; Celebrities; Everybody *Magazine.*

Fickle

People who are fickle are people who change their minds all the time about everything, like maybe one day they like chocolate ice cream the best and the next they like only mint chocolate chip; or one day they have a crush on their neighbor, and the next, poof! GONE.

(Almost.)

(Due to circumstances — and BFFs — outside of their control.)

Everyone is sometimes a little bit fickle, I suppose.

See also BFF; Crush List.

Fish

Slimy animals that live in the sea and breathe through the cracks that run along the side of their heads.

I have a recurring nightmare that one day I'll be swimming and a teeny-tiny mini fish will nibble on my arm or hair or any part of me and I'll have a heart attack and drown. I am more afraid of decorative, dime-sized tropical fish, like in *Finding Nemo*, than I am of man-eating sharks. True fact.

My wrists are starting to cramp up from typing this. I hope I don't get carpal tunnel syndrome, which afflicts people who type too much, and renders them unable to record their own histories such that they die alone and unrecognized and poor and then they have to lie in their unmarked grave forever, knowing no one knows anything about them. Or, worse, their bodies are thrown into the sea and eaten by small, carnivorous *fish*!

There. You thought I forgot this entry was about "fish," but I didn't.

Now you are scared too. And if you aren't, you have to ask yourself, "Why NOT?"

Freckles

A freckle is a buildup of melanin in your skin, which makes it appear to be dotted with a marker. See how enriching it is to read my encyclopedia? Probably you can go ahead and drop out of school now, because this book is enough to educate you for life.

My mom says that sometimes freckles go away when a person hits puberty. I hope this is true with every cell in my whole body. Please, please, please let it be true! On the other hand, surely people will notice when my freckles suddenly vanish overnight, and I'm not entirely sure I want the whole world to know the exact second that I hit puberty. Humilio![62]

See also Aaron-Martin, Isadora (Tink).

Friend

A friend is someone who you can count on, no matter what. Friends are better than family because family can't always be counted on to have your back, yet you continue to be stuck with them, regardless. Your friends can be counted on because if they don't have your back, you can shout at them and never speak to them again.

Even though sometimes shouting at your friends is impossible, and you don't want to never speak to them again.

Not that I am talking about anyone in particular or about anything that has happened.

I'm not.

Or maybe I am, just a little bit.

See also Anderson, Freddie Blue.

---

62. "Humiliating."

G

Gadzooks

"Gadzooks" is the only swearword that we're allowed to use at home. Basically, I live in a cartoon. I thought Freddie Blue was going to choke to death from laughing last time she was over and Dad dropped the spatula on his foot and screamed, "GADZOOK IT!"

The exception to this family rule being, guess who? You are right! *Ding ding ding!*[63] Seb swears his head off all the time, and we can't get him to stop. So there the rest of us are, all "gadzooks" this and "gadzooks" that, and he is properly using all the four-letter words available to mankind.

Apparently, when I fell off the skateboard on the train track, I screamed, "Gadzooooks!" right before I hit the ground. I hope Kai didn't hear it, or if he did, that he's now had it wiped out of his memory by passing aliens on a UFO.

See also Autism; Boarding, Skate.

Ginger

In Great Britain, according to my dad, "ginger" is the word used to describe people with red hair. For some reason this is also a terrible insult. I'm not sure why. When Dad is teasing Mom, he tells her she is ginger, although she isn't really even a redhead. Her hair is actually a very glam, slightly reddish blond color.

---

63. There is no prize for being right in this instance because the answer was obvious. But you DO have the satisfaction of knowing you were right, and that's better than being wrong! Right? Right. See? SATISFYING.

Prince X is not a ginger. But I would probably still love him, even if he was.

I wonder if Prince X reads *Everybody* magazine?

I bet he does. Will Prince X see a picture of . . . me?

OMG.

Girls

Girls are people who are . . . not boys.

I am a girl. Obviously.

But what I mean to write about are the girls at school. The *groups* of girls. The *gaggles* of girls. The clubs I don't feel I get to join because me and Freddie Blue, we've always just been kind of on the outside.

It never bothered me, but it always bugged her. The thing is that girls — at least the ones at school — don't like me. I don't know why not. I'm pretty likable once you get to know me.

Even Seb has more girls who are friends than I do. He used to blurt out things that most people consider rude, but he considered factual, such as "You look really fat in those pants!" Boys didn't care, but girls did. Now he doesn't do that much anymore and he's cute and smart, so girls are drawn to him.

Next year at school, Freddie Blue and I had planned to reinvent ourselves and be super friendly to all the girls all the time, not in an annoying way, but a way that would make us pops. I had been sort of looking forward to roaming the school in a glam pack of girly-girls, friendlily tossing our hair and laughing, less popular kids trailing in our wake and hoping we grace them with a smile or a piece of sugarless gum.

Now that I think about it, though, I might prefer to stay

on the outside, looking in. I don't even like chewing gum. It's much too spitty for my tastes.

See also *Cortez Junior.*

Glam

Word meaning "spectacularly fab!" Short for "glamorous."

Sometime last year, Freddie Blue and I made a pact to start using a word that no one ever uses and to use it all the time to see how many people copied us. "Glam" was our first. I've noticed a lot of people are using it now. So, success is ours! I am currently campaigning to make our next word "scintillating," as in "Gosh, what you are saying about Mexican iguana frogs is so scintillating!"[64] but Freddie Blue says that being obnoxiously smart just makes people want to stuff you into confined spaces, such as refrigerators or old wells.

Still, I think it's a great word, especially — only — if used in the properly sarcastic tone.

See also *Anderson, Freddie Blue; Bullies.*

Grabs and Grinds

Grabs are when you are boarding and you reach down and grab your board. Grinds are when you slide down something on your board, but you don't slide on the deck or the wheels, but actually on that metal bit that goes between the wheels.

Kai taught me that. At Drop Mac Park.

What happened was that I went to DMP looking for Ruth. And she wasn't there. But Kai was there with about eight other boys.

---

64. Yes, that is sarcasm.

I didn't know what to do, really. I didn't want to march up and start talking to him. (Actually, I did, but I was too shy.) So I just started doing the only thing I knew how to do, which was to swoop back and forth on the curvy ramp.

After a while, I forgot he was there, to tell you the truth. I just got into the feeling of swooping back and forth. I even tried it with my eyes closed.

And then when I opened them, there was Kai, staring at me.

"Dude," he said. "You're pretty good."

I laughed. "No, I'm not!" I said. "This is my second time ever. I mean, third. But the first time doesn't count because . . ." I trailed off, because I was embarrassed. I hoped he'd forgotten. He grinned.

"Yeah," he said. "Wow. It's your second time? That's, like, rad." He dropped his board and started tipping around on it. "I could show you some stuff." He shrugged. "If you want."

"Yes!" I said. Then I felt like an idio because I sounded so eager, so I said, "You know, I don't have a lot of time, so just for a second."

"OK," he said. "Um, well. You gotta start with a grab. You grab your deck like this when you jump." He demonstrated.

"I can't jump!" I said. "I can just . . . swoop."

"Oh," he said. "Well, swooping is good." He grinned again. "Swooping! But it's not as good as grinding."

He threw his board up on the railing and then there was this horrible metal-on-metal sound, and he stood up on it and slid down. That's when I figured it out.

He wasn't teaching me stuff, he was showing off.

Almost like he was trying to get me to *like* him or something.

But that can't be right, because he's Freddie Blue's. Or at least, he will be soon enough.

"Try this," he said, and he put his hand on the part of my shoulder where my T-shirt sleeve was rolled up, to show me how to stand. All the blood in my whole body ran to where his hand was, all at once, and I got light-headed and jumpy all at once. I flinched without really meaning to.

"Um, sorry," he said, and moved his hand.

He showed me a bunch more stuff, but I wasn't really paying attention. I was just thinking about how he touched my shoulder and how it felt. Nothing like a dead fish. Which is weird, because I remember when he held my arm after I fell, which feels like a billion years ago, how cold and grot it was.

"Um," I said.

"What?" he said.

"Nothing," I said. I started rolling again on the board. I wasn't sure what to do, exactly, but somehow I managed to bend over and grab the board and do a lame sort of a hop.

Then I ran over my own finger.

"OH, MAN! Are you OK?" he yelled.

"I'm FINE," I yelled back.

I don't know why we were yelling, as we were only four feet away from each other. Then we looked at each other and started laughing. I laughed so hard I had to get off my board and hold my stomach. It just got funnier. I kept thinking, "Stop laughing!" which made me laugh harder, but he was laughing just as hard! I'd never met a boy who laughed like me, laughed like he couldn't stop.

It was pretty great.

So: "grab" and "grind." The only real boarding words I know.

See also Boarding, Skate.

Grandma

The great Isabella Martin lived for eighty-three fantastic years, which was just not enough. Grandma was born on the side of a road in New York City. True story. Her mom was out shopping and BOOM, there was Grandma, right on the sidewalk in Times Square. Who is born in Times Square? What could be cooler? Grandma was so glam. She liked to refer to herself as "constantly surprising, right from birth." Which she was.

When Seb was being diagnosed with autism, it was a strange time on Planet Aaron-Martin, i.e., at home. He had always acted different and it wasn't until I was six that Mom and Dad decided that maybe there was a capital-*I* Issue. Seb was eight. (That's late for an autism diagnosis, FYI.) What happened was that he started going under his desk at school and barking, and they were forced by the school to have him tested. It was like that. They had just thought he was "willful" and "unique" due to his brilliance.

While all this went on, I became invisible at home. This is because I was small and polite and not howling at the moon. Grandma was the only one who could see me. She always took me seriously and let me talk about how sometimes I was scared of Seb, even though if I showed that I was scared, Lex got mad. It was a mess, but that was nothing to do with Grandma.

Grandma is the only person who insisted on calling me Isadora. I liked it when she did it. She said "Tink" sounded like someone hitting the side of a glass with a spoon, which she enjoyed at weddings, but not as a name for her granddaughter. Her house up the street always smelled like perfume and meat loaf. It sounds gross, but it was a very comfortable scent. Grandma was the best. I'm crying now just writing this. I can't believe she died! She wasn't even very old. She died during an operation to replace her knee. She had thought she was going to wake up as the bionic woman, and instead she didn't wake up at all. I was ten. I shake my fist at the heavens when I think about how she's dead and how many much more unpleasant people are still alive.

Grandma was my best friend and best family combined, which just made her the best.

See also Apple.

Grounded

I do not have to tell you what it means to be grounded. I only mention it because I am struggling to come up with G words that are captivating enough to warrant a mention in the Encyclopedia of Me.[65]

I have been grounded more times than I can count, from crimes ranging from Not Actually Crimes (e.g., the rescue of Mr. Bigglesworth) to things that may, in fact, BE crimes, such as sneaking into movies that are for mature audiences, or stealing the Aardie costume and putting it in FB's mom's bed with her, so that when she woke up in the morning and stared right at it, she screamed for forty-five minutes and then called the police.

Really, FB's mom should not be allowed to call the police. She does it with the kind of reckless abandon that ties up the police force and distracts them from whatever real crimes might be happening in this city. If you think about it, she's the one who should be punished, not me.

---

65. Words I can think of but have no bearing on my life whatsoever: gravel, gristle, gravy, Google, Greece, gravity. I will work hard at endeavoring to somehow become involved with any or all of these things for future editions. Encyclopedias — in case you don't know this — always have lots of editions, so I could theoretically update this book every year for my ENTIRE LIFE. Except I won't, because that seems like way too much work, and also I already have a really great idea for a Dictionary of Disasters that I'd rather write than rewriting this.

Besides, everything is usually Freddie Blue's idea. I just go along for moral support. Because that's what BFFs do, right?

See also Aardvark; Anderson, Freddie Blue; BFF; Couch, Itchy.

Growing up

One of the steps on the road between being born and getting old and dying. The part that includes all the "responsibility" and things like "jobs" and "bills."

Sometimes at night when I'm supposed to be asleep, I hear Mom and Dad worrying and/or arguing about what will happen to Seb when he graduates from high school (if he graduates) and grows up. How will he go to college? How will he get a proper job? My parents are unable to imagine a future for any of us that does not include college, which is funny because Mom only recently went back to school and Dad never did.

Dad says, "Let's take it one day at a time." Which is fine for Seb apparently, but he'll often give *me* a bad time about what I'm going to be when I grow up, which is a writer, which Mom and Dad say is not a "real job" so I need to have "a backup plan." My "backup plan" is to marry Prince X, which I would never be dumb enough to tell Mom and Dad! So instead I lie and say that I plan to go to law school. Everyone in the world thinks that "law school" sounds impressive, but I think it sounds painfully dull and horrific and therefore is parent-approved and a good answer. If you are looking for an answer to supply to your own parents, please feel free to steal mine.

See also Aaron-Martin, Sebastian (Seb).

Hairless Cats

Cats. With no hair.

I don't know that much about hairless cats, but I can't leave out Hortense, our family pet, who you already know a lot about. Hairless cats are sometimes also called "Canadian Skinless Cats." I'm not making that up. It's true. Being Canadian ought to make Hortense extra polite, but I do not believe that is the case. Hortense can be very ornery.

This photo of a hairless cat looks exactly like Hortense (or a handbag) but it is not Hortense (or a handbag).

I can tell you that — unlike regular old cats — hairless cats like baths. Hortense takes a bath once a week. Well, when I say she "takes a bath" that implies that she just hops into the tub and washes herself, when in fact it is my job to do it. I don't mind, though, because she likes it so much. If you put a regular cat into the bathtub and started washing her, she'd as likely as not scratch your eyes out with her razor-sharp claws. Hortense lies back like she's having a day at the spa. And she purrs.

Hortense is just *not* a regular cat, although she *does* have razor-sharp claws that she uses more frequently than she should, just never in conjunction with a bath.

Halloween
The last day of October, during which everyone dresses up and demands candy from the neighbors or goes to a party and screams when they put their hand in a bowl of spaghetti labeled "brains."

Last year for Halloween, Freddie Blue and I dressed up as dice. It was *wildly* funny. We did this whole thing where people would pretend to toss us and we pretended to roll around and we'd land on a different number each time. Actually, now that I've written that down, it sounds incredibly stupid, so you'll just have to take my word for it when I say that it was hysterically funny. Freddie Blue peed her pants, but you couldn't tell at all because she was wearing a box.

See also *Anderson, Freddie Blue; BFF.*

Haywire
Another word for "out of control."

Lex is in a band called Haywire. If by a "band," I mean "a group of boys who never actually practice but sometimes scream into microphones during parties or at 'talent' shows, which they have never won." Originally, it was meant to be a band for Lex and Seb, both, but Seb hates music. Especially the kind of music that Lex plays. He says it makes him feel like he's been put into a blender with a bunch of nails and broken glass and tinfoil and then blended at high speed.

He is not wrong.

So Lex is on his own. Secretly, Lex thinks that one day

Haywire will be famous and will make billions of dollars and he will have enough money to take care of Seb forever, like when we are grown-ups and Mom and Dad are dead. I know this because I read it on the laptop. I guess he was trying to write a blog but didn't realize that the Internet was involved and never got around to uploading it during his allotted thirty minutes. His attention span is quite short. The file was called "haywire.doc." How could I know it was private? When he caught me reading it, he deleted it and everything else on the laptop's hard drive too. He was grounded for a week, which did nothing to get my stuff back. I am still mad.

Haywire is also how Seb gets when he is melting down. "Meltdown" is the correct word for "going haywire," according to Charlotte Ellery, who is a big fan of using only the right word for anything, so if any of us say, "Seb went haywire," she sighs and looks depressed, like she can't believe we never listen. Then she says, "Actually, what you mean is that Seb had a meltdown, as is common among people with autism."

Honestly, I don't see what difference it makes.

Worse, I'm the "trigger." The Haywire Trigger. Maybe Dad should call me that instead of the Peacemaker. Because it would probably be more true.

Like yesterday, Seb went haywire. And it was my fault.

I was writing my book when the boys came tumbling into the room, knocking over the mail, a glass of milk, and a table lamp,[66] much like two unattractive ponies who have accidentally had a double-shot espresso.

"What are you so happy about?" I said.

---

66. It's the fringe-covered gypsy lamp that Mom bought in Paris when she was traveling with a dance troupe. It's truly the ugliest lamp in the world and is not (unlike what she believes) beautiful just by virtue of being French. No one bothered to pick it up.

"We're going to be in *Everybody* magazine!" said Lex.

"Give me five, Seb, my man, my bro, my brown, my MAIN FAME."

Seb slapped his hand. "European green crabs are now living at our beach," he said.

"Gosh," I said. "That's scintillating, Seb."[67]

"What I wouldn't do to see a Chinese mitten crab," he said. "Want me to draw you a picture of one?"

"Hey," said Lex. "You can tell that to the people from *Everybody* magazine. About the crabs."

"Really?" said Seb. "Cool. Maybe I could catch one for them, if I can find one. They're hard to find. I wonder if they'd wait if I took a long time to find one."

Then for some reason, I said, "*Everybody* magazine! Gosh, that's exciting. Imagine all those hundreds of cameras snapping your picture, Seb. Over and over again. Picture after picture after picture. I can't imagine a crab would like that."

I knew it was mean, but still, Seb did not freak out.

"Pictures?" I repeated. "Of you? With a camera?"

Seb shrugged and said, "You're crazy, Freckles. Must be a freckle in your brain. Freckle-brain." He laughed his I-am-a-weird-maniac laugh.

Lex laughed too. They have the exact same laugh. It's like being trapped in some kind of nightmare echo chamber of bullying brother laughter. "Freckle-brain, good one. Hey, I wonder if Freckles does have freckles in her brain. That's hilarious!"

"Shut up," I said. "You're bullies."

"Bullies who will be in *Everybody* magazine," said Lex.

"Don't call me names," said Seb. "Don't call me a bully."

---

67. See?

Then Dad came clomping into the room, wiping grease off his hands. "I heard you talking about *Everybody*!" he said. "This is going to be so great."

"Whatever," I said. "Big deal."

"It IS a big deal," he said, grabbing me off the couch and whirling me around the room and then throwing me back, nearly breaking my neck. "I'm getting the video camera! Let's interview each other about how it feels to be famous." He turned the camera on and started this pretty bad voice-over about how we're going to be in *Everybody* magazine. And then.

Then.

The minute the camera hit Seb, he started an A-1 haywire meltdown freak-out. Whatever Charlotte Ellery wants to call it, it doesn't change what it was.

Which was terrible.

I won't say what he said, but it was a lot of swearing and yelling. At me. At everyone. When he gets like this, he's said that he actually doesn't even really see anyone else, but it sure seems like he does. Then he started hitting himself on the head with one of the encyclopedias. I think it was *S*.

It was really hard to watch, but also hard to know what else to do. Sometimes when it happens, I feel like I become part of the wall. I am invisible. And I can't move. I can't look away. What happens to Seb seems totally private, but he does it in such a berserko way that it's completely public, so you look. Even when you shouldn't. Even when you don't want to.

Dad tried to wrestle the book out of his hands, and the rest of the pile of encyclopedias teetered and fell in a cloud of gold dust. The fan hit the floor and Hortense jumped and meowed so loudly, everything paused for a second while we watched her climb up the drapes. Then Seb let go of the book, pushed Dad off, and ran up the stairs into his room. He was sweating. His hair was soaked.

He slammed the door so hard I could hear Lex's signed, framed poster of LeBron James smashing on the floor. Then I heard Seb throwing more stuff around. I could see Lex's jaw working, but he didn't say anything.

Dad sighed and put the camera down as though it weighed a thousand pounds. For a second, he leaned on the table. It almost looked like he was going to cry. Lex went, "I'll go."

And Dad said, "No, I'll do it."

"I don't mind," said Lex. "No big."

"Lex!" shouted Dad. "I'm going."

"Fine," said Lex. "Whatever. Do your thing." He sat down on a chair and started tipping it backward.

"Stop it," I mumbled.

"Don't tip the chair," said Dad. Lex ignored him.

"DON'T TIP THE CHAIR!" Dad repeated.

"STOP IT!" I yelled. "It's not Lex's fault!"

"HE'S TIPPING THE CHAIR!" yelled Dad.

"BUT HE ISN'T WHY YOU ARE MAD!" I shouted.

"Hey," said Lex. "Forget it. It's fine. I'm not tipping. See? Nice work, Peacemaker."

"Don't call me that," I said.

"Guys," sighed Dad. "Oh, forget it."

We listened as Dad went and knocked on Seb's door and Seb screamed, "Go away! Get the #^&@^&# out of here!"

Dad called, "Go ahead, guys, go outside."

"But . . ." I started.

"GO," he said. "NOW."

Dad gets way stressed out when Seb's in his rage cycle. I should also mention that Dad handles Seb completely differently than Mom does. Mom's done a lot of research and has all these elaborate steps that she follows, and the step she'd take right then would be to ignore Seb entirely. It's part of the chart that she has attached to the fridge.

Dad is the opposite. He always goes in and tries to hold on to Seb and hug him and go on and on and on about how much he loves him until Seb snaps out of it. Mom gets so mad when he does that. She says he's positively reinforcing the behavior.

Anyway, I didn't need to be told to go twice. I followed Lex out the door. "Whooo!" I yelled. I don't know why I yelled that. I think I was just so glad to not be in the House of Haywire anymore.

Lex glared at me. "Yeah," he said sarcastically. "It's a total celebration. I'm going to the beach. Are you coming or are you just going to be a freak?"

"I'm not a freak," I said. "I'm coming."

"Whatever," he said.

"Want to get ice cream?" I said.

"No," he said. Then he totally stalked off without me.

"Fine," I yelled after him. "Go!"

Which is why I went for ice cream by myself.

Which is why I saw Kai.

Which is why what happened, happened.

I am not prepared to write any more of this story right now. You are going to have to wait for the letter *I*, which I realize is probably going to be on the next page, but I am just not willing to write about what happened quite, quite yet.

See also *Aaron-Martin, Sebastian (Seb); Autism; Ellery, Charlotte.*

Heights

Until I fell in love with the Tree of Unknown Species, I was totally and completely terrified of being high up. I was more afraid of heights than I am of elephants or even being murdered in my sleep by a mask-wearing criminal with claw gloves.[68]

Now I am not at all afraid. It went away, just like that. I can't remember why I was scared before. It's weird how that happens, how one day something can scare you so bad that your legs won't hold you up, and then you try it. And then everything changes, and it turns out you are OK, after all.

Mom says that I'm still afraid, I'm just pretending not to be, but I think that's just because she might be a little bit jealous that I'm completely cured and she is not.

Hickey

A hickey is a bruise that you get when your skin gets sucked very hard, either by a vacuum cleaner or by a mouth (your own or someone else's). You can give yourself one by putting your forearm into your mouth and sucking really hard. Freddie Blue and I give ourselves hickeys sometimes in class if the class is very boring. Once she had fourteen hickeys on her arm. It looked like she'd been punched repeatedly by someone with a tiny fist, such as an elf.

Apparently, boys like to give you hickeys on your neck, but honestly I don't see how this could even happen, unless they are pretending to be vampires and you are pretending to like it.

---

68. I inherited my fear of heights from my mom, who is so afraid of heights that she once froze on top of a stepladder while changing a lightbulb, and I had to call Dad at work to come home and help me to get her down. True story. Ask him. Don't ask Mom because she'll say it didn't happen, but it DID.

Howl

A really loud noise made by twin brothers during full moons, which they think is hilarious and usually causes at least one passerby to scream and run away.

I don't actually remember when this started — it seems like the boys have been doing this stupid howl for my whole life, probably because they have. Lex says it helps Seb to work out all his stuff, to stand on the front lawn and just howl like a banshee at the moon. Seb says that he does it because Lex is actually a werewolf and the only thing that keeps him from eating the entire family is this stupid and annoyingly loud ritual. When I was little, that scared me to death, but now I know they are just kidding around. They never miss a moon.

I guess I don't mind it. I'm used to it, looking out my window on moony nights and seeing them there, heads thrown back, howling like psychos. It's actually sort of funny.

See also Aaron-Martin, Sasha Alexei (Lex); Aaron-Martin, Sebastian (Seb).

I

Ice Cream Incident, The

Ice cream is a frozen dessert enjoyed by everyone. Go ahead, show me someone who does not like ice cream. You can't, can you? Because everyone likes it. Because it is delicious.

This entry is not really about ice cream.

It is about kissing.

It is a long-ish story. Be prepared. Maybe get a snack and a cold drink! Find a comfy place to sit, like maybe a hammock.

Yes, this is the story that began with *Haywire*. If you have forgotten what happened in *Haywire*, I will wait while you go back and reread that entry. I have time.

Done? OK, then.

So Lex stomped off to the beach without me, and I headed into the ice cream shop. The very best ice cream shop in the world, as I may have already mentioned. I have two words: WAFFLE. And CONES. I was looking forward to seeing if they had my favorite of all flavors, which is called Sparkly Unicorns and Happiness. It has chocolate and tiny peanut butter cups and big swirls of caramel and marshmallow and colorful sprinkles. Basically everything you can put in ice cream that tastes good is in there.

Kai was outside the shop, eating a huge cone of about eight different scoops, most of which looked like chocolate. At first I was nervous, then I went right away to excited to see him, then I noticed who he was talking to, and within a split second, I went right to downright annoyed. He was talking to a big gang of girls from my school, including, but not limited to, the horrifically awful Stella Wilson-Rawley. I glared at her ferociously, totally forgetting that I was going to practice being über-friendly at all times.

"Hey, Tink," said Ruth Quayle.[69]

"Hello," I said, without opening my mouth, which made it come out funny, like a small growl. She gave me an alarmed look. I tried to smile but I did not feel like smiling.

"Tinky Tinky," said Stella, and smirked.

"Grak," I mumbled, which wasn't the least bit witty but was all I could come up with.

I was about to push by her when Kai noticed me. He gave me this huge, manic, crazy-guy grin and shouted, "THERE you are."

Which made me slightly happy. But then, before I could even say, "Hi," which is what I was going to do, but in a voice that was just slightly frosty and unwelcoming, he grabbed me and then he

. . . *kissed me right on the mouth.*

With his mouth!

Which had melted ice cream bits on it! And saliva!

I repeat: HE KISSED ME ON THE MOUTH! WITH HIS SLIMY MOUTH!

I was so stunned that all I could do was gawp at him like a fish that has been tossed onto the beach by a rogue wave and cannot breathe air and is dying. Your first really meaningful kiss is supposed to be amaaaaaazing and mine was just plain shocking. SHOCKING. I didn't have time to mentally prepare!

---

69. Ruth Quayle was friends with SWR? How was that possible? I was shocked to my core. Not that RQ and I were BFFs or anything; obviously FB had that job forever and always in my heart, but I did feel a bit sick and, honestly, betrayed. Even though it didn't make sense. Feelings rarely do, or so I'm learning.

I thought I liked him! But then I didn't! And then I did again! And now I just wanted to run away, screaming!

But why?

My heart started pounding like someone trapped in an elevator who is about to plunge to a terrible demise. I couldn't get my breath. He then whispered something in my ear.

"WHAT?" I said loudly, because I didn't hear him. I couldn't hear anything. Well, that's not true, I DID hear SWR saying, "Ew."

"Thanks, you SAVED me," he repeated.

I can hardly remember the next bit because my head was spinning like a Tilt-A-Whirl. But I must have somehow gone in, ordered, and paid for my Sparkly Unicorns and Happiness cone because the next thing I knew, I was marching directly out the back door of the shop. Alone.

As in, with no one following me.

Not Kai the Kisser. Not Ruth, my supposed new friend. Not *anyone.*

I kept marching until I got to the beach, but by then, I felt light-headed. From the SHOCK! And my ice cream had melted all over my hand, giving me that gross sticky-finger situation that I hate. I was tragically forced to throw away the cone. I threw away Sparkly Unicorns and Happiness! Could things get worse?

I thought about it. I guess it would be worse if, for example, a passing great white shark — and yes, they DO have those here — could suddenly become demented and throw itself onto the beach, snapping its jaws at everything that moved, chomping off my right leg below the knee before belly flopping back into the bay. Worse, no?

Maybe not, actually.

At least that wouldn't be *embarrassing*. Or *awkward*.

I sat and ran sand through my fingers and stared out to sea. Crab traps bobbed up and down on the waves, and kayaks paddled by in colorful flocks. Every once in a while, someone dove in and shouted from the cold. Finally, Lex came up behind me and grabbed my shoulder, scaring me half to death. I was obviously totally still in shock, or I would have smelled his approach and been ready for the assault.

"Time to go," he said.

We walked home slowly. I could feel my legs again, but I wished I couldn't because they were itchy from the sand and also felt like lead. I sighed dramatically, in a universal signal of, "Ask me what is wrong!"

"Stop doing that, you're bugging me," Lex went, and then he punched me hard on the arm.

"THAT HURT!" I shouted.

"You're a total pain," he said. "I don't need this. I'm not your babysitter. Why do I always have to look after everyone?"

"I'm not a baby," I said. "And you aren't looking after me. I go to the beach alone all the time."

"Whatever." Lex shrugged, putting his iPod on. The music reverberated loudly around his head in a cloud.

I hated Lex right then for not asking me what happened. Why do other people get nice siblings who they can confide in about things and I get . . . LEX AND SEB?

Talk about unfair.

When we got home, the house was quiet. Lex went and made himself and Seb sandwiches. I did not want a sandwich. I did not want anything. My lips felt weird and tingly, like maybe I was going into anaphylactic shock.[70] I sat down on the hall floor. The floor is tile and it was nice and cool against my skin. It helped, sort of like how an ice pack helps when you hurt your knees trampolining on them in the middle of the night during sleepovers.

Half of me was going, *Wheee! He kissed me! A cute boy kissed me! KAI kissed me!* The other half of me was going, *Ick! Ack! Ick! Ack!* Kind of like a ticking clock, or more like a ticking bomb. Punctuated every now and again with stabbing feelings of fury! Betrayal! And rage! None of which I really understood!

And the combination was dizzying.

I dragged myself to my room and called Freddie Blue.

"She's not home, Tink," said FB's mom. "She's gone camping with her dad this weekend."

"Camping?" I repeated. "Freddie Blue doesn't camp."

Her mom laughed grimly. "I know, right?" she said. "Well, I'm sure she's having an adventure, if nothing else. Her biggest adventure yet, no doubt."

"But!" I said.

"I'm sure she would have invited you, but her dad was taking her with some of his friends and they probably didn't have room," she said quickly.

"I don't care," I lied. "Just tell her I called."

---

70. Anaphylactic shock is when you get a bee sting or eat peanut butter and you are super allergic, SO allergic that you have to stab yourself in the leg with a needle that looks like a pen. In case you didn't know this, I can tell you that the main symptom is that your lips and tongue get all tingly, which I know because my dad gets that if someone's wayward dog licks him at the park and then he has to stab his thigh with his pen-needle, which is really pretty cool if it also didn't involve having to have a dramatic-near-death experience from a puppy's smooch. The people who own the dogs in question always feel super bad when Dad does that in front of them, and they should. Those friendly dogs are like loaded pistols!

Camping!

Life was so unfair.

I lay back on the cold tile, which had stopped helping, and I cradled the phone like it was a tiny kitten on my chest.

And then it rang.

"Hey," said Kai. "May I please speak to Isadora?"

I knew it was him, right away, but for some reason I said, "Hang on a sec."

Then I held the phone away from my ear and screamed, "TINK!"

Then I pressed the OFF button very, very softly, like I didn't want anyone to notice that I did it.

He didn't call back.

I don't know why I did that.

I got up off the tile floor and went down to the basement. Dad's bike was glittering clean; it looked finished. It looked like an artist's version of a motorcycle and not like an actual motorcycle. I walked by it, careful not to touch it and leave fingerprints, and grabbed Seb's board from the storage room. Then I headed down to Drop Mac Park. Swooping was obviously the only answer. Maybe swooping is always the answer, in situations where ice cream is not.

I don't really have much more to say about ice cream other than that, if you think about it, it's really pretty good for you. It's made from milk! Calcium! Have some. Your bones will thank you.

See also Camping; Haywire.

Irony

Irony is when something happens that is funny only because it's twisted in some way. For example, it's ironic that I had a crush on Kai and then he kissed me, which made me NOT have a crush on him, but now thinking about the kissing and thinking about Kai gave me back the crush. Actually, that isn't ironic; I'm just trying to work some things out and sometimes it helps to write them down.

J

Janowicky, Austin

My first kiss. Kind of.

Surprised? Because you thought Kai was my first kiss? Nope. Sorry.

Kissing games do not count. But if they did, then technically Austin Janowicky gave me my first kiss.

It happened during a game called "Three Minutes in the Closet" at my and Freddie Blue's birthday party (Virgorama!) last September. Drawing Austin Janowicky's name was the "Three Minutes in the Closet" equivalent of losing. Happy birthday to me! It was the longest three minutes of my life. The awkwardness was so intense, I'm surprised I wasn't crushed to death by it. It was like a giant concrete block of awkward. Worse, Austin stunk. Mostly like garlic and tuna fish, but also of worse things, like bad breath and feet. For the rest of the school year, his buddies teased him about making out with me, like he'd done it voluntarily and also like it was something really terrible. I honestly think I got the worse end of that bargain. At least I'd brushed my teeth!

Freddie Blue got to kiss Damian Kato, who is/was among the cutest of the boys in our class. I was admittedly jealous. She wore her hickeys like a badge of honor. But I'm over it because Damian Kato is now known as BB Big Barf, due to the fact that he threw up violently during the school's performance of *The Wizard of Oz*, right on the Cowardly Lion. (He played the Wizard.)

Freddie Blue still claims that the kiss "took my breath

away." I mean, honestly, who does she think she is? Scarlett O'Hara in *Gone with the Wind*?[71]

See also *Books; Bullies; Hickey.*

Jealousy

Jealousy is a sickly green feeling that comes over you when your BFF tells you that she *loves* the boy who just kissed you in the ice cream shop. It is the worst feeling in the world, akin to having all your body dunked into a puddle of slug slime and being forced to eat the eyeballs of a sheep.

I was up in the Tree of Unknown Species, writing.[72] The tree was so beautiful. My favorite, like I said. I don't know if I liked it more now that it was Kai's tree or if I liked it less because it felt like it was less mine.

Probably neither. I mean, what makes it great is that it is easy to climb because the branches are fat and solid and densely arranged so as to make convenient footholds and handholds. The first part, before the branches start, is actually a bit tricky, so I have to pull myself up using a rope that I found in the carport. Now that the tree is Kai's and not the neighbors-who-are-never-home, I hope no one tells me I have to stay out of it or stop climbing it. That would be the worst.

I heard Freddie Blue Anderson's familiar galloping run up the driveway. "Tink! Tink! TINKER BELL AARON-MARTIN!"

---

71. *Gone with the Wind* is another one of my favorite books. Read it. Do not be fooled by the ridiculous cover. There are lots of different covers because it's been printed a billion times, so pick one without a sunset picture of a man kissing a woman. That's the worst one. The book looks and sounds boring, but I promise it isn't and you will love it. However, if you do not love it, it is not my fault, it just means you have poor taste in reading material, and I cannot be blamed for your shortcomings.

72. Well, not actually writing, but "thinking obsessively about Kai and the kiss," which is really part of the writing process. Thinking about your own life, I mean, not necessarily thinking about Kai specifically.

she shouted. "I AM BACK! I HAVE SURVIVED THE WILDS! TINKY! TINNNNNK!"

I ignored her, not because I wasn't happy to see her, but because she knows that anyone who calls me "Tinker Bell" deserves to trip and fall on a samurai sword that someone has accidentally dropped, pointy-end up, on the driveway.

"WHERE IS MY TINK?" Freddie Blue shouted.

"I DON'T KNOW!" Seb shouted.

"DON'T SHOUT AT FRANK!" Lex shouted at him.

"She's probably up that dumb tree," said Seb.

"She's so weird!" giggled Freddie Blue. "Right, Lex?"

I peered down through the leaves. "I don't think so," said Lex. "Also it kind of sucks to say that about your best friend, right? I mean _____."

Was Lex defending me? I didn't have time to think about it before Freddie Blue appeared below me. "There you are," she said. "What are you doing? Trying to spy on your boyfriend?"

"No!" I said. "I don't have a boyfriend. I'm not spying on anyone."

"I'm coming up," she said.

She didn't need the rope because she could reach the branches with her bare hands. Obviously, she had a growth spurt when I wasn't paying attention. I mean, I was always aware she was taller than me, but *BAM*. Now she's officially tall. Model-tall. She did a pretty impressive somersault over the biggest branch.

"This reminds me of when we were kids," she said, settling in just above me, her feet dangling near my face.

"Totally," I said. I was feeling prickly. I should have been happy to see her. I missed her, after all. But "when we were kids"? I didn't want to say, "Last summer, you mean?" which is what I was thinking. "How was camping?" I asked instead.

"OMG," she said. "It was totally the best adventure ever. And you aren't going to believe who was there. Guess! Come on, guess!"

I shrugged.

"Stella!" she shrieked. "Stella Wilson-Rawley! They just like showed up there on Saturday night! And you know what? I know you hate her, but she was actually, totally, totally the most awesome fun. We slept in a tent by the river and there were cougars in the woods, IsweartoGod we heard them, and we were laughing SO hard because what if we were eaten by a cougar! Hilair, right?"

I squinted up at her. The sun was right behind her head, making her head look like a giant black hole. "Um," I said. "Seriously? Stella?"

She laughed, like it was the funniest thing in the world.

"I don't think it would be funny to be eaten by a cougar," I added. "It would probably be really painful and gory and scary." There was a lump in my throat. *Do not cry*, I told myself. *DO NOT CRY.*

But . . . STELLA? Stella, who draws mean pictures of me on bathroom walls? Stella, who mocks my hair? Stella, my Worst Enemy EVER?

"So what did I miss here?" FB said. "It's like I've been gone for a billion years! Look at all my mosquito bites! The mosquitoes were, like, totally insane crazy. Stell got bitten so many times, she practically scratched her legs right off!"

My smile felt like something brittle that was about to drift off my face and crumble on the ground like a dead leaf. "Karma" is what I wanted to say, but didn't.

"And OMG, she told me the funniest thing ever, you aren't even going to believe this," said Freddie Blue, suddenly swinging around and dropping backward so she was dangling from her legs with her face near mine. "She said that she saw you and Kai *kissing* at the ice cream shop. I mean, AS IF, right? I told her she was a screaming nutbar, and she was killing herself laughing. She's as crazy as a crate of chimps!"

"Really," I said. "Well. That's sure . . . crazy. Wow."

"Well?" said Freddie Blue. "What do you mean, WELL? If you kissed Kai, you'd have told me already, right? And besides, I know you don't like him. And even if you did, well, it's not like he'd just suddenly start kissing you, right?"

"I do sort of like him," I whispered.

"What?" she said. Her face was tomato red. "I can't hear anything! The blood is all in my ears! Woooo!" She swung back upright, nearly falling off the branch and crushing me to death. Her foot bumped my ear.

"OW! Be careful," I said. "That hurt." (It didn't. But it COULD have!)

"I'm OK!" she said. "I'm OK! Wow, I'm seeing stars, though. Neat. I never really knew that happened, I thought it was just an expression. Anyway, the stars when we were camping were AMAZING. You wouldn't have believed it. There were millions of stars. You never really see them from here. Stella says it's because of the light pollution. Hey, did you know she's really smart? She's got an IQ that's like a billion or something. It's the highest in the school. She isn't allowed to tell anyone what it is because they might get all insecure and jealous. Mr. Hamm swore her to secrecy."

"Super," I said. I stared down at Kai's house. *You kissed*

me! I thought, looking in his window, even though I couldn't see anything due to the angle of the sun. *YOU KISSED ME!*

"Anyway, what are you doing up here?" she said.

"I'm working," I said. "Thinking is work when you are writing a book."

"What's your book about, anyway, kiddo?" she sighed.

"FREDDIE BLUE," I said. "It's an encyclopedia. You already know that."

"Duh," she said. "I knew THAT. I just forgot, I guess. Are you almost done?"

"Never mind," I said.

"Huh," she said. "OK, be that way. So what's new? I mean, other than kissing Kai in the ice cream shop." She started to laugh violently, instantly getting the hiccups. *Hic. Hic. Hic.*

"Don't pee," I said. "You'll get me all wet."

"Gross," she said. "Don't be *hic* mean. Tell me what *hic* you did while I was gone. It's been ages. Have you been in the tree the whole time? Tinkers, you've GOT to be more sociable if we're going to be the *HIC* It Girls of our class. You know that." She burped. "There," she said. "That always fixes it. No one knows that, Tink. Except me." She smiled in the way that someone would smile if they'd just cured cancer or won the lottery, or both on the same day.

"The *Everybody* magazine thing is tomorrow," I said, to change the subject. I wanted to talk about it because I wasn't at all ready. And I didn't know what to do to get ready. Was readiness even required? What would FB do?

"It's tomorrow?" she said, like she was all excited. "You're soooooooo lucky."

Just then we saw Kai wheeling down the sidewalk toward our (OK, *his*) tree. The skateboard wheels made their gorgo ball-bearing-ish type noise on the pavement.

"I don't know why you don't like him," said Freddie Blue. "You still don't, right? I mean, nothing's changed? Even though you're all into boarding now?"

"Right," I said, even though just looking at him was making my hands shake. In the best way.[73]

He kissed me! Did I mention that? Kai *kissed* me!

"You know what?" Freddie Blue said. "He's a totes awesome boarder and I like his name. He's soooooo cute too, if you like the messy look."

"If you do," I parroted. I was having a hard time talking, to be honest.

"I do," she said dreamily, staring at Kai with the moo-moo eyes she usually saves for Seb and Lex. "I think I really do."

"What?" I said.

"I think I'm actually in love with him!" she squealed in a whisper, which only she can do. "My heart is totally racing!"

"So's mine!" I wanted to say. But I didn't. Because mine stopped racing and fell right out of the tree and rolled down the hill, where it was squashed flat by a bus. If Freddie Blue liked Kai again, I might as well be a piece of dryer lint being blown away by a strong wind.

She said, "I'm in *love*! Oh, this is awesome! It's exactly like falling, Tink. You'll understand when you're older. I just knew it would be like this."

---

73. In my experience, there are only three occasions that cause hand shaking: 1. Cold, 2. Anger, and 3. Totally Out-of-Control Crushes on the boy next door.

Which made me want to stick a sizzling-hot safety pin directly into the center of my palm.

Or hers.

FB was staring at Kai in a way that she probably imagined was "starry-eyed" but actually just made her look like she was having a seizure. "Well," she said. "I totally like him. I'm so glad you decided not to like him, Tink."

"Uh-huh," I said. There was a lump in my throat the size of a tumor. The sun glinted on her golden highlights and she looked prettier than she ever had before. What did I do? Did Freddie Blue just steal my boyfriend?[74] Or did I just hand him over without a fight?

What is wrong with me?

"*Grrr*," I said in my throat.

Freddie Blue started climbing down the tree, her hair shimmering in the wind.

"What is that sound?" she said from below me. "Did you hear that? I thought I heard a dog growling."

"I didn't hear anything," I managed to choke out. What was I going to say? "I was growling at you for stealing my not-boyfriend-who-kissed-me-in-the-ice-cream-shop?" I don't think so.

"See you, Tinkster!" she yelled from the ground. "I have to go call Stells and fill her in!"

"Uh-huh," I said. "Uh-huh." I swallowed. My throat hurt, like it was closing tight around the lump. Kai was gone. Freddie

---

74. NOT that he is MY BOYFRIEND. I get that. I know he kissed me for a reason and not because he liked me. I just thought maybe he did like me, after all, and that maybe he kissed me because he wanted to, but maybe I'm just making up a big story around something that didn't mean anything to anyone and I don't even know why I'm still talking about it and I'm going to stop NOW. I promise.

Blue was gone. It was just me, in my tree, feeling a thousand times more alone than I ever had before. And sort of sick.

With jealousy.

I was jealous about camping. Jealous about Stella. And 100 percent extra super jealous that Freddie Blue was going to win the Boyfriend Race, and not just with ANY boy, but with the boy who I was hoping would be mine: Kai.

Jealous, jealous, jealous.

Jealous.

"Jealous" is also one of those words that does not fit its meaning. The real word for "jealous" should have a lot of *k*'s and *h*'s in it and hard sounds, like a mouthful of chewed glass. The word "jealous" itself sounds more like the name of a dessert made from Jell-O and something delicious.

Unlike what jealousy actually is, which is the ugliest, worst feeling in the world.

See also Anderson, Freddie Blue; BFF; Boyfriend Race, The; Camping; Crush List; Everybody *Magazine.*

K

Kai

The boy next door. Blue-haired. Boarder.

In trying to write this entry, I've realized that I don't know his last name.

How could I have a crush on someone when I don't know his last name?[75]

Obviously, I don't have a crush on him at all and so it's perfectly OK that Kai is Freddie Blue's number one crush, and so he can't be mine.

There is nothing else I can say about Kai that you do not already know, as everything I know about him I have already written in this encyclopedia, thus guaranteeing that I will never let anyone read it, ever.

Seriously, did I say *you* could read this?

STOP RIGHT NOW.

See also Boy, Blue-Haired, Who Just Moved in Next Door; Copwell Beach; Crush List; Ice Cream Incident, The.

Karate

The sport of kicking wood and/or other people and breaking it/him/her.

My brothers have both taken karate, and as a result, Lex can chop a piece of wood in two with the side of his hand. Seb

---

75. I read somewhere that if you don't know what color someone's eyes are, then you don't love them. Not if you just can't tell, but if you say, "Oh, I LOVE so-and-so" and someone else says — and no, I don't know why they would, but just say hypothetically that they do — "What color are his/her eyes?" and if you don't KNOW, then you aren't really in love. Also, you look like a total doofus going, "Actually, I have no idea! Maybe blue! Or brown! Probably one or the other, or possibly green!" I do know that Kai's eyes are brown. That's something I know for sure. Which doesn't mean that I love him! It just means that I am very observant, which is a good skill for a writer to have.

sometimes karate kicks the door when he's mad. Once he put a hole in the wall with his foot, then got stuck there.

Neither of my brothers still takes karate, and there is still a gaping hole in the drywall downstairs to remind us of why this is the case.

Karma

Karma is when you do something unforgivable to someone else and then something rotten happens to you. Maybe you are riding your bike and you accidentally scrape the side of someone's car with your handlebars and you don't stop. Karma will fix you by inserting a pothole into the road in front of you, causing you to fall over your handlebars and scrape your nose on the pavement,[76] regardless of the fact that the owner of the car probably deserved to have it scraped. Karma is probably also at work when you steal your BFF's crush and destroy her completely, whether you mean to or not. I mean, who knows what karma has in store for someone like *that*?

I have obviously stacked up some bad karma because today is the *Everybody* photo shoot and I have a pimple in my nose cleavage[77] that is the same size as my right nostril, but because of where it is located, it is actually pushing my nostril over, giving me one normal nostril, one half nostril, and one giant boil. That's right. A nostril-sized pimple.

"Impossible!" you say. And you are wrong. It is possible.

It is so large, it hurts. I think it might have its own heart because I can feel it pulsing. A nostril-sized boil is a perfect

---

76. Yes, OK, fine, this did happen to me. But the car belonged to Mrs. O'Malley. As I'm sure you understand, my instinct was not to ring her doorbell and explain the situation. Rather, it was to pedal away quickly. My nose still has a scar if you look at it in certain lights.
77. That crack between your nostril and the rest of your face, otherwise called Nostril Valley.

beginning to any day, especially a day when you are going to be photographed for a national magazine. Glam!

"Thank you, O Mighty Fate!" I said out loud after I finished examining my nose in the mirror. I should add that Fate is in charge of Karma, and tempting it is stupidly asking for capital-T Trouble. I stomped down the stairs for breakfast. *Stomp, stomp, stomp.* No one was still at the table, which was littered with filthy dishes covered with egg smears and toast crusts. Gross. I made a smoothie and drank it on the Itchy Couch, with only Hortense for company.

"We're going to be famous," I told her. She stared at me through slitted eyes. "Cats everywhere will want to be your friend," I said. "They won't really like you, though. They will just be using you because you're in a magazine." She licked her paw scornfully and blinked.

"Fine," I said. "Be that way."

The room was still and empty.

"I'm going out!" I shouted. No one answered. I left my empty smoothie glass on the kitchen table with the rest of the mess. Mom was going to have a fit when she saw that disaster area, and I know I should have tidied it up. I just . . . couldn't. I could only hope that the fickle hand of Fate wasn't actually going to punch me directly in the solar plexus.

I marched myself directly to Freddie Blue's house. I didn't have a choice. Even with the Kai situation bubbling and boiling in the background and twisting my stomach into knots, the truth was that I still needed FB. She would be able to help me. She might be the only one who would *want* to help me.

FB lives exactly eleven and a half blocks away, which is very close when you are in an air-conditioned car, but may as well be in outer Swaziland when you are walking in a heat wave.

By the time I arrived, sweat had trickled into my inflamed zit, swelling it to the size of a piece of fruit, such as a cherry or even a kumquat. It stung. I would have cried, but I didn't have enough moisture left to make tears.

Freddie Blue's mom let me in. I pretended to not notice her noticing my nose, but I know she did. Her eyes were wide with shock. "Hello," I said. "Excuse me." I stomped past her and up to Freddie's room, ready to have her make me laugh and feel better and pretend she didn't notice the fruit-like growth on my nostril.

"Hey!" I said. "Check this thing out on my nose."

Freddie Blue waved at me, with her now patented[78] Swatting Away an Annoying Fly hand-flappy gesture.

"What are you doing?" I said. I may have gotten the signal wrong, I thought. Maybe she was choking on a fish bone, or worse! "Are you OK?" Then I noticed that she was on the phone, mostly because she started pointing at it frantically and mouthing "HANG ON" in this overly fake, weird way that would have been funny if it weren't so rude.

I flopped down on Freddie Blue's perfect bed to wait. Her bed was the most comfortable bed in the world, and the prettiest. It looked like a bed in a catalog and not like a real bed at all.

I closed my eyes and tried to not listen to what she was saying, which was impossible. I cracked my eyes open and looked at her. She was making more wild hand gestures, as if she were signaling that there was an earthquake coming and I should run for my life. I nodded politely and went back to closing

---

78. It's only patented because she keeps doing it to the point where it has become her signature gesture. I do not know if she is aware of this or not, but I'm sure she is. Actually, I'm pretty sure she practices it in the mirror. It is getting very refined for an offhand gesture.

my eyes and trying not to listen. She was rhapsodizing about a purple top that she saw in a store when she was shopping with her dad that was "totally to die for, like death on a stick gorgeous."

I opened my eyes and rolled them at no one in particular. Death on a stick? What?

Finally, she hung up and went, "Now, Tink, what's up?" As though I was just the next thing on her list. The way she was looking at me reminded me of how the school secretary, Mademoiselle Oiseaux, looked at me when I was sent to the office — a blank look that said, "I am a professional and you do not interest me, you teensy speck of human dust, and I am also French and very sophisticated!"

It hurt my feelings, I don't mind telling you, both when Mademoiselle Oiseaux did it and then when Freddie Blue did it.

"I . . ." I started. "I don't know. I guess I should go. I mean, it's the photo shoot." I shrugged, like it was every day that a national magazine popped over to take photos of me and my insane family, and not like I'd come all the way over here so she could help me how to figure out how to *be* and what to do.

"Oh, kiddo," she said. "Don't look so bummed out! We'll make you look super glam and I know just the —"

Then her phone rang again. And she held up one finger — EXACTLY LIKE MADEMOISELLE OISEAUX WOULD — in a gesture that said, "Hang on, someone more important wishes to communicate with me regarding purple articles of clothing! Oooh la la! *Je suis le* best of *le* best!"

I got up from her bed, where I'd been sweating a dent into her perfect white comforter. I pulled it smooth a bit and then I turned and ran out of the room, down the stairs, and out of the house.

She didn't come after me. I waited just to see if she would. I mean, I thought she would.

And she didn't.

It occurred to me that I was often running out of rooms, alone, and not being followed.

I started to run again, but I couldn't run for very long because it was super sticky, icky hot and I didn't want to actually die.[79] Finally, I slowed to a walk. But instead of walking home, I went to Drop Mac Park.

I wished I had a board, but I didn't. So I found a patch of shade and just listened to the soothing sounds of boards clattering up and down the ramps. Watching other people skating was almost as fun as doing it myself.

I wished Kai was there because I thought maybe he'd get it. He'd get why I was upset. Wouldn't he?

I watched and listened until my heart stopped racing and I felt like I wasn't breathing through a straw. I felt OK.

It was just a zit.

It was just how Freddie Blue is.

It was just a stupid photo that no one would see.

It was *just*.

I'm more scared of karma than I am of anything else. Maybe all this is happening because I deserve to have bad stuff happen to me. Maybe I did something really awful once, and I don't even know what it was, and now it's all coming back to me like a nicely wrapped Christmas parcel full of sadness.

---

79. Don't take this the wrong way, but I am super curious about what happens when you die. I don't want you to think I am suicidal, because I'm not, but I'd like to try dying for, say, ten seconds, just to see if it's like a LIGHT or HEAVEN or just a bunch of nothingness that's like a bog of black paste, sucking you in and down into a void where you lie, bored senseless, for eternity.

You'd think I'd remember if I'd done something that terrible, though, wouldn't you?

See also Anderson, Freddie Blue; BFF; Crush List; Drop Mac Park; Everybody *Magazine*; Kai.

King, Stephen

The author of many, many scary books that you should not read after dark when you are alone, unless you want to be so frightened that for the next fourteen years, you dream about man-eating strawberry pies.

See also Books; Dark.

Kissing

The act of pressing your mouth on someone else's and squishing it around in a way that is a lot better than it sounds.

I have nothing to say about kissing that I haven't already told you. You are obsessed with kissing! It's none of my business, but you might have a problem.

See also Ice Cream Incident, The; Janowicky, Austin; Kai.

Knife

A sharp, bladed thing usually used to cut meat or cheese or to spread butter on toast or even to sharpen pencils in a pinch when the sharpener is lost, which pencil sharpeners always are. Also, the way in which we here at the sophisticated Aaron-Martin household start our car. Resulting in a frantic search each morning for the one specific knife that fits in Mom's ignition, in addition to the usual frantic search for her glasses and her keys.

K

Koan

A koan is a riddle that you can't solve. It's a Buddhist word. My mom is a Buddhist, which I may or may not have mentioned before. What it means is that we have a statue in the garden of a very fat, nearly naked man with an unusual hairstyle, and she frequently mutters things under her breath about choosing not to suffer.

Until I met Kai, I did not know how a koan applied to real life. Now I think that I do. Here is the unsolvable riddle: Why do I sometimes like-like a boy with blue, tufty hair who in no way resembles Prince X, who I always thought was my true love? And why do I sometimes act weird around him and feel like all I want to do is get away from him?

It's not really a riddle because there is no highly amusing answer that makes you gasp and clutch your sides, going, "Oh! I should have known! A NEWSPAPER! How hilair!"

In this case, the answer to the koan is _____. A Buddhist would find that funny. Because it's an answer that is not an answer! Buddhists are very much into answering questions with blanks, I think, which may or may not make Lex the world's first accidental Buddhist.

I actually don't understand Buddhism at all.

See also Kai.

L

Lame

A word meaning "worthless," "weak," or "otherwise awful."

Things that are lame can sweep through your life like a bad weather system, raining lameness down on every single one of your lame surfaces until you are so soaked with lame that there is no hope of anything ever being unlame ever again.

Lame, lamer, lamest, and lamosity are all related words. When something is extra lame, it's important to double the word: lame-lame. The lamosity of this entry is trumped only by the lame-lameness of my lame existence.

As in, "Wow, that photo shoot was lame-lame." Or "Golly, that photo shoot was a swirling swamp of lamosity." Or the like.

See also Everybody *Magazine.*

Leg Shaving

I started shaving my legs when I was pretty young, like eleven. This is not because I'd hit puberty, but because I am a very hairy person.

Shaving my legs is the first thing that I did before Freddie Blue did. She did not have bad enough leg hair to need to shave until this year.

The first time I shaved my legs, I cut them so badly I thought I'd have to go to the hospital for a transfusion, which is when they fill you up with bags of someone else's blood to make up for all the blood you lost from your cut-up legs. Someone else's blood equals someone else's DNA. Then what? Do your own cells start to mutate?

Obviously, people have transfusions all the time and do not metamorphose into anyone else, but it would be much more interesting if they did. If that happened, I would immediately sign up for a transfusion from someone who had truly awesome hair, tall genes, and good karma.

See also Karma.

Lips, Phillip

Photographer for *Everybody* magazine, guaranteed to be unlike anyone you've ever met before in your life, unless the people in your life are all insanely theatrical, annoyingly ingratiating photographers from Seattle with comically over-blown lips.

"CALL ME LIPS!" he said at least twenty times after he flung open the front door without knocking and marched himself directly into our living room, where I happened to be lying on the Itchy Couch, sweating and minding my own business, while all around upstairs, I could hear my family crashing around in a panic of "getting ready."

"Uh," I said. Which is all I could say. Because I couldn't think of anything except his lips. He had the biggest lips in the world. They looked like a lip-shaped helium balloon that had randomly landed on his face and would float him upward into space if someone were to let go of the string.

"You are a gorgeous little thing!" he shouted in my face. "Kudos!"

"Um," I said. "Thanks, I guess."

"You should be a MODEL!" he shrieked. "Too short, what a shame! A shame! But kudos! The hair! KUDOS! Your eyes! LOVE them!"

"Uh," I said.

"She could use some makeup," said my mom, appearing gracefully out of thin air, looking as cool and unruffled as anyone who was just screaming, "WHERE ARE MY GLASSES? PUT THAT CAT IN THE BATHROOM AND LOCK THE DOOR!" can look.

"Not very chatty, is she?" he said to my mom, who nodded and smiled. She looked so glam, she could have been on the cover of the magazine and people would have bought it by the millions. He turned back to me. "Off you go, sweetie, go get changed! Angel here will help sort you out!"

Angel was in charge of the clothes, which made sense, because she was wearing about twelve layers of them. She smelled like lemons and moved and talked so fast, I could hardly keep up. She was a human hurricane! A gale force! I swear, I could feel the air whooshing around me!

I emerged from the whirlwind wearing a puffy shirt.

A puffy PIRATE shirt.

A puffy YELLOW PIRATE SHIRT.

Not that anyone would notice what I was wearing. Like Pip's lips, it was impossible for anyone to look at anything that wasn't the zit on my nose.

"Tink," said my mom. "We HAVE to do something about that monster zit! Come to the bathroom with me."

At that second, the phone rang.

"Hello?" I said.

"It's me," said Freddie. "Look, where did you go? I'm sorry I was on the phone. It was, like, super important."

"What," I said. "Ever." Mom began gesturing wildly at my nose. I ignored her.

"Don't be mad," FB said. "I just had to tell Stella[80] about

---

80. Yes, THAT Stella. Please rate the relative horribleness of your BFF striking up a friendship

this fabu glam purple shirt my dad is going to get me for Tuesday."[81]

"Gosh, how terrific," I said, with as much licorice-y sarcasm as I could muster. "I have to go because there is a photographer here from *Everybody* magazine waiting to take my picture."

"Oh," she said. "Great! I'm right outside your house. I'm coming in."

"Don't!" I said. But it was too late. There she was.

"Wow, Tink," she said, peering at me so closely I could smell her minty breath. "That is a huge pimple."

"I know," I said frostily. "You should go, it's family only. Um, a closed set. You know."

"Don't be silly, Tink!" Mom laughed. "Of course she can stay."

"No, she cannot," I said.

"She could be in the picture," said Lips. "She's very pretty. Kudos! Too bad she isn't the sister!"

"NO!" I shouted.

"Why are you shouting?" said Lex, wandering in casually, looking like he was about to go strolling on a Caribbean beach. Why he got to wear sophisto clothes and I had to look like a buttercup-yellow pirate who was about to burst into a merry song was a mystery to me.

"Go away!" I said, to no one in particular.

"We have to shoot while the light is still good," said Pip the Lips. "Outside, I think. Let's go!"

---

with your WEE (Worst Enemy Ever) on a scale of one to ten. If you said TEN, you win a lovely parting gift. If you said anything OTHER than ten, go take this book immediately to the recycling or delete it, if you happen to be reading it on an e-reader, because YOU DO NOT GET IT OR UNDERSTAND ME IN ANY WAY and so you are wasting your time. Thank you.
81. Tuesday, in case you are keeping track, is our first day back at school.

"I can't stay," said Freddie Blue. "I'm meeting someone? Someone who is a *boy*."

Lex laughed. "Nice work, Frank," he said. Then for no reason that I could ascertain, he did an armpit fart. To her credit, Freddie Blue looked slightly disgusted.

"Aren't you too young to date?" said my mom.

"Date?" I said.

"Oh, it's not a date," said Freddie Blue. "I'm just . . . it's just Kai. See you." And she was gone, slamming the door behind her.

My heart fell all the way through my body, out the soles of my feet, and through the floor to the basement, where it got on Dad's Harley and rode away forever. I let Mom put seven layers of face paste onto my zit, effectively molding me a new nose out of foundation. I looked completely ridiculous but I no longer cared. I didn't care about anything: the zit, the shirt, the world, Pip's lips. Nothing.

I was too depressed.

Too depressed to even be amused when the camera appeared and Seb, who apparently can change his mind about more than one thing, said, "Cool, is that a Nikon blah blah blah 19238 XLDSL whatever?"

Because apparently, when I wasn't looking, Dad promised to buy him his own incredibly expensive and fancy camera as a "reward" for putting up with the photo shoot, which the rest of us ALSO have to put up with, with no reward, because we don't need rewarding, as we do not have autism.

Stab, stab, stab. That is the sound of me stabbing something painfully into something. I don't even know what (or who) to stab in this instance. But I would like to say, for the record, that I would also like a fancy camera.

If anyone asks.

Which they won't.

So then I spent the afternoon pretending to enjoy Frisbee and cold drinks with my family in oddly posed, frozen tableaus.

"FREEZE!" Lips shouted. "Oh, that's perfect. Kudos! I'm just going to . . ." Then he would walk over and artfully rearrange every single person's limbs. It was very trying for all of us, especially He Who Cannot Be Stressed.

That's right. Seb.

So it was just a matter of time before Seb accidentally threw a Frisbee into Dad's eye, hard, and while Mom was bending over to see if he was OK, Dad dumped his pretend cold drink on her hair. But the pretend cold drink was made out of some kind of icky gel, which ruined Mom's hair. Like, really ruined it. As in, she'll probably have to cut that goo out of her hair with shears.

Then Seb started hopping around. "I'm done," he said. "I'm done."

"KUDOS!" shrieked Pip the Lips. "YOU ARE ALL SO FABU! Especially you boys! And Mom! And Dad!"

"Gee, thanks," I mumbled, quietly on purpose so he couldn't hear me.

"Gee, thanks," Seb mimicked. Loudly.

"Don't mimic me!" I said.

"Don't mimic ME!" he said.

"Don't mimic ME," I yelled.

"Don't yell at me!" he yelled back.

"Everyone calm down," Mom said. "We have to enter into our stages."

"Tink!" yelled my Dad. "You are the Peacemaker!"

"That's so stupid, Dad!" I yelled. "I'm just a kid!"

And then I held my breath until I fell over.

"I'm done," said Lips just as Seb decided to take off running somewhere. Nowhere. Anywhere. Who cares where? "Kudos to you all! Will send you proofs! Much love! *Besos, besos!*"[82]

Lex took off after Seb.

"Thanks so much for coming," said Mom.

"Will my black eye be edited out?" said Dad. "I mean, if the shot you use was post-injury?" He laughed wryly as though to say, "This isn't funny, but I'm such a good sport!" when I know he really was worried that he was finally going to be in *Everybody*, but looking like a victim of a terrible crime and not like a pseudo-movie star.

Pip the Lips appeared not to hear the question. Or maybe he was just choosing not to answer. Which meant the answer was, "No! The black eye will not be edited out!"

"Dread," I said. "Dreaded, most dreadful, dreadest."

And I wasn't just talking about the shoot, I was also talking about FB. And Kai. FB and Kai TOGETHER. Where did they go? What were they *doing*?

I went inside. Something was making me dizzy. The sun or the breath holding or the pretending. Or maybe it was just something else. Something to do with a certain BFF whose initials were FBA.

Probably not, though.

See also *Autism;* BFF; Everybody *Magazine; Haywire; Karma.*

---

82. Spanish word for "kisses," which I know because I love Spanish. If you are looking for a language to learn, try it! It's the best. If only I could speak Spanish all the time, I think my life would be a lot prettier and more romantic.

Lurk

A skateboarding word that means "looking around for really awesome places to skate that are not really meant to be skate-boarding parks," which I learned yesterday when Ruth called and said, "Hey, Tink, want to go lurk?"

And I said, "Sure!"

Except I had no idea what she meant, and so when I met her at the corner, I didn't have my board. I looked like an idio, which was fine, because I'm used to looking like an idio. Ruth just laughed because she thought I'd forgotten and then went on to tell five different stories about how she has also forgot-ten really obvious things, such as to put on her shoes before school. Then she came back home with me so that I could get my board. I think she never once stopped talking, except when she did three cartwheels in a row on the sidewalk and finished with a round-off. She is a very flippy person.

It actually used to be that I couldn't decide if she was hilarious or just weird, but now that I know her better, I'm going to say "totally and completely hilair."[83] And I don't care what FB says.

We ended up at an empty swimming pool next to the old community center. It had a deep curve that was perfect for the swoop, in a dizzying-drop kind of way. We rolled back and forth for ages until finally an elderly woman, who I'm pretty sure was Mrs. O'Malley's evil twin, came along and shouted,

---

83. I laughed so hard that I almost peed my pants, which has never, not even once happened to me from laughing. But the funnier thing (in a not actually funny way) was that when that happened, it made me think of Freddie Blue (Queen of the Pee Pants) and then right away I felt bad that I was lurking with Ruth and not FB. I felt like a bad friend, and also like RUTH was bad for taking me away from FB, and then the mood changed horribly and I ended up pretending I had a headache and going home, even though *lurking* was the best fun ever and I did a perfect ollie. OK, NOT a perfect ollie. But something that, from a distance, if you didn't know better, you might have thought was an ollie-like move.

"I'm gonna call the cops on you rabble-rousers! You have no respect for community property!" As if the swimming pool, which was cracked and featured graffiti and ragweed, was going to be further damaged by our mad skillz.

Another word for "lurk" is "going on a skafari," which is really more awesome but didn't fit alphabetically. I am nothing but devoted to the art of encyclopedia writing, so I had to fit it in here. You're welcome.

See also Boarding, Skate.

M

Magazines

A soon-to-be-antiquated glossy book produced monthly or weekly, consisting nearly wholly of ads and pictures of celebrities in their bathing suits kissing their boyfriends/girlfriends du jour while enjoying relaxing beach vacations that they are sharing with the 103 paparazzi who are photographing them for the magazines. Magazines will go the way of the dodo soon because everyone has the Internet and it is much quicker to get instant, up-to-the-minute celeb facts from the Web than it is to wait for someone to bother to print up something that you only have to recycle later.

Now that I've been a part of the world's worst, ugliest photo, I want nothing more to do with magazines. In fact, if I find out tomorrow that magazines are gone forever, I will celebrate with a small party where I invite all my friends and we drink Kool-Aid and eat white cupcakes with strawberries perched daintily on the top.

And now I have one more reason to hate magazines, *Everybody* in particular, but I am sure they are all Purveyors of Evil, so I'm willing to lump them all in together in one giant, sweeping generalization of lameosity.

One word: *Interview.*

Here's what happened:

I was in the kitchen, blending up frozen hunks of organic strawberries, mangoes, and bananas for a smoothie,[84] when

---

84. This is truly the best smoothie of all time. You also need some high fat, very tasty vanilla-flavored yogurt, some milk, and a large handful of ice cubes. Blend until PERFECT, as in "no ice chunks." Enjoy!

Dad came into the room looking pretty pleased with himself. "Hi, Tink," he said.

"Hi," I said. "What are you being all happy about? Tell me right now."

"I just finished the interview with the *Everybody* writer for the piece that's going to go with the pictures," he said. "It went really well. I think you're going to love it. The reporter was so nice. I really felt like a celebrity. Isn't that funny? Who would have thought. I'm right chuffed, actually."

"I highly doubt that I'll like it," I said.

He went on like I'd said nothing. "Your mom did such a good job too. Oh, and the boys were stars! Really brilliant. You never know what they are going to say. Unpredictable sorts, as you know. But, man, I'm just . . ."

"I guess they didn't want to talk to *me*," I said. I was pretending not to be hurt, but I was hurt. I WAS HURT! I am part of this family too! I said it out loud, "I AM PART OF THIS FAMILY TOO!" But he continued blithely on.

"There wasn't even a single outburst," he said. "Seb was just right on about everything. Yes! Can't believe it, Tink. So great."

Maybe I'd been struck mute in the night, I thought. But that couldn't be, because I could definitely hear my own voice. "Horse," I said. "Cow. Pig. Donkey." Yep, I definitely heard myself, yet Dad was still oblivious. I contemplated this while noisily blending my drink to an absolutely perfect, iceless smoothosity.

"We'll have the picture proofs tomorrow," he said.

"Whatever," I said. I poured him a glass of smoothie.

"Thanks!" he said. I smiled at him as sweetly as possible and we drank our smoothies in companionable silence that I didn't bother to fill, because there was clearly no point.

"I can't believe we're going to be in *Everybody*," he said wistfully. "Who would have thought it?"

"Mmf," I said.

And now YOU are welcome to hate *Everybody* magazine — and all magazines — as much as I do.

See also Celebrity; Everybody *Magazine; Fame.*

Malg

The opposite of glam. Also, glam backward. This word, "malg," is not catching on as quickly as "glam," although I predict that it is only a matter of time before it sweeps the nation.[85]

See also Glam.

Martin, Jenna (Mom)

Dr. Jenna Martin is my mom. She is a doctor in real life, as you know, although she looks like someone who would play a doctor on TV, and not like an actual doctor, which really is grossly unfair, if you think about it. You should either BE a doctor or PLAY a doctor on TV, but it is a terrible gene-pool discrepancy if you get to do both. Mom is a massive success at everything she does, from arranging her hair on her head, to her career, to her mystifying ability to win every board game she ever plays. Mom has never NOT succeeded, and she cannot even begin to understand how someone could just be straight-up terrible at something, such as life or ballet.

Most times, when I introduce people to my mom, they say to me, "Oh, are you adopted?" I wish this was a lie for dramatic effect, but it's true. It has happened on at least seven different

---

85. Which will probably happen sometime around the first of Never, and/or when this book becomes a bestseller. That would be around the fifth of Never. Either way, sometime in the first week of Never, would be my best guess.

occasions. Luckily, I have a Patented Tink Aaron-Martin Stare down for just this occasion, which involves making half my face look unbelievably sad and the other half angry and scornful. When I say "half," I mean a top/bottom split, obviously, as it would be impossible to split your face vertically and have two different facial expressions on it.

Most of the time, I'm glad that Mom is my mom and not, say, FB's mom, who is flaky and often forgets to cook supper and/or offer supportive, loving advice to FB about how to be a good BFF. Mom could stand to be a little less quick on the "YOU'RE GROUNDED" button, but mostly she's OK. She is really, really, really amazing with Seb. Sometimes. I know Dad means well and tries his best, but Mom is really magical with him when he's haywire. Seb is crazy about Mom. He'd do anything for her. He says she's the only one who really gets him, and he's probably right.

I remember once I asked Mom if I was going to be autistic when I grew up, like Seb.

She said, "No, Tink. Absolutely not."

That "No" made me feel fixed. Like she'd cured me with her "No"! I'd been worried, to tell you the truth. But she has a way of saying things that made them seem like very obvious and true facts. So while she didn't literally cure anything, because I didn't need "curing," she did, sort of, cure me anyway.

Mom makes really good caramel popcorn and terrible lasagna. We don't have lasagna very often, though, so it's really no big deal. And we don't have caramel popcorn as often as we should, if you ask me.

See also Ballet; Grounded.

Mega Mall

Like a regular mall, only much, much, much bigger, sometimes containing more than one of the exact same store, and up to six separate Starbucks. Embarrassing bastions to consumerism and pretty pointless places to hang out, but everyone does anyway, because where else can you go and just BE without having to do some kind of activity that requires more energy than sitting down to a big Diet Coke and a plate of fries?

I was in the Tree of Unknown Species, thinking about Freddie Blue Anderson and NOT thinking about Kai at all, even though I happened to be looking at his house at the time, when his mom pulled into the driveway, got out of her van, and proceeded to unload half the mall out of the back of it and into the front door.

Back-to-school stuff, I thought, and my heart dropped all the way to the bottom of the tree and boinged back up again, nearly knocking me to the ground from the impact. And at that exact second, I came up with the most brilliant, if awful, plan in the world to patch up my poor, damaged friendship with Freddie Blue and get back-to-school clothes at the same time.

The Mega Mall.

It would be an ADVENTURE. And an ADVENTURE is all we would need to get back to being just regular Tink and FB, like we always had been, BFFs 4eva, etc. We would not let a boy come between us! Even if he was the only boy I might ever really, really like! Even if he did hang out with FB during my moment of fame! And even if FB still hadn't told me what happened! It would all be perfect again!

Instead of what we had now, which was just an awkward love triangle where two of the points didn't even know they were part of the shape.

I climbed down the tree and marched into the house, tripping over Hortense and knocking over those stupid encyclopedias, which always seemed to be in the way. I found the phone stuffed between the cushions of the Itchy Couch and I called Freddie Blue.

"Hey," she said. "What up, sister?"

"Don't talk like that," I said. "It's sort of racist. You are the wrong color to call me 'sister.'"

"Oh, don't be so sensitive," she said. "It's boring. You are not the only nonwhite person in the world, you know."

"OK, OK," I said. There was a silence.

"I know, I know," she said. "You are dying to ask me about Kai and what we did. Well, guess what? It's a secret! My lips are sealed like an envelope."

"I don't care what you did," I lied.

"Oh," she said. "Are you sure?"

"FB," I said. "I'm sure."

"Well, sigh," she said.

"Look," I said. "I have an idea! It's for an adventure. We need an adventure, FB. We just do."

"I guess," she said. "I've been bored, I have to tell you. Bored, bored, bored."

"Um," I said. "OK. The idea is that we go to the mall and . . ."

And I told her.

My Big Idea.

My Really Big and (in retrospect) *Incredibly Stupid* Idea.

"Tink," she said. "You are totally an awesome geni."[86]

I hung up and right away began to get ready to sneak out into the night. Except it wasn't night, it was day. But "sneak out

---

86. "Geni" is a perfectly excellent example of how you cannot shorten certain words without sounding like a total idio.

into the day" just doesn't sound as good. And it wouldn't even be sneaking. But again, "sneaking" sounds more exciting, no?

It felt like sneaking, so it's really the same thing. My heart was already pounding like crazy and I was dripping with flop-sweat, which is the sweat you have when you are about to do something that is quite likely to fail dramatically. But I didn't care. It was awesome to be embarking on something with Freddie Blue. Like she and I were a team again! Like no boy was confusing everything! Like the old days.

It was the perf plan. MY plan: We were going to — on purpose — get locked in the department store at the Mega Mall overnight. We'd be able to try on all the clothes and shoes and even sleep in the beds that are all made up in the furniture department, while watching the big-screen TVs. They sell food on one floor, so we wouldn't go hungry. It was foolproof! We couldn't possibly get caught.[87]

We went to the mall at noon, for lunch. And to do our research, which mostly meant that we ate too much junk food and giggled. Even though I was desperate to ask her what happened with Kai, I didn't. Because I didn't really want to know, in case it wrecked *this*. I was seriously happy to be giggling with Freddie Blue. It felt right.

It felt normal.

Especially when she started to laugh when I tried to start a flash mob in the food court, and her Diet Coke came spraying out her nose, which hurt, so she started to cry, which was good — she said — because it stopped her from peeing in her pants.

"Flash mob!" she whispered, and we started laughing again. She probably would have peed that time if I hadn't

---

87. "We can't possibly get caught" is a sentiment once uttered by every idio who is now rotting away in the prison system for the rest of time, FYI.

suddenly heard a really familiar voice shouting, "ISADORA! WAIT UP!"

Freddie Blue didn't even turn around, because why would she? I think she's forgotten it's my name. But I turned around. My hands were insta-shaking. And there was Kai, waving like mad. He came over and he was all, "What are you girls doing?"

I couldn't look right at him. All I could think about was the ice cream shop and how one minute he was just standing there and the next minute, he was kissing me. *KISSING ME.* And then, next thing I knew, he was hanging out with Freddie Blue. All of a sudden, I wished I'd pressed her for details. Why didn't I? I was desperate to know! Why didn't she just TELL me? She knew I wanted to know! What kind of BFF was she?

And now was he looking at her funny? Was he looking at her at ALL?

He was mostly looking at me.

I could feel myself starting to blush from my feet up. My tongue felt like it had been stung by a bee. "Oh," I said. "You glbkr, we were just gjlkjw."

"Huh?" he said. "Are you OK, Is?"

Is! No one had ever called me a nickname based on my actual name before. I felt swoony. I glanced at Freddie Blue, thinking I'd give her the OMG HE IS SO CUTE look, when I realized that she was blushing. And smiling in a way I haven't seen her smile before. She bit her lip and flicked her hair back dramatically.

"Hey," I said, "what are you —"

She interrupted, "We were looking for little clothes for Tink. Because she's so . . . little. It's hard to find cool stuff in kids' sizes!"

"Freddie Blue," I started to say. But it didn't come out. Instead, I think my mouth just hung open in a way that suggested I might be dying, accompanied by a wheezing sound. I coughed to cover it up.

"Huh," Kai said. "I just grabbed some new jeans. I had to take back a bunch of stuff my mom bought this morning that was so hid. Like, hideous. You know? Unless I wanted to go to school looking like a junior stockbroker. My mom has NO idea. What can you do?"

He waved the bag in our faces and we were both so flustered that at the same time, we both said, "They're nice!" even though obviously we couldn't see them through the bag. I shot Freddie Blue my newly Patented Tink Aaron-Martin Stare of He Kissed Me First So I Have Dibs Even If You Tried To Steal Him When My Back Was Turned, which she didn't interpret right.

"You look weird," she said. "Are you getting a headache, Tink? We should get you home. But then we can't do our thing. That we're going to do." She looked at Kai and winked in a super-theatrical way.

"What are you going to do?" he said.

And before I could stop her, either with a look or by reaching up and clamping my hand over her big mouth, Freddie Blue had invited him to join us on our adventure, our TOP SECRET adventure, MY adventure.

While she talked (and talked and talked), I couldn't help but notice that she was taller than him. They just didn't look right together. I didn't think it made sense that he was her number one crush AT ALL.

"I think that . . ." I started to say, but then I stopped. I didn't know what I thought.

"Is it OK if I come too?" Kai asked. "It has to be OK with Isadora," he said firmly to Freddie Blue. "What do you say, Is?" He looked into my eyes and the cold bits of fear that were all around my heart melted instantly, like butter in the microwave.

"Yeah." I shrugged. "Sure. It will be . . . fun!" I was feeling something. Something I couldn't really describe, mostly because I didn't know what it was. Whatever the halfway point is between terrified and excited and confused and happy and upset and mad and giddy. I thought about how FB and I had each told our parents that we were sleeping over at each other's house. The oldest trick in the book! And how my mom had said, "Good! Have fun, you deserve it. I know things have been hard for you."

She was being so nice. I felt bad about the lie. I really did. But it's not like I could have told her the truth, even though I wished I could have.

"We're going to hide in the bathrooms," said Freddie Blue. "Just before closing."

"I think they check the bathrooms, though," said Kai. "I have a better idea."

Which is how we came to be hiding in the center of the round racks of sale clothes in the clearance section when the lights went off. We waited for what felt like seven hours, breathing in the horrible plastic smell of the awful material they use to make blouses[88] for elderly women. It was SO quiet in there, the quiet was like a blanket blocking out all the air, making me feel like I couldn't quite breathe. And I couldn't move.

---

88. Do you ever notice how the word "blouse" is never used to describe clothing on anyone under the age of eighty? Why is that? They are "shirts" until you are seventy-nine, then *poof*, they grow up to be "blouses"? How does that work?

Finally, I heard Freddie Blue pushing the clothes aside and tumbling onto the floor. "TINK!" she yelled. "KAI! COME OUT COME OUT WHEREVER YOU ARE! Hey, this is so great, we can play hide-and-seek and stuff." She giggled.

"Don't pee," I murmured. But for some reason, I still couldn't move. I stood there in the dark with all the toxic-smelling clothes pressing around me like a horrible predator's hug, and it occurred to me that I wouldn't be able to leave the store now, no matter what. What if something were to happen? The doors were all locked and probably had an alarm on them. We were trapped!

I started wigging out, trying to remember to breathe out through my mouth and in through my nose, when Kai stuck his head through the cushion of clothes.

"BOO!" he shouted.

"Ha-ha," I said flatly. I was still trying to figure out the whole breathing thing. In, out. Out, in. Too much, not enough.

I pushed the blouses aside and squeezed out, breathing deeply of air not polluted by plastic. I knocked some stuff onto the floor because I was hurrying. But picking things up gave me something to do, so I didn't mind. All of a sudden I felt really self-conscious and shy and like my arms weren't attached properly. I could feel Kai staring at me, and I sort of liked it and I also sort of didn't.

When I was done, we all stood there for a minute looking at each other like, "Wow, we did it!" After our eyes adjusted to the dark, it was really not so bad. The racks of clothes looked somehow smaller when there was no one else in the store. The EXIT sign glowed red. Everything was echoey and cave-like.

"Wow," said Kai. "This is . . . I wish I'd brought my board."

"Me too," I said.

"Oh, Tink," Freddie Blue laughed. "You don't have a board."

. "I do, sort of," I said. "I mean, I have Seb's."

"You do?" She stared at me. In the low lights, her eyes looked sad, but I'm sure it was just an illusion. "I didn't know that." She shrugged and kind of shook like Hortense does when she gets out of the bath. Then she screamed, "Whooo! Yahoo!" and started jumping around.

"Freddie Blue!" I said, like I could call her back to her normal self. She totally ignored me, and pulled a mannequin down and pretended to dance with it, all wild arms and legs.[89] I wanted to tell her to *shhh*, but I couldn't. I mean, she wouldn't have listened.

I looked at Kai. He looked . . . puzzled, I guess. He raised his eyebrows. I shrugged. "Woohoo!" I said halfheartedly, so it didn't seem like Freddie Blue was as crazy as she was acting.

"I don't think . . ." he said. Then he shrugged.

"What?" I said.

"Nothing," he said. He was standing so close to me, I could feel how warm his breath was. I shivered. He smelled like toothpaste and a bit like dryer lint, warm and dusty.

I started to walk, just to be doing something. Freddie Blue danced exuberantly over to the shoe department, singing. She seemed to know exactly what she was doing. She went right through the swingy, employee-only doors and vanished into the back part where all the sizes are stacked.

I couldn't believe she did that. Kai and I silently sat down on chairs and waited. It was awkward but it also wasn't.

---

89. I don't know if you read the book *Where the Wild Things Are* when you were a kid, but the way she was acting reminds me very much of a WILD RUMPUS. Watching a WILD RUMPUS is sort of embarrassing, like you feel like you should look away and yet also you know that the WILD RUMPUS is being put on for your benefit, so you are also obliged to watch.

Somehow the silence fit, or maybe Freddie Blue was just being noisy enough for all of us. Finally, Kai blurted, "I saw you and Ruth at the old pool."

"You did?" I said. "Why didn't you come and, um, lurk? That would have been OK."

"I don't know." He shrugged. "Look," he said. "I'm kind of . . . feeling . . . bad about the whole ice cream thing? Because I . . . you seemed really mad or something? And so I just want to, like, say sorry right now, and I'm really sorry, Is. I am. I don't want it to be, like, awkward."

It doesn't sound sweet when I'm telling it now, but when he said it, it was all I could do to not run through the swingy door and report it all word for word to FB. Of course, she wouldn't be happy for me now, would she? She might do something weird, or loud, or make it something dumb instead of something great. I sighed.

"You're still mad," he said. "Great."

"No!" I said. "No, not mad. It's OK. Really. Don't even . . . it's fine. I wasn't mad. I mean, I was. But now I'm not." I smiled, really smiled. "I'm not mad, Kai," I said. "Awkward is the worst. Let's not be awkward."

"Oh," he said. "Cool, because I was going to ask you —"

But I don't know what he was going to ask because just then, Freddie Blue came leaping back through the swinging door, which flapped open and shut behind her like one giant hand, clapping. She had so many boxes in her arms, they were spilling out and falling on the floor.

"Grab some!" she yelled. "Tink, help me!"

I picked up a box of sparkly green sandals.

"Oooh, aren't those just to die?" she shrieked. "They look like mermaid shoes. So awesome."

"Mermaids don't have feet," I pointed out.

She glared at me. "Give them back," she said. "You're just jealous that you didn't find them first. I think they are glam to the max!"

"Sorry," I said. Even though I wasn't.

"They could, like, wear them on their hands maybe?" said Kai.

"Not funny," said Freddie Blue, shoving them onto her feet. She teetered around on them up and down an aisle. They looked completely ridic.

"Glam," I lied.

"I love these sooooo much," she said. "If they were a boy, I would totally make out with them. They make my ankles look so super skinny."

Kai bit his lip. I could tell he was trying not to laugh. I looked away. I knew if I looked at him, then it would be him and me having a joke at FB's expense, and I couldn't do that. She was my BFF, after all. Even if she was acting completely insane and annoying me to the max.

The even dumber thing was that Freddie Blue was lying. Everything she was doing was a big, fat lie. She was not really having fun, I could tell. She was just pretending to have fun, like she was auditioning for a role in a movie as the zany, fun girl, only she was a terrible actress and the audience was getting uncomfortable and wanted to leave the theater. It was fake fun!

I was not having fun either. I felt like I was trying to act normal, and by trying to be normal and be myself, I was acting like someone else entirely. I breathed in through my nose and out through my mouth, then reversed that because I'd forgotten which way around it was supposed to be to be calming. Either way, it wasn't working at all. I was just getting more anxious.

"I'm hungry," said Kai. "Can we find some food or something?" He pretended to eat a shoe. I smiled, but Freddie fell on the ground laughing.

I wondered if maybe she'd inhaled too many blouse fumes. Maybe she needed medical attention! She definitely needed *some* kind of attention. And a lot more than her share.

Kai walked toward the food department. The store sadly lacked a café, but it did sell candy and whatnot. I waited until he was a bit ahead of us and I grabbed her arm. "Hey," I whispered. "Calm down, OK? You seem a bit . . . crazy."

"CRAZY?" she repeated. "You think I seem crazy? I'm just having fun, Tink. You could try to have some too. This was your idea, remember? It isn't an adventure if you just stare and look annoyed, you know. It's just . . . dumb. And BORING."

"I . . ." I said. "Sorry."

"Boring is worse than anything," Freddie Blue declared. "Boring is worse than dead."

Kai yelled, "Are you guys coming? I'm starving."

"OK, OK, keep your shirt on," said FB, grabbing my hand. "Come on, Tink."

We climbed up a nonmoving escalator. It felt odd to use an escalator when it wasn't working, like somehow time had stopped.

"Hey, Isadora," said Kai. "What's your fave candy here?" He waved at the wall of candies. I stared at them. In the dark, they all looked the same.

"Licorice," I said finally, and he handed me a little bag of licorice jelly beans that he'd weighed on the scale.

"Hey, Kai," said Freddie Blue. "Did you know my real name is Frederique?"

"Yeah, that's what I figured, Freddie," he said. "Do you want me to grab you some stuff?"

"Skittles, please," said FB. She smiled. "You're so cool, Kai, to grab those for me."

"Whatever." He shrugged. "They're right here."

He weighed them and then wrote down the weight on a little piece of paper and put it in his pocket, like he was doing something secret. The way he did it seemed like he didn't want me to ask, so I didn't, but I bet he was thinking exactly what I was thinking: If we wrote down how much we ate, we could pay for it tomorrow.

Somehow. I wasn't exactly sure how. But I smiled at him for real.

I chewed on those jelly beans until I started to feel sick, which was almost right away. There was nothing to drink and I was parched. This adventure was turning out to be pretty icky.

"Let's go watch a movie or something," Kai suggested. He was holding his stomach, so I guessed that he felt totally sick too. (He ate a bag of licorice allsorts, so I'm not surprised he felt sick. Those are the most disgusting candies in the universe.) Freddie Blue, on the other hand, seemed totally unaffected.

"Aw," she said. "That's boring. I want to explore! Come on, it's an adventure! We can watch movies at home." She yawned with exaggerated boredom. "Borsk," she said. "That's my new word for boring," she added. "Totes borsk."

"Oh," said Kai. "But we aren't at home."

"Exactly!" she said. "So we should explore. Right, Tink?"

I shrugged. Personally, I was dying to watch a movie *with Kai*. And explore what? We were locked in the department store, sure, but we'd pretty much seen it all when it was open. There wasn't much left to see.

"I kind of want to watch a movie," I ventured.

"Ugh." She rolled her eyes so hard they nearly stuck at the top of her sockets. "You two are lame." She turned on her heel and flounced off. "Catch you lame lamers LAMER," she shouted. "I mean, LATER."

I giggled. I knew she was mad. I should have cared, I guess. But it all seemed fake! Super extra fake with a side of fake! And I just wanted to sit next to Kai and see what happened next. We looked at each other and raised our eyebrows in a look that said, "Well?" and then I started to laugh for real, only it was sort of a mix of a laugh and a cry, but I don't think he could tell. I'm pretty sure he thought I was just howling with laughter. I wiped my eyes.

"Yeah," he said, and scratched his head. "I don't know."

We tiptoed over to electronics. It was so shadowy in there that "quiet" just seemed much more right than "loud and screaming." Unfortunately, they hadn't thoughtfully set up a couch or something in front of the TVs. I guess they didn't want people resting there instead of shopping. We had to sit on the floor. Kai was pretty quick to figure out how to get the DVD player working, but the only movie we could find without breaking open a new one, which seemed a bit too much like stealing, if you ask me, was *Finding Nemo*.

"I hate fish," I whispered.

"Why?" he whispered back.

"Um," I said. "Well. I don't know. Because of their little mouths?"

"Their little mouths?" he said. He frowned. "That makes no sense! The little ones don't even have teeth! What are they going to do, like, nibble you to death?"

I laughed. "I know!" I said. "It's dumb. But sort of, yes! Nibble me to DEATH!"

Then he laughed too. "Their little mouths!" he said again.

"No!" I said. "Seriously, in Malaysia they have these foot bathtub things where you can pay to stick your feet in and the fish . . ." I could hardly finish the sentence. "The fish EAT the dead skin of your feet! Ack!"

"The dead skin?" he repeated, wiggling his eyebrows at me.

Then we were both laughing so hard that we flopped over, and somehow he was leaning on me. I could feel his heart beating against my shoulder. I froze for a second, then I sat up and put the movie in.

In and out, I breathed. Out and in. Mouth, nose. Nose, mouth.

As soon as the movie started, the funny feeling I'd been having all night crashed over me like a freak wave, the kind that sweeps innocent beachgoers out to sea, never to be seen again. Was he going to try to hold my hand? What if he did? What if he didn't? What if Freddie Blue saw? What if she didn't see? What if she still had a crush on Kai? I wanted to fast-forward to the moment just to see what was going to happen, and then rewind it back and do it again slowly and in a not-so-entirely-freaked-out-way.

Not that anything was going to happen.

He wasn't going to kiss me or anything.

Right?

We watched quietly for a while. I was super-extra-not-comfortable, but I didn't want to move. It was like moving would have drawn too much attention to me or something. I sat frozen in place while he moved around. He lay first on his front, then his back, then his side, then he sat up, then he lay down again. Both my legs went to sleep and started to tingle. I worried where Freddie Blue was.

"I wonder if Freddie Blue . . ." I said. "I think we should maybe go and —"

"Huh?" said Kai. "Hang on, I love this part."

I looked at the screen. The Dad fish was yelling at the Nemo fish, not because he was really mad, but because he was so happy he had found him. Kai sniffed.

"Are you crying?" I said. "Seriously?"

"No!" he said. "I just . . . no. I mean, I think it's . . . he found his kid, that's all. And he's all, like, so happy to see him. You can tell how much he loves his kid, right? It's just . . . what? Don't look at me like that! I'm not crying!"

"I'm sorry," I started. But I didn't know how to finish it. I felt kind of like an alien who had just landed here on Earth, and even though I spoke the language, I didn't know how to put sentences together. I wanted to say something perfect, to make him feel better. "I like Ellen," I said. "She's funny."

"Yeah," he said. He reached over, like he was going to hold my hand.

But then.

He suddenly sat bolt upright. I thought he must have heard something. "What?" I said.

And he leaned right into my face. And he kissed me.

"!" I said. Not that "!" is a word, but if it was, that's what I would have said.

Instead I said, "What's with you and the kissing?"

"I don't know," he said. He looked embarrassed. "I'm sorry."

"No!" I said. "Don't be sorry! I like it! I mean, I like you! I mean —"

But I didn't have time to say anything else because at that exact moment we heard voices. Loud voices. Not just Freddie Blue, but someone else. And Freddie Blue sounded scared.

My first thought was *Gadzooks, it's an ax murderer!* But if it was an ax murderer, Freddie Blue wouldn't be talking, and she was talking a lot. Kai and I looked at each other and I could tell that I was blushing all the way past the roots of my hair. I hoped he couldn't see it. If I blushed any harder, I'd likely spontaneously combust. And that would be harder to hide.

We didn't move. I didn't move because I couldn't, due to the fact that my legs were asleep. And he didn't move because he was scared. I could tell he was. I didn't blame him, with parents like his. I'd be grounded, but it would be worse for him. His whole body curled inward and cringed.

"I'm sorry," I whispered.

He shrugged. His face got a little tough and the voices got closer and closer. And the next thing we knew, a really bright flashlight was shining at us and a voice was saying, "You kids are in so much trouble."

"Uh-oh," I said.

Kai grabbed my hand, hard. I somehow got to my feet and so did he. I could see that Freddie Blue was crying like mad, but when I caught her eye, she winked at me so I knew it was all part of her act.[90]

Why we hadn't thought about security patrols, I had no idea. We aren't dumb people! We are gifted! We go to Cortez! With the combined "gifted" thoughts of all three of us, you'd

---

90. Everything seemed like it was an act with her lately, and this was just like the grand finale or something. I didn't know whether to clap or cry, really.

think we would have come up with "security guard patrols."
But apparently not.

And then it was too late.

As you've probably guessed, my mom and dad were not
very happy to be woken up at midnight with the news that their
daughter was at the police station, which is where they took
us because they apparently had had a lot of trouble with kids
sleeping in the store lately and they were going to make "an
example" of us. I was super scared. Kai and I were both crying.
Freddie Blue took a different approach[91] and was saying things
like, "My dad is a judge, he'll get me off the charges!"

I can only guess that no other major crimes were occurring
and the police were borsk[92] and needed something to do. After
they brought us sodas, I felt less scared. Clearly they weren't
going to throw us into cells with hardened criminals and drunk
college students. All they were going to do was call our parents.

Oh, and also the store manager to see if the store wanted
to press charges.

Which, luckily for us, they didn't.

Dad got there first, before Kai's parents and Freddie Blue's.
I waved to them as I left. I couldn't do anything else. "Bye," I
whispered. Kai didn't even answer. He was staring at his shoes.

I felt terrible.

Dad was furious. I knew that because he kept saying, "I am
furious!" If I was going to pick better words for what he was,
I'd choose "incandescent with rage." Dad doesn't usually get
that mad, but his hands were shaking.

---

91. I'm not sure this was the best tactic, as it looked like mostly what she was doing was annoying
and offending the police people. I'd say "policemen" but one was a woman, so that wouldn't be
entirely accurate, and I am nothing if not married to the facts.
92. I really don't see "borsk" catching on in place of "bored." It just doesn't work, although I feel
like I should use it just out of loyalty to FB.

"You are grounded, kid," he said. "I can't believe you would think that was a good idea. What a stupid, stupid thing to do."

"I'm sorry," I muttered. Because I was sorry. I really was.

"I can't believe you'd be so irresponsible," he continued. "And lie to us. And even think of doing something so silly to begin with. You are the Peacemaker in our family! Not the Troublemaker! There is a world of difference between the word 'peace' and the word 'trouble,' Tink! And who is that boy?"

"Er, he lives next door," I said. "He's Kai. Kai is . . . just some kid." Even saying that, I felt disloyal. He's not just some kid! He might maybe be my boyfriend! I wished Mom had come to get me because I could have told her about Kai. She would have understood.

"And I hear the store is a mess," he went on. "You're lucky they aren't pressing charges. How dare you? Seriously, how dare you? I wouldn't have expected this from you, Tink."

I wanted Dad to stop talking. I wanted to be alone in a quiet room to try to figure out what I was thinking. I knew it was a dumb thing to do. But no one got hurt, right? Not that I'd have said that to Dad. I wouldn't dare.

"I'm sorry, Dad," I said again.

"Uh-huh," he said. "Sorry you got caught, or sorry you did it?"

"Sorry for all of it," I said. I closed my eyes. I hadn't gotten what I'd wanted from the adventure, which was to be normal BFFs with FB again. If anything, that whole thing had gotten worse.

But I'd gotten something else. And maybe it was what I'd been looking for all along.

Maybe it was sort of like my dream came true. In a way that made a lot of people mad, sure, but still . . .

It happened.

Kai kissed *me*.[93]

See also Adventure; BFF; Boyfriend Race, The; Crush List; Fish; Grounded; Kissing.

Mesopotamia

I know nothing about Mesopotamia, but when I think of an encyclopedia, it's the first thing I think of. I have no idea why. If you are really curious about the details of Mesopotamia, you should go to a garage sale and purchase your very own set of gold-edged books, which contain the answers that you seek, plus millions more.

Encyclopedias are really pretty awesome,[94] you know.

Mohism

A Chinese philosophy, sometimes also called "School of Mo," which makes it sound like a movie spoofing something serious. Basically the idea is that you should love everyone *exactly the same amount*: your mom, your brothers, your teacher, the guy at the bus stop with the waist-length beard, Mrs. O'Malley, whoever. ALL THE SAME. Which is ridic, because you can't really choose how much you love a person. It's not a *decision*. Sometimes you meet someone, and you're like, "Oh, hello, you seem nice enough, maybe we'll be acquaintances who say hello in the hall sometimes or share a pen if one of us forgets ours at

---

93. I think this means that I won the Boyfriend Race, but I don't want to say that out loud in case I jinx it, and actually the whole Boyfriend Race feels embarrassing and dumb and wrong now and I don't even know what I was thinking when I thought it up. I'm sure glad I never said it out loud or wrote it in an encyclopedia or anything.

Oh, wait . . .

94. Yes, I know that everything in encyclopedias is on the Internet and in a more modern and updated way, but it's just not the same because you can't flip the Internet open at random and learn something fascinating about Mohism, for example.

home," so you don't love them at all. And other times, you'll meet someone and you'll think about them all the time until you suspect you might be going a bit crazy and then they'll kiss you in an ice cream shop and then call you, and you'll hang up on them, and not see them again until you spend the night with them in the mall, where they will kiss you again, and you'll keep thinking about it over and over again, and then you would know that if you went to the School of Mo, you would flunk out entirely and be asked to never set foot on the campus again.

See also *Ice Cream Incident, The; Kai; Mega Mall.*

N

Name

The label you are given to differentiate you from the other seven billion people on the planet.[95]

I happen to think that your name is one of the most important things about you. For example, when you hear the name "Freddie Blue," you imagine a pretty girl who is fun and popular. When you hear the name "Tink," you probably picture either a tinker[96] or an animated fairy. You hopefully have a perfectly exquisite name, like Grace or Indigo or Sienna. I really like the name Sienna. If I got to pick my own, I think that's what I'd pick.

Of course, I didn't get to pick my own. Which is why I was named after a very famous dancer, Isadora Duncan, even though a dancer is the last thing I'd want to be. And Tink? No one would choose to call themselves Tink, I don't think. I wouldn't. I mean, I wouldn't NOW. Obviously, I DID ages ago, when I was four and told everyone they were to call me Tinker Bell because I preferred it to Isadora.

Who lets their kid choose a name from a Disney movie?

My parents, that's who.

If/when I ever have kids, I'm going to think carefully about their names and make sure to give them really good ones. Then I will actually take the crazy and novel approach of calling

---

95. If you have anything like a regular, normal name, it is very likely that more than one other person shares it. It is impossible for there to be seven billion unique names. It just is. Don't question it! It's true, because you read it in an encyclopedia. So there.

96. Someone who tinks. Actually, I don't know what a tinker is, come to think of it.

my kid by that name instead of renaming them something that sounds like the sound of a coin dropping on a hardwood floor.

See also Aaron-Martin, Isadora (Tink).

Napping

The act of sleeping at random times during the day.

I stopped napping when I was two, just like everyone else. On the other hand, I have started again now that I'm nearly constantly grounded. It's the kind of napping where you wake up feeling sick and groggy and like you're lying under a blanket of wet, foggy wool. My muscles are going to atrophy! It can't be healthy. I think Mom and Dad did not properly think through this form of punishment.

Napping would be a lot more pleasant if my brothers didn't keep waking me up by continuing their passionate hobby of full-body-contact Wii playing. The shouting at two P.M. when you are sound asleep is completely uncalled for, IMHO.

See also Grounded.

Nemo, Finding

Animated movie about a clown fish who gets lost and ends up in a dentist's office.

AKA my favorite movie of all time, although I formerly hated this movie due to my fear of fish. Now I will love this movie forever. I think I will buy it. No, better yet, I will buy it for Kai for his birthday! Actually, I don't even know when his birthday is. Or what his middle name is. Or whether he likes egg salad sandwiches. Or his last name even.

I don't know anything about him. Not really.

And he doesn't know anything about me. Not yet.

I hope he wants to find out more.

Does he?

And if he does, why doesn't he just call and ask? I'm grounded, not *muzzled*.

So maybe he's just not that interested.

Maybe he doesn't want to know me, after all!

And just as quick as the shock you get when you stick your finger in an outlet accidentally while trying to plug in your straightening iron, I am in a terrible, awful, no-good mood now. It has nothing to do with *Finding Nemo*, I just mention it because I don't want you to think I'm just happily jotting down encyclopedia entries and nonchalantly ignoring the fact that I'm trapped in my house with a hairless cat who has more affection needs than anyone can satisfy, and my phone isn't ringing. And it could be! It works. I just checked.

See also Grounded; Fish; Kai; Mega Mall.

Norway

A country in Scandinavia where, like Alaska, there is snow and probably bears and lots of thick, woolly sweaters. The major difference being that in Norway, skateboarding was illegal until 1989.

1989!

Think about it!

Outrageous!

Or at least, that's what Ruth Quayle said when she phoned me, proving to me that my phone worked AND I was allowed to talk on it. She managed to fit in a dozen different topics in about fifteen minutes, including the thing about skateboarding in Norway, a complicated story about Claymation and filmmaking, the strange pasta her mom was making for supper, and something about how if you lick a slug, your tongue will go numb. I didn't have to say anything, which was a relief, because I had nothing to say.

"Want to go to Drop Mac?" she said. "I have totes designed this awesome sail for my board. It is going to be seriously gnarlicious."

"I can't," I sighed. "I'm grounded."

"WHAT?" she yelled. "That's totes outrageous! School starts next week! You are being robbed of your last week of summer! What did you DO?"

So I told her.

Maybe because I was lonely and grounded and upset, I ended up telling her the entire story, including the kisses — she gasped and said, "I totes knew he liked you!" — and about Freddie Blue and how she was acting.

"Freddie Blue Anderson is a big phony now," said Ruth. "She used to be totes funny and now she's just a big Stella-clone."

The way she said it was so matter-of-fact, my blood ran cold. Because maybe she was right. But it couldn't be true! Could it?

"She is not," I said frostily and hung up.

I flopped back on my bed, which was rumply and uncomfortable, and watched Hortense slinking her way invisibly across the floor. She had a way of doing this, like if she moved super slowly she'd be camouflaged, that was so dumb it was funny.

Then I picked the phone back up. I could call FB. I could — I WANTED to — call Kai. But instead I called Ruth back, mostly because her number was right there on the call display. And also because I felt bad. "I'm sorry," I said. "I didn't mean to hang up on you."

"It's OK," she said. "I shouldn't have said that. I guess I didn't think about it. I know you, like, like her. So whatevs. It's probably just a phase or whatever."

"Yep," I said. "Probably. I mean, I know her pretty well. So."

"Yeah," she said. "So. Anyway, forget it. Look, call me when you're ungrounded. I've got to go sail this thing. Wish me luck!"

"Luck," I said, and hung up, feeling more alone than ever. Outside, the sun blistered down and the breeze lifted the leaves of my (Kai's!) Tree of Unknown Species, flipping them back and forth between darker green and silvery green. It was so pretty, my heart ached. Ached because it was trapped in my chest, which was trapped in my room, which was trapped inside forever and always.

For all I knew, being grounded was illegal in Norway. It probably was.

"Oh, Norway," I sighed. I flipped open the N volume to take a look at the pictures. It looks pretty there. You should go.

I would, but I'm grounded.

This bear is saying, "Welcome to Norway!" But what he means is, "Oh, you don't speak bear? Well, too bad. WELCOME TO MY STOMACH, TOURIST." (Norwegian bears are very similar to Alaskan bears.)

See also *Boarding, Skate; Grounded; Hairless Cats.*

NT

NT is an abbreviation for "neurotypical," and it is the word that people with autism use to describe people without autism. This gets very confusing because autism is a "spectrum" and depending on who you ask (e.g., Dad), "everyone is on the spectrum," meaning that no one is NT.[97]

Charlotte Ellery says that we are all NT in this family — and she tested us just to make sure — except for Seb. Dad despairs when she says that, because he is going to stick to his idea that everyone is autistic no matter what anyone else says. "NT is just the far end of the spectrum, then," says Dad. "But we're all on it somewhere."

"Fine," says Charlotte. "If that's what you want to think. You're all on it, shoved right up at the far end labeled NT." Sometimes Charlotte is hilair.

What Seb wants to know is what is going to happen when there are more autistic people in the world than people without autism. Will autism then be neurotypical? Because technically it will be more typical than not? In that case, then what will the rest of us be called?

It's a great mystery, Seb. I'm sure we'll get to the bottom of it eventually, but in the meantime, it's like the Stonehenge of questions: an unsolvable mystery. A koan.

See also Autism; Ellery, Charlotte; Koan.

---

97. He is not the only person in the world who believes this, just the only one in this house. Mom and Seb think he is wrong. And Lex and I do not care. Our not caring unites us more than any sport or TV show or music ever could. Oh, and we also like the same music, in case you were wondering.

O

Obsessive-Compulsive Disorder (OCD)

Obsessive-compulsive disorder is when you have to do something a certain way or you'll feel crazy inside, like your brain is in the washing machine on a spin cycle and can't stop. So you do things to stop it, like sanitizing your hands a million times, or touching your nose before you turn right.

Charlotte Ellery says people with autism often have a touch of OCD and that Seb is no exception. (It was Seb who said that about the spin cycle on the washing machine. I stole it from him, but it's not like he's going to read this anyway, so I don't have to credit him, but I will because I'm nice that way.)

It's true, he does wash his hands a lot. He always has sanitizer in his pockets, both of them, in addition to in his backpack, tucked into the side of his shoe, and in a little dispenser that attaches to the zipper on his hoodie. Once I caught him sanitizing his boots after he stepped in dog poop. I wish he didn't have to do that. I mean, I understood about the *poop*, but there is something about his face when he starts sanitizing that makes me feel like what he really needs is a hug.

However, Seb loathes hugging and if you hug him, he is likely as not to practice a karate chop on your forearm that will require surgery to repair. Don't say I didn't warn you.

See also Aaron-Martin, Sebastian (Seb); Autism; Ellery, Charlotte.

O'Malley, Mrs.

Mrs. O'Malley, as you well know, is the mean old woman who sits outside smoking on a bench and insulting us if we walk by, while keeping her sad, mangy miniature pugapoo, Mr. Bigglesworth, prisoner against his will in her purse. I very much doubt anyone really knows Mrs. O'Malley. She's not exactly someone who welcomes new friends with her open smile and laughing eyes.

I think the only pleasure that Mrs. O'Malley gets out of life is derived from thinking of new insults to throw at passersby. This makes me both sad and happy. Sad, because that's pathetic. And happy, because thinking of new insults to throw back at Mrs. O'Malley gives me a goodly amount of pleasure too.

See also Arms.

Ollie

The coolest skateboarding move ever, where you jump WITH the board, but without grabbing it first. So you're just rolling along and then, using only gravity (!), you and your board leap into the air. Together. Somehow, the board stays glued to your feet, even though it seems like it wouldn't or shouldn't. Ollies are both hard to explain AND hard to do. Trust me.

See also Boarding, Skate.

Oreo

A cookie that is black on the outside and white on the inside, best eaten by separating the halves and scraping the icing out and throwing it away, as the icing is disgusting.

I like Oreo cookies, but I don't love them, due to the icing factor. In fact, I have almost nothing to say about them, but "Oreo" is approximately the only other word I can come up with that begins with O, and seeing as I have nothing but spare time, I do not want to neglect any of the poor little letters of the alphabet. Even the ones that don't start any good words.

I will try to think of more O words and may return to add more entries, breaking my own just-made-up-right-now rule about not going backward. But unlike Seb, I can break my own rules without it being a federal case that I first need to plead in front of the Supreme Court of Me. In fact, forget it. This is my encyclopedia! THERE ARE NO RULES!

So there.

Oxen

Large, hairy animals, likely with a great deal of excess saliva dripping off their curly-haired mouths. I have never seen an ox, but I would imagine they smell just terrible, and I am as affronted by bad smells as I am by spit. They are probably also quite drooly, what with their huge heads and furry faces.

Honestly, I'm a bit afraid of all large animals because they look like they might trample me to death and not even notice.[98] Being trampled to death is my number four fear, after heights, brain tumors, and being nibbled by fish, but may have been bumped to number five by my new fear that has just jumped into my head just now: Kai doesn't really like me after all and instead is just a compulsive kisser with impulse control problems.

See also *Elephants; Fish; Ice Cream Incident, The; Kai; Kissing.*

---

98. Here is some helpful information for you: If you're being trampled by a herd of elephants, you should play dead because an elephant will not step on someone who is lying down. Apparently they have no compunction about standing on someone who is sitting up. I don't know whether oxen prefer to trample people who are sitting or lying down, but I don't want to be the one to find out either. You'll have to do your own testing, and let me know what you find out so I can update this encyclopedia with the correct information.

P

People Magazine

A half-celebrity, half–"normal person" magazine — sound familiar? — copies of which also flop listlessly on every surface of this house, much like The Magazine That Can't Be Named.

Superior to the other, similar magazine in every way, *People* magazine has never been known to destroy entire families by publishing a photo of them looking completely demented, such as the one that was in today's *Everybody*. A photo that featured two manic-looking twin teenage boys, a beat-up father, a mother with something resembling a giant octopus of slime in her hair, and a small girl who was almost entirely hidden by a large shrub, under which a cat imitating a wrinkled-up handbag was perched. The proximity of the cat to the girl and the weird angle of the shrub, combined with the girl's huge and puffy shirt, makes her look like a human who has been shrunk in the wash and then tossed into a regular-sized scene for giggles. You can be assured that the entire family in that photograph is now in very, very dark moods, and it is best to not mention *Everybody* magazine in their presence.

In related news, I've just read the terrible, no-good, very bad article in *Everybody* magazine that accompanied The Worst Photo of All Time, and I have to go now and cry into my pillow about the fact that not only will I not be made popular by fame, I will likely be the laughingstock of the school and referred to only as "Arrrgh, matey!" (thanks to the shirt) or "Freckle Peckle" (kindly contributed by Seb in a lovely quote about how "coping with a Freckle Peckle is more difficult than 'coping with autism,' dude."[99])

I have just now made a commitment to being tough and impermeable to meanness, so I refuse to let the article bother me in any way, even though it really, really does.

From now on, the only magazine I will ever read will be *People*, my new favorite.

See also Everybody *Magazine; Magazines.*

People Who Don't Call after Kissing a Person for the Second Time and on Purpose, Not by Accident

Otherwise known as "bad people," these people do not warrant a mention in this encyclopedia. Go back and strike from your memory any mention of any such person that might have been previously mentioned in this weighty tome.

Oh, bollocks, as Dad would say.

I am going to call *Kai*. This is ridic! It's almost 2020, for goodness' sake, which — if not the start of a new century — is at least the start of some decade where it is perfectly acceptable for girls to phone boys and say "hey" without the girl feeling like she should be waiting for the call. I don't know what is going on here, except maybe there is something in the atmosphere that is making me act like someone who is not the real me.[100]

If only I had the Internet so I could e-mail him or IM him or write on his wall instead, which would be so much less personal and nervous-making than an actual real live CALL.

---

99. Which is beyond mysterious, not that he'd call me Freckle Peckle, which he does all the time, but that he'd say "dude," which he has never ever said as far as I know and sounds much more like Lex. Was Lex pretending to be Seb? Do I hate Lex? Or Seb? OR BOTH?

100. Not that I have ever been in this situation before, because I haven't, but if you'd asked me before this all happened, I would have given you the Tink Aaron-Martin Patented Stare of Outright Confusion, and then I would have said, "Why would I be waiting for someone to call me? I would call someone if I wanted to talk to them. What a dumb question." Oh, life, you are so funny sometimes.

I'll work up to it. Soon.

I don't know what I'm so afraid of.

See also Kai. Kai. Kaiiiiiiiiii. Oh, stop it.

Phone

An instrument that I suppose is electrical that allows you to talk to people by pressing a piece of plastic and metal against your ear after first dialing their number into a keypad. An antiquated invention that few people use, preferring as they do the asynchronous[101] conversations they have on the Internet, where they can not bother answering and not be considered rude. The exception to this is that sometimes your BFF calls you on the phone up to ten times a day! To the annoyance of your brothers! Until suddenly, something happens in your friendship, and just like that, she stops.

See also BFF.

Prince X

Prince X is, well, a prince. I can't tell you which prince! Because it's a secret. Not really. But it is. The thing is that if you knew which prince, you would laugh at me until your face turned purple and you began gasping for air, much like you would if you were choking to death on a piece of bubble gum that was lodged in your esophagus. So I'm not going to tell you.

And you can't make me.

---

101. "Asynchronous" means "not in sync" or "syncing at different rates," which basically means that you can have a conversation with someone at a different time than they are having it with you. Charlotte Ellery says that having autism is like being asynchronous while the rest of the world is in sync, so that it takes longer for Seb to figure out what is what and to respond or catch up than it would an NT. I do not know why I bring that up now. I just like the word "asynchronous" because it is a word that commands respect from your listener, being a word that they are not likely to know, such that for the rest of the conversation, they are wondering how quickly they can get to the Internet to look up what it means so they know what you are talking about.

Sometimes, I write small, non-embarrassing plays featuring myself and Prince X. Who am I kidding? It's the most humiliating hobby of all time, but each time I promise to stop doing it, I come up with an excellent idea for a new one and do just one more. If anyone ever saw one, I'd die. Or I would will the earth to open up a giant crack that would swallow everyone who saw what I had written and they would be destroyed or spat out in Australia, and I would be able to survive with my head held high, knowing it would be very unlikely that I would run into them at ballet or in the line to buy a large cookie in the cafeteria at lunch.

If I were going to write a play about me and Prince X, it may or may not be something like this. I wouldn't read it, if I were you. Although I hear Australia is nice at this time of year.

Scene One opens with Prince X sitting in the library. Enter stage left, a young, very beautiful girl (that's me, but with enough makeup on that I look beautiful, not just like my regular frumpy self). Prince X looks up. At that moment, a huge earthquake shakes the building, and Prince X is trapped under a heavy shelf of books, which the beautiful girl hero-ically lifts to save him.

Prince X: *You saved my life! And you're cute. We should marry.*

Me: *It was nothing! Don't worry about it! You don't have to marry me. I'm too young anyway. My mom would kill me.*

Prince X: *But I want to! You're the most glam girl I've ever met.*

Me: *Swoon.*

Prince X recently became engaged, but I am not going to write that part into any of my plays. I'm sure it's just a passing thing and won't last, or at least that is what I am hoping for and sometimes requesting of the Buddha in the back garden, as I do not attend the School of Mo and cannot bring myself to love all princes equally. He really is my one and only.

Although I'm not entirely sure that I don't like Kai just a smidgen more than Prince X, after all.

See also Kai; Mohism.

Pugapoo, Miniature
A tiny dog that results from crossing a tiny poodle with a pug. Looks a lot like a dust mop or a reggae singer. A sadly neglected and horribly unkempt pugapoo looks like a tiny pug with a 'Fro.

Would you keep this dog in your purse? Seriously? WOULD you?

The miniature pugapoo is the ugly friend of the dog world and probably is BFFs with a pretty dog, such as a Weimaraner, and likely always feels too short and too hairy in comparison. Although the truth is that the pugapoo is a much more fun and lovable dog and the Weimaraner is just pretty much acting like a jerk, if you ask me.

See also Arms; BFF; O'Malley, Mrs.

Q

Quayle, Ruth

Ruth is easily both the funniest and also the most excitable thirteen-year-old girl I know. She has peculiar, sticky-uppy hair and sometimes wears clothes that look like she maybe grabbed them from her dad's laundry pile and didn't notice. She has more energy than a whole fleet of kangaroos and hardly ever stops talking or jumping around from foot to foot, except when she is skating. She is an awesome boarder, but she says she is likely to only keep it up for a little while longer, as she is getting bored with it and thinking of starting a new hobby: making horror films using Claymation. It's hard to know if that's true, or just a passing thought that she has said out loud. She is very much a think-it/say-it simultaneously kind of person.

Ruth's best quality is that she neither cares nor notices what other people think.

It bugs me a lot that Freddie Blue doesn't like Ruth.

It bugs me a lot that Ruth doesn't like Freddie Blue.

It bugs me a lot that I'm still *grounded*.

I was thirsty, so I went downstairs for some water and sat on the Itchy Couch to drink it in the path of the fan, which was really just blowing hot air around and making it hotter. I picked up the phone and hung upside down from the couch.

And without thinking about it, I dialed Kai's number! I did! Just like that! I wasn't even nervous!

It rang.

And rang.

And rang some more. No answer. No answering machine either.

"Lame," I said out loud. I hung up, gulped down some water, and looked at the big pile of encyclopedias. I missed Freddie Blue. I did.

I dialed her number.

"Yes?" she said slowly. Like she was mad or bored or both.

"It's me," I said. "Tink."

"Oh," she said. "I thought you were Isadora now."

"What are you doing?" I said.

"I'm just getting ready to go out with some friends," she said. "Why? What are you doing?"

"Nothing," I sighed. "Writing my book. I'm grounded, remember?"

"Your mom is so harsh," she said.

"Well, we did break into a department store and made a mess," I said. "It was kind of worse than the trampoline thing."

"I guess," she said. "But you didn't hurt your knees. Hey, Tink?"

"Yes," I said.

"I gotta go. Some people are waiting for me. Talk to you . . . later." She hung up.

I sat on the Itchy Couch for a while and watched the water bead up on my glass. It was scintillating, in that it wasn't even slightly interesting. Lex came in and started chomping loudly on an apple.

"Hey," he said.

"Hey," I said back.

"Sucks to be you, I guess," he said. "It's like _____ outside."

"I know," I said. "That's very supportive, thanks."

"Just trying to be _____," he said. He yawned. "Well, see you."

"Bye," I said. I closed my eyes. Was the highlight of my day really going to be talking to Lex while he ate an apple in four huge bites?

Why, yes. Yes, it was.

I should have called Ruth, especially as this is her entry in my encyclopedia. But by then, my energy for the phone had run out and I needed to have a nap to store up some more nerve for trying Kai again later. So I didn't.

Sorry.

See also Grounded; Phone.

Queen

The head of a country, if the country is a monarchy, which only about five or ten countries in the entire world actually are. If you marry a king, you get to be queen. But if you are already a queen, and you marry someone, he only gets to be a prince. I think that's how it works. Don't quote me on that.

If I marry Prince X, then one day I'll be queen of a very obscure country in Europe that you would not be able to find on a map, even if you had to find it in order to get an A in geography. As Queen X, everyone will love me, and I'll have a hairless cat that will popularize the breed so that poor old Hortense isn't the only one in a thousand-mile radius. Prince X and I will have adorable children, and if they inherit my freckles or Afro, we'll be rich enough to just have them all fixed up.[102]

See also Afro; Freckles; Hairless Cats; Prince X.

---

102. Yes, of course I'm joking. Obviously freckles and Afros will be made insta-glam by our trendsetting royal family and people will be racing to their plastic surgeons to have freckles added. And Afros will be so totes pops that even FB will have one. (I can't wait.)

Quince

I think that quince might be either a fruit or a sort of jam but am too lazy to look it up, so if you are interested in further exploration of the subject, you'll have to check elsewhere. Like on the Internet, which I'm sure you have instant access to at all times because your mom doesn't lock her office door, and/or you have a BFF who you can call without worrying if she's too busy with her other friends to check facts for your book.

I apologize to you, my readers, for this lameness of my knowledge about quince and for forcing to do your own fact-checking. (You may want to double-check all the facts you've read here, now that I think of it.)

See also Computer; Lame.

R

Remorse

"Remorse" is the feeling you get after you do something regrettable, such as trying to spend the night in a shopping mall or allowing yourself to be dressed in a jaunty yellow pirate shirt and posing in a national magazine.

My life is positively dripping with remorse. If remorse was melted cheese and my life was really soft white bread, nicely toasted, then together it would make a really delicious sandwich. If you like melty cheese. Which I do.

UNLESS "melty cheese" means "remorse," in which case, I do not.

What?

See also Everybody *Magazine; Grounded; Kai; Lame.*

Respite Care

Respite care is kind of like a hotel for people with autism and with other things too, where they go stay in a house with other people who are enjoying a nice weekend away from their family.

Respite care for Seb is one of Charlotte Ellery's "pet projects." She thinks we should be shipping Seb off every other weekend so we can focus on "other things" or "each other." But she doesn't *know*. She doesn't get it. She thinks you can just put your family away somewhere when they bug you or get on your nerves. And that's not how family works.

At least, that's what Mom and Dad say. And I guess I agree.

I mean, think about it. It wouldn't be fair.

Would it?

Without Seb, what would we do? What would HE do, without us? Would it really be different? For us or for him? Would he like it? Would we? Would he feel like we were trying to get rid of him? Would we be?[103]

I guess Mom and Dad would have to fight about something other than "You Are Handling Seb's Autism Wrong!" Like maybe the Care and Feeding of Tink Aaron-Martin, for a change.

Maybe that wouldn't be such a bad thing, after all.

See also Aaron-Martin, Sebastian (Seb); Autism; Ellery, Charlotte.

Room

A place with four walls and at least one door. Sometimes a window, if you are lucky.

Number fifteen on my list of life goals is to one day have a room in Paris, where I can look out the window at the Eiffel Tower. I have never been to Paris, and Mom says that I would hate it and never really want to live there, but I do not think she knows me as well as she thinks she does. I may very well be deeply Parisian on the inside.

I like my room because it has a view of the Tree of Unknown Species and . . . other things. Which makes it acceptable.

---

103. I do not know the answer to any of these questions. These are just some of the million things that come up when Charlotte Ellery dares to whisper the words "respite care." Funnily enough, the only one who doesn't get defensive and weird about the subject is Seb, who shrugs and says, "Fine by me. I could use a break from Lex, he's a total pain in the ____." When he says this, Lex looks so sad that I want to slap Seb for hurting his feelings, when we all know Lex does tons for Seb that Seb doesn't really get because he doesn't really think too much about Lex's feelings, as I've mentioned. Anyway, it's complicated. Like a pile of jumbly blocks stacked precariously on a foundation of Seb. If the jumbly blocks were "emotions" and Seb was . . . Seb.

For now.

Forever, at the rate I'm going.[104]

I was about to stare thoughtfully out the window and describe in detail what I could see from here, which is mostly just the branches of the Tree of Unknown Species.

And then I noticed Kai was on the lawn! Waving his arms around! Like someone who wanted to get my attention!

I opened the window and yelled, "HI!"

"HI!" he yelled back. He was just about to say something else when my mom's car turned into the driveway. Kai ran away, his blue hair bobbing sweetly in the breeze. He was running toward the tree. Was he climbing it? My tree?

I heard my mom clip-clopping across the porch. (Mom loves shoes and wears fancy high heels on days she can "get away with it," i.e., days when she is not actively delivering a stuck baby.) The door closed and then the *clip-clop* was in the kitchen and then the stairs and then, *bam*. There she was.

"What are you doing, Tink?" she said. "It's not appropriate for you to be shouting to your friends out the window. This is supposed to be punishment, remember?"

"How can I forget?" I said. "I've been wrongly accused!"

"No," she said. "You haven't. You confessed AND you were caught red-handed. So now you are paying the price for doing the crime."

"But Kai did the crime too," I pointed out. "And he's outside." I snuck a look out the window. I wasn't sure, but I

---

104. I can hardly wait to write my first English assignment when I get back to school, which will no doubt be "Where I Went on My Summer Vacation." I bet my answer is unique. MY ROOM. I'll probably get an A, a sympathy-because-you-had-a-terrible-summer A, but still an A.

thought I could see him, partially hidden by the leaves of the tree. My heart skipped six consecutive beats.

"I'm not everyone's mother," she said, tucking her hair behind her ears. She looked really tired.

Before I could stop myself, I went, "Yeah, well, I wish you weren't mine."

She snapped her head up and looked at me. I could tell I'd hurt her feelings. A lot. But I also didn't care. I didn't. Well, I guess I did. I felt bad about it, especially when she stomped out and said in a cracking voice, "You can come down for dinner in an hour."

"Whatever," I said.

"Tink," she sighed, from the doorway.

"And my name is Isadora!" I shouted. "Why doesn't anyone ever call me Isadora?"

"Because you told us not to, remember?" said Mom. "Because you said you didn't choose it."

"I didn't choose 'Tink' either," I said frostily.

"Actually," she said. "You did."

"Well, you shouldn't let a four-year-old pick her own name!" I shouted. "And I said Tinker Bell, not TINK. And it was nine years ago! I'm allowed to change my mind!"

"TINK," she said. "I've had enough of this." She clip-clopped down the hall.

"It's ISADORA!" I yelled. "Now," I added. "I mean it!"

"Isadora," said Seb, sticking his head out into the hall. "Isadora is a bore-a." He started laughing really hard and stupidly, clutching at his sides. "Isadora Isabora," he chanted.

"SHUT UP!" I screamed, and I slammed my door. I went over the window and looked into the tree. There was no one there. The tree was as empty and alone as my heart.

Do you want to know what the view from my room is? Really? Well, I'll tell you. It's bleak. Bleak, bleak, bleak. With an extra helping of BLEAK thrown on the top for good measure.

See also *Grounded; Kai; Name.*

S

Sarcasm

Sarcasm is irony with a twist and a shove. Dad says that, like licorice, sarcasm is an acquired taste. He also says that only smart people appreciate irony and sarcasm.

I love sarcasm. And I enjoy licorice. Draw your own conclusions.

School, First Day of

Today was the first day of school.

I wore my new dark jeans (capri length!) and a sleeveless T-shirt that had a fake wrap front. The shirt was gray. I thought it looked skater-cool in the store, but I realized, too late, that it looked like a washrag that had cleaned a hundred cars and had subsequently been thrown into the trash. Which was good, in a way. It said, "I am not trying to please you, fellow students at Cortez Junior. I am too cool to obsess about what I'm wearing." Which was ironic because I was obsessed with what I was wearing.

As I got ready, my brain was all abuzz with thoughts, which felt like flies swarming my gray matter. They were mostly things like: Why am I so scared? What is wrong with me? Do I look OK? Should I wear makeup? Maybe I should cover my freckles, and then I won't be called Freckle Peckle? Does anyone even really read *Everybody* magazine? Yes? Should I run away to Slovenia and change my name to Natalka Novotny? Or to Quebec to join the cast of the Cirque du Soleil? Or to China to make plastic toys in a large factory? All of which sound better than going to F.E.C.E.S. for what will probably be the worst day of my life.

In addition to things like: Will Kai talk to me? Why didn't I just call him again? What is wrong with me? Will Freddie Blue talk to me? Do I want her to? Will Ruth be my friend? Will I have any friends? Will I have to eat my lunch alone, leaning on my locker, pretending to be super engrossed in a book?

I concentrated on breathing. In and out. Out and in.

I tried to reassure myself: Nothing would happen.

Or.

No one would talk to me.

Worse, teachers would talk to me and would want me to speak to everyone about autism. I'd become the autism mascot and would be trotted out at basketball games like the Aardie of the autism world.

I yelled good-bye to my family, which was mostly ignored. I don't want to talk about it, but Seb was super stressed. The morning was full of the sound of slammed doors and broken eggs. The house stunk of sanitizer, which wasn't a bad smell and made my sinuses feel clean, but still indicated that Seb was teetering on the edge of haywire-dom.

I stepped outside. It was a windy day and even the air smelled like fog and back-to-school. The leaves on the Tree of Unknown Species looked like they changed color from green to yellow overnight. I went and stood under it for a minute and looked up through the leaves at the sky. I didn't have time for climbing. And maybe climbing was for little kids, anyway.

I was growing up.

I was in the eighth grade now! This was serious business! I reached out and touched the smooth roughness of the bark. "See you, tree," I said.

Then I ate four Oreos for strength.[105]

---

105. Zero out of ten doctors recommend a hearty serving of Oreos for breakfast!

Seb and Lex burst through the door. "Calm DOWN, man," Lex was saying. "It's the same school, the same kids. Just relax. Dude, you just . . ."

"I'm FINE," yelled Seb.

They blasted by me in their matching Prescott hoodies. "Good luck!" I yelled.

Lex waved. Seb didn't even turn around.

"Tink!" yelled Mom from the back deck. "You're going to be late! I'm not driving you!"

"OK, OK," I said. I took a big breath and held it for as long as I could, which was all the way down the driveway.

I walked the long way, past the 7-Eleven and ice cream shop, past the abandoned fall beach where garbage left over from summer was being tossed around by the wind. And then, just like that, I was on the steps of Cortez Junior, out of breath and as sweaty as a wet mop. Perf.

I sighed and looked around. It was so crowded! But I didn't recognize anyone, except Wex Stromson-Funk.

"Yo, Plank!" he called.

"Freckle Peckle!" one of his buddies shouted.

I stopped dead in my tracks. NO. Not more than one bully! Was Wex contagious? I refused to take it!

I marched right up to Wex and said, "Look. I am rubber. You are glue. Anything you say bounces off of ME and sticks to you, geni."

He stared at me, mouth agape. His face was completely blank. Wex was the T. rex of mankind. All mean and spastic, but with no brain and absurdly small arms. Except, obviously, he had normal-sized arms. If only he had tiny ones, he probably would have been a nicer person.

I said, "I'm sorry, I don't have time to wait until your lone, tiny brain circuit shorts out. I must go."

"Uh," he said. "Did you call me Jeanie?"[106]

And then I saw Kai. He was standing behind Wex, but close enough that they'd obviously been talking. Had HE been the one who called me "Freckle Peckle"? I refused to believe it, but, at the same time, was 100 percent sure it was true. My heart broke into a billion shards, which shot around my body in my veins and arteries, stabbing me everywhere at once, like a zillion bee stings.

"Kai," I said. I worked hard at lacing each letter of his name with a layer of ice. I squinted at him. "Hello."

Then I turned my back and walked away. I was scared he wasn't going to answer. Or scared that if he did, he'd say something mean. Was he FRIENDS with Wex? My legs were shaking like wet dogs.

What had just happened? What?

I pushed my way through the crowd until I found a bathroom.[107] I looked at myself in the mirror. Conclusion: a mess. I tried to twist my hair back into shape but it was hopeless. So I did what people do in movies, which was to splash a bunch of water on my face. Cold water.

In movies, apparently no one wears mascara. Normally I don't either, but I did today because I thought it might make me look sophisto.

---

106. It is probably very hard for you to imagine why Wex Stromson-Funk was at a school for gifted people. He was not VERY gifted. At least, not outside of math. Being good at math can get you into good schools but it does not — repeat, does NOT — make you smart in any necessarily meaningful way. JEANIE. Ha ha ha. Oh Em Gee.

107. Always look for a bathroom when you don't know what else to do. That is a useful tip. If I wasn't already almost through the alphabet in this encyclopedia, I would seriously consider making this an advice book, because it is full of good tips like this one. If by "full of good tips," I mean "has one or two bits of advice that might be useful if you are ever in exactly the same situations that I have been in."

Which it did! Good news! But only if "sophisto" also means "looking like you've been punched in both eyes by someone with black paint on his small round fists."

I cleaned myself up as well as I could with some very rough paper towel, which gave my face the look of having a bad wind-burn. Did I care? I did not.

Then I went back out into the fray to look for Freddie Blue. I can't explain why, except to say that it was like Freddie Blue and I were wrapped up together in strands like cobwebs, and no matter how hard I pulled (or how hard she pushed) to get out of the web, I was still in the web. And the web wasn't a bad thing; it was the web that I knew. And the web had been fun for my whole life! And I didn't want things to be different. Just being back at school made me want to crawl right back in and get firmly stuck in the place where I belonged.

Which was with FB. Even if she was a bit spidery lately.

Then I saw her! She was waving her arm in the air and yelling, "Here! OVER HERE!"

Everything was going to be OK! Cue birds singing! Happy music! With ukuleles!

Except then when I got closer to her, I realized she wasn't even talking to me. She looked right past me! Like I wasn't even there!

I watched as she ran up to Stella Wilson-Rawley. She was talking in an extra-loud, fakey voice, but I still couldn't make out what she was saying due to the ringing in my ears.

You know how they say that when you die, your whole life flashes in front of your eyes, like a fast-forwarded movie, all odd angles and random flashes of things you'll never know again? It was almost like that, as I fell out of the web of us. I could see bright flashes of kidnapping Mr. Bigglesworth or knee-jumping on the trampoline or just all the times we lay on the Itchy Couch and ate raw cookie dough and laughed ourselves senseless about Hortense, or climbing the tree, or even the way she mooned around after Lex, and when she gave me her red balloon at her seventh birthday party after I accidentally let go of mine and it got tangled in the telephone wires.

Then I noticed that she and Stella were wearing *matching outfits.*

I gasped out loud, from shock and horror. It could only have been the stick-death purple shirts! They were hideously and truly malg.[108] They looked like the kind of shirts that a teacher would wear, all collared and ruffled, if the teacher was ancient, partially blind, the owner of eight cats, and the star of an episode of *Hoarders.*

"My eyes, my eyes," I murmured. "I am blind!"

"I bet you wish you were," said Ruth, appearing next to me out of nowhere. "What are they wearing? They look like orchids on a wedding cake! Orchids with heads! And unsightly shoes!"

I looked down. Both FB and SWR were wearing bright pink kicks. They were so bright, that even after I looked away, the image of them was still burned into my retinas.

"You should have called me last night," I said to Ruth. "We could have worn matching garbage bags and really set some serious trends."

She snorted. "Yeah," she said. "SORRY. Hey, do you want to go to Drop Mac after school? You've got to see the sail I made for my board! It is so fun, it's ridic!"

---

108. Malg is *glam* backward, in case you have forgotten and/or are too lazy to refer back to the Ms. And it is only just now when I write it down that I realize that even the WORD "malg" is malg. I am never going to use it again. I am putting it in the casket of Freddie Blue Anderson memories that I am going to bury in the dirt and never think of or speak of again.

"Yep," I said. I was flooded with relief. FB was not talking to me and I was still OK.

Even so, I stared at her as she disappeared into the crowd. Maybe if we were in the second grade, matching would be acceptable. But now that we're almost thirteen? NOT. I was glad not to be part of their little club! Exclamation mark! Even seeing them makes me feel embarrassed to be alive![109]

I dragged myself through the rest of the day. After school, I waited by the front steps for Ruth, feeling sad and forlorn. I stared at my too-white shoes and tried to imagine what I had done to make FB ignore me. I mean, shouldn't I be the one who was mad? Was she even *mad*? Or was she ignoring me because I just didn't matter anymore?

Then I noticed that Kai was rolling toward me on his board. The ball-bearing sound on the pavement made my heart soar. And! He was smiling! And before I could stop myself, I blurted out, "Kai! Hi!"

He said, "Hey." I could tell he was trying to sound casual, but he was also grinning. A lot.

I grinned back. "Want to come to Drop Mac with me and Ruth?" I said.

"Sure!" he said. Then he added, "So you're, like, sort of famous now, I guess. I mean, I saw *Everybody*. My mom didn't believe that I knew you. She thinks that magazine is just, like, celebs and stuff."

"I'm a celeb," I said, pretending to be affronted.

"Um," he said.

"I'm kidding!" I said. There was an awkward silence. I

---

109. In addition to feeling entirely left out and miserable and actually sort of heartbroken for the sad mess that my life has so quickly become.

tried to fill it by laughing, but it came out weird, like a tiny little "ha" in a cavern of silence. He fidgeted around with his board, finally dropping it and doing a couple of little flips on the stairs. Then, before I could stop myself or even think about it, I blurted, "Why didn't you call me?"

"I don't know," he said, after a second of staring at me. "I kind of figured you were famous now and that you wouldn't . . . I mean, I did call you a couple of times, but when your brother said you were, like, too busy to talk to me, I thought you probably just . . ."

"My brother said that?" I said.

"Yeah," he said.

And then it all made sense. Reader, if you don't have a brother, do not get one. That is my best advice to you. Take it. You won't regret it. Also, you will likely get all your calls.

"So, like, why weren't you in the article?" he said. "That IS stupid. But you, um, looked pretty dope."

"Thanks," I said. I was smiling so hard, my face hurt.

"Are you OK?" he said.

"I'm good," I assured him. "I'm totally good." His eyes looked especially brownish-gold today.

"Hey," I said. "Can I ask you something sort of personal?"

"Um," he said. "I guess." He squinted up at the sun. I could tell he was nervous.

"No!" I said. "It's not like that. Like not really, really personal. I just . . . I wondered what your last name is."

He looked at me and then laughed in a great gust of laughing that practically knocked me over.

"What?" I said. "I don't know your last name!"

"OK," he said. "It's . . ."

"What?" I said.

"It's Neck," he said.

"NECK?" I said. "What kind of last name is Neck? I mean, OK. I'm sorry. That was totally . . ."

He shrugged. "Yeah," he said. "People get a lot of laughs out of it. It's just a name." He scuffed his foot on the ground. "So."

"I'm totally sorry," I said. "I was just —"

"Don't worry about it," he interrupted.

Ruth rolled up behind him, smacking him on the head by mistake with her backpack. "Ohmigosh! I'm sorry!" she said. "Tink, are you ready? What a crazy day! I can't believe how many new kids there are! Where did they come from? Did a gifted alien ship land on earth and dump them in Cortez?"

I laughed. "What?"

"Where did they go last year? It's like they appeared out of nowhere! Look at that one!" She pointed to a girl going by who had green hair and seven piercings in her ear. "ALIEN."

I laughed harder. "She is not! You're crazy!"

Ruth dropped her board and did a perfect spin. "Don't blame me when they suck you up into their ship, then. Let's skate."

And then they were gone, swooping down the hill on the music of ball bearings, and I was left standing there thinking, *What? They left me! Alone!*

"HEY, WAIT UP!" I yelled, running to catch up.

And you know what?

They did.[110]

See also BFF; Bullies; Cortez Junior; Kai; Quayle, Ruth.

---

110. Sometimes, to get what you want, you have to just ask for it. That is helpful tip #201! Or so. I haven't been counting, but if you have, feel free to send me a letter with the correct number and you will win a prize. The prize will be this book. But you already have this book, so all in all, it might just be a waste of a stamp.

Shoes

Protective outer coverings for feet, sometimes leather or plastic or canvas, usually with hard or bendy bottoms that save your feet from becoming ragged, bleeding stumps when you step on broken glass or live animals.

I have four pairs of shoes, but I prefer to wear flip-flops if I can get away with it, for comfort's sake, although they suck when worn while on a skateboard.

My feet are so freakishly, hideously small that I usually have to buy my shoes in the kids' department. I hope you are generally happy with your normal-sized feet. You should be.

Skiing

A sport that involves snow and skis, and whizzing down mountains dressed in glam outfits and goggles, swishing enthusiastically in giant S curves that throw sprays of pretty snow in the direction of passersby. Everyone knows this, but this is an encyclopedia so I have a responsibility to include important facts and related trivia. I do not know who invented skiing. Probably someone Swiss who lived near or on the Alps.

Skiing is popular among rich people all over the world, such as Prince X.

I am almost sure that I would be good at skiing, given half a chance, making it one of a million sports I would rather do than ballet, which tragically is about to start up again and I haven't yet had the gumption to tell Mom that I'm out. That I'm done. That I, Tink Aaron-Martin, am quitting.

But I will.

Probably.

See also Ballet; Prince X.

Spanish

The second-most commonly spoken language in the world, or at least it was in 1976 when this encyclopedia that I'm reading was printed.

And my favorite language.

¿Hablas español?

Kai is also in my Spanish class. This is a huge coincidence that points to the intervention of fate. *¡Muy bueno!*

This is a picture of a Spanish dish called "paella." It looks delish. (And although the idea of beach shells in my meal is a teensy bit disgusting, they also look quite glam.)

Stealing

The act of taking something that you didn't pay for and or ask for, or deserve for that matter, something that belongs to someone else. And keeping it.

I'm not a Moral Superstar Who Always Makes the Right Choice and Is Frequently Held Up as a Model of Respectability,[111] but stealing anything, even the idea of it, makes my

---

111. I do not know anyone who would fit this description either, but maybe there is someone out there who is completely perfect and never does the wrong thing. If there is, this person is probably really annoying to be around. Think about it.

throat vibrate strangely in a way that suggests I'm about to be sick. Don't tell Freddie Blue, but I went back to the department store at the Mega Mall the next day and paid for the food we ate, even though I didn't have the exact amounts. I gave them $14, because it is all that I had, and I'm sure we did not eat $14 worth of candy.

I think they thought I was crazy because they hadn't said we had to, but I think they just forgot to say it. It was pretty obvious to me.

Also, I'm scared of karma, as I believe I mentioned earlier, back in the *K* section that you should have been paying more attention to. Just kidding.

See also Karma; Mega Mall.

Stuck Yawn Syndrome

When your body feels like yawning, so you open your mouth to have a good, satisfying yawn, but instead of having that happen, the yawn refuses to come out and settles deep into your lungs instead, making you feel like you can't breathe properly even though you obviously are breathing. If you weren't breathing, you would be dead before long.

If this happens to you, you are not "nutso as a bag of nails,"[112] (which FB actually said to me when I told her about it a long time ago), you have just accidentally hyperventilated and need to find a brown paper bag, stat. Only brown paper works. Breathing into any other color of paper bag is useless, so do not bother trying it.

See also School, First Day of.

---

112. Another Freddie Blue–ism that makes no sense whatsoever and suggests she isn't as smart as she thinks she is. I never really noticed before how so much of what she said was just plain dumb. I think it was a case of being too close, sort of how if you are looking at someone all the time, you start to not notice what they look like, and it's only when you go away and then come back that you really can see them properly.

Swooning

Swooning is just another name for fainting,[113] except it sounds more graceful. Say "swooning" out loud right now. See? I can see why it isn't used much anymore, as it's silly to use such a graceful word to describe crashing to the ground in a dead faint, invariably knocking things over on your way down.

See also Boarding, Skate.

---

113. Which I only just recently found out. Don't tell anyone this, but before Mom told me that a faint and a swoon were the same thing, I imagined a swoon to involve a sort of swooping to the ground, like a flying squirrel on a strong draft of air. I know it doesn't make sense, but not everything has to make sense in order for you to believe it is true. I think I've proven *that* by now, if nothing else.

T

Teachers

People who opt to spend their working hours teaching instead of doing something fun, like writing books or sitting in the branches of a tree whose leaves are slowly turning gold and red or perfecting their ollie in an empty swimming pool.

I have no idea why anyone would want to be a teacher. But lots of people do, at least they must, because there always is a teacher at the front of every room in the school. I was actually going to write a list of all the teachers that I have this year, and then I realized that that would simply bore you clear out of your mind and straight into another book. I wouldn't want to do that. What if something really good happens in the last seven letters of my alphabet?

Tipping, Chair

The act of tilting your chair backward while sitting on it and attempting to balance it on the back two legs without falling over and cracking your head open on the hardwood floor, i.e., an activity that boys seem to find endlessly entertaining and the best way to make Mom and/or Dad furiously angry in the space of 0.2 seconds.

Which is how it started at dinner, with the tipping.

Mom and Dad were already mad. I don't know why, not exactly, but it had to do with Seb. He'd been sent home from school early for causing a disturbance with the fetal pigs they were meant to dissect in biology. I asked Lex what Seb did and all he said was, "Tink, you can't set a pig free when it is dead and in a bucket of formaldehyde."

Mom and Dad were eating in a way that suggested they were only barely able to chew greenery in each other's presence. This may not make sense to you, but I can always tell. It's like Mom chews in a very determined way that makes her teeth click. And Dad very obviously smiles in a way that suggests that he's not happy, but rather boiling inside like a cauldron of fury, his jaw bubbling back and forth.

Seb seemed fine. Just like he always is. He was drawing. He's allowed to draw at the table, naturally, when the rest of us are not.

"How was school?" said Mom, helping herself to a big heaping bowl of broccoli. It had melty cheese on top, which improved it 100 percent, especially if you ate only the cheese and left the broccoli alone.

"Fine," I lied. It was a lie on a lot of levels. Now that school was in full swing — which basically happened on the second day — it was a lot of work, for one thing. For another, I was feeling weird about Freddie Blue. And Kai had been so great, teaching me skateboarding stuff, but it's not like he was my boyfriend. Not that I wanted him to be!

Yes, I did.

I wanted him to be my boyfriend!

I chewed my broccoli furiously.

"What did you do?" asked Dad.

"When?" I said. "Nothing!"

"Whoa," he said. "Someone's cranky."

"I'm not cranky," I said. "You should talk."

"TINK," said Mom. "Don't be rude. I don't know what is going on in this family." She sighed and put her fork down. "Honestly," she said. "What next?" She rubbed her temples.

"Whatever," I said. "What was the question?"

"He asked what you did at school, dummy," said Lex. "It's not a hard question. Aren't you supposed to be gifted or something?"

I glared at him. "I am gifted," I said. "I didn't answer because I didn't want to baffle you with too much brilliance." He snorted. "Anyway, nothing happened at school." I rolled my eyes. "You know, school stuff. Classes. Lunch."

"Oh, great," said Dad, like he was listening, which he clearly wasn't.

"Remember, ballet starts up again tomorrow," said Mom. "Have you found your leotard and made sure it still fits? You didn't grow, did you? Did you know that people grow more in the summer than any other time?"

"Yeah, like Tink is ever going to grow," said Seb. He laughed and nudged Lex.

"Bwa ha ha," said Lex. "She was, like, grounded all summer, so she's all sun-deprived and stunted."

"Oh, that's hilair," I said.

"Boys, be nice," said Mom. "Tink, you didn't answer. Are you all ready?"

"Yes, fine, whatever. It's fine," I snarled. A lump formed in my stomach and started growing, like a conk[114] on a tree. I no more wanted to put on pink tights and a black leotard than I wanted to, say, have my arms removed by a saltwater crocodile while innocently walking along the banks of a river in Australia. I was not a pink tights and black leotard person!

---

114. A "conk" is a kind of fungi that grows on trees and sticks out like steps, or in some cases, like gross, protruding tree brains. Conk is also a hairstyle favored by some black men who reject their Afros, especially in the 1950s, when it was cool to do so. Now it is not cool, as the Afro is symbolic of your general Africanness, which is a conclusion I've recently come to.

I've actually decided to start loving my hair. I bet you didn't see that coming, did you? That's part of what separates my encyclopedia from regular old boring ones — sometimes it's going to shock you to your CORE.

I was a baggy pants and sneakers sort of person! A skater! Not a dancer! WHY COULDN'T MOM SEE THAT?

"Did you try on your whole outfit?" Mom sighed.

"Yes," I lied. "It's FINE, MOM."

"*My* day was awesome," said Lex. "Blah blah blah."[115]

I chewed my cheese. Soy! Foiled again.

"Need bread," I murmured.

"Me too," whispered Lex, and winked. "MMMM, good broccoli, Mom," he said. "I'm just going to get some _____. From the _____." Luckily, as he rarely finished his sentences, no one asked him to. He got up and wandered into the kitchen. I heard the bread box open and close.

When he came back, he slipped a piece onto my lap. Sometimes he's OK. Squishy, white contraband bread was the best. Dad must have bought it because Mom would never allow something without nuts and seeds to cross her threshold. I rolled it up into a neat ball and popped it into my mouth.

Mom and Dad didn't notice because they were busy listening to Seb. Seb was explaining how the field at the new school is awesome because it's prime snake territory, and he is starting a club for snake collectors and he was anticipating a lot of interest, and there were four types of snakes to be found in the area. Oh, and yeah, he was sort of also a celeb now, did we know that? Kids at school were being really friendly, especially the girls, and he was thinking he'd let them join the club too, if they showed a real interest in snakes and weren't just after him now that he was all famous.

I choked on the bread. I could have died! No one even looked up.

---

115. I say "blah blah blah" to save you from the boring details, which translate in English to, "I'm so popular! Everyone likes me! I am ____!"

"That's good," said Dad, to no one in particular.

"How nice," said Mom at the exact same time. "Does this broccoli taste sandy to you?"

"No," said Dad. "It's fine."

Then Lex started tipping his chair.

"Don't tip your chair," said Mom.

"Sorry," said Lex. "I was just _____."

But then Seb tipped his chair too.

"SEB," said Mom. "Don't you tip either."

Lex stopped. Seb didn't.

"Hey," said Lex. "I stopped so you have to stop too."

"Don't," said Seb. "I'm autistic." He smirked.

"Give me a break, dude," said Lex. And he reached over and tipped Seb's chair straight again.

We all went back to eating — the broccoli really needed a lot of chewing. But Seb was . . . It's hard to accurately pinpoint how he was haywire, he just was.

I guess we should have seen it coming. I don't know if anyone else did. Maybe they all did and I was too busy thinking about Freddie Blue and/or Kai to notice.

Seb tipped again. Chewing with his mouth open. Loudly.

"Don't tip your chair, Seb," said Mom. "Close your mouth when you chew."

"Don't tip your chair, Seb," mimicked Seb. "Close your mouth when you cheeeeeew."

"Seb," warned Mom. When he starts mimicking, Mom always gets mad. It just gets under her skin. You'd think he would have learned by now not to do it, but apparently that's one of the somethings that he can't learn.[116]

---

116. I don't know if I mentioned this before, but one of the things that Charlotte Ellery says all the time is that we have to stop trying to teach Seb to be more like us, and just get that he is how he is

"Seb," mimicked Seb, tipping his chair so far it fell over. His feet kicked the remainder of the broccoli casserole off the table and the dish smashed. He lay on the floor with a little smirk that suggested he was not hurt, but wasn't going to get up either. "I'm OK," he said. "A-OK."

"I've got it!" said Lex, leaping up so fast you'd think he'd been waiting for just that moment to happen. "I'll clean it up!"

"Leave it," said Mom. "Seb can clean it up."

"No," said Seb from the floor.

"Seb," said Mom calmly. "Get up and clean up the mess you made."

"I don't have to," said Seb. "I'm not a normal person. You can't put normal expectations on me!"

Mom whirled around to Dad. "See?" she says. "That's JUST what I'm talking about. That's what you've done by telling him something so stupid! He just uses it as an excuse!" She turned back to Seb. "Seb, up. And clean up that mess right now."

"I'll clean it up," said Dad.

"Don't you dare," said Mom. "Seb needs to learn to take responsibility."

I could feel myself starting to cry. I couldn't help it. At this point, even *I* wanted to clean it up and it had nothing to do with me. The awful tension was turning my stomach upside down.

"Don't YOU start crying, Tink," Mom said in this exasperated voice. "I thought you were the big Peacemaker."

"That's not fair!" I shouted. "I don't want to be your stupid

---

and can't be "taught" to be us. We are ourselves, and he is himself, and he will do stuff his way, no matter how many times we tell him not to. At least, I think that's the gist of it.

peacemaker! And I didn't have a very good week either, so thanks for ASKING."

"Wah wah wah," said Lex. "You're a bigger pain than Seb."

I pushed back my chair and ran up the stairs to my room.

"Tink!" Dad called.

"Leave her," said Mom.

I closed the door and turned off the light. It wasn't dark, but I liked it better in the dim half-light than in the full brightness. After a few minutes, I guessed Seb must have gotten up, because I could hear crashing and banging, i.e., the sound of Seb throwing stuff around in his room.

I started to cry again. I wasn't crying about Seb, not exactly. I was crying about a bunch of stuff, like all the bits and pieces of my life that felt broken had all bunched together in my throat like a giant popcorn ball and were stuck there and I was choking. I cried and looked out the window at Kai's house and saw the light in his TV room come on, and then the TV. So then I cried and watched his TV with the sun setting over the beach in the distance and the seagulls circling.

Then after a bit, I felt OK again. Like I'd swallowed the popcorn. Sometimes crying is the right thing to do. It cleans everything up, like how storms make the whole outdoors feel clean once they've passed.

Maybe that's how Seb felt after an episode too.

I felt like I could breathe. I actually felt sort of good. I wasn't the PEACEMAKER! I said "No"! I didn't hold my breath and fix everything! I totally understood what people meant when they said they'd been empowered. I was strong! I could set boundaries! I COULD SAY WHAT I WANTED!

But then that whole thought melted away, because of what happened next.

As I watched out the window, I saw something. Something weird. Seb was getting into Mom's car. Into the driver's side.

And Seb couldn't drive.

But it was the way he was getting in that was troubling, the way he was hitting himself while he did it, flailing at his own head and torso. It sort of looked like he was trying to punch his way out of his own skin.

I stood up and pulled the blind at a better angle so I could watch. Mom was trying to stop him. Dad followed them out and stood on the lawn, shouting.

I held my breath. Like I could make peace from up here even though no one could see me. The shouting got louder. Seb locked the car doors and Mom was hammering on them and Dad was shouting. I opened the window as far as I could so I could hear better just as Seb jumped out of the car, shouting, "WHERE IS MY KNIFE? MY KNIFE?"

He shoved Mom aside like she didn't weigh anything, and she fell over onto the driveway. Before she could even get up, he was back, waving something in his hand, and he got back into the car and I realized what was happening because my brain suddenly flashed to how Mom used a knife to start her car. And I remembered Dad saying just a few days ago, "I'll get it fixed, honey. I will. But in the meantime, at least no one will be able to steal it!" And I remember we all thought that was funny.

Oh, it was hilair.

I wrapped the blind cord tight around my finger and watched as my skin turned purple. I didn't want to see what happened next, but I couldn't stop looking either.

The car started up so loudly, it sounded like a car at a racetrack, roaring to life. It lurched forward and then stopped again, really fast. There was still a lot of noise. It took me a minute to realize what the noise was, which was screaming. It took me a minute longer to even see Lex running toward the car, and then I saw him in front of the car, holding out his hands like he could stop it. Like Superman. And then he was standing in the driveway. And then the car roared and lurched again and Lex was gone.

And then I was out the window and sliding down the roof and somehow, I don't even know how, climbing down the drainpipe so fast that later I would realize my hands were all bleeding and torn up.

Lex was lying in the driveway.

He didn't move at all.

I was totally sure he was dead, and I was screaming my head off.

But then he sat up. Sort of. He kind of went up on one elbow and said, "Man, Peckle, that is so loud."

Then he fainted. I guess it's a family thing.

I suppose someone called 911. It's all a blur to me, because then there was the ambulance and then Lex and Mom were gone, and it was just me and Dad and then we realized that Seb was up the tree, making this kind of keening sound like an animal might make, and Dad was saying, "Go inside, Tink, go to bed or something. Do something. I need to help Seb."

So I did. It was like I had no idea what to do with myself and that was the only thing that anyone suggested, so I did it. I washed my hands and put Band-Aids on the cuts. Then I climbed into bed in my clothes and without brushing my teeth or anything. I thought I wouldn't sleep, but I did. I slept so much that I missed school, actually. I woke up at noon.

"Tragedy," said Mom, "does that to some people."

Lex's leg was broken in three places and also some of his ribs. He's going to live. But it's more than just that his bones were broken. It was like in that split second, our whole family was just crushed flat under the weight of that car. Like the car was the autism that we'd all lived with forever, and we'd just been running along in front of it or beside it, and it had never occurred to us that it could actually crush us.

Or maybe it was sort of crushing us all along, but it took this tragedy to make us notice.

See also *Autism; Haywire; Knife.*

Tragedy

Something terrible that happens that shakes you to the soles of your shoes. Usually a natural disaster, such as an earthquake. But sometimes not.

This shouldn't be an entry in my encyclopedia. This spot should be taken up with more regular words like "Tiger" or "Tapir" or "Tap Dancing."

But I'm putting it in because of what happened with Lex. You can't blame me, can you?

This is my life. And this is my book. And it was our tragedy.

At least, it was tragic to everyone but Seb. I know he felt bad, in the way that he does, but he didn't seem to *really* feel bad.

Charlotte Ellery was summoned the next day. She sat down on the Itchy Couch and we all gathered around. I felt like I was waiting for something important, like she was going to say something that would wrap it all up into a neat little bundle and make it so that I'd be able to see the whole thing differently. Safely. Charlotte Ellery had always made autism safe somehow.

But instead, she said, "What a mess, Seb."

He got all defensive and said, "It's not like he's dead."

"Right, he isn't dead," said Charlotte. "But he's really, really hurt."

Seb started swearing. He got up and jumped onto the back of the couch, so he was standing over Charlotte, and then jumped down over her onto the ottoman. He slid off and started shifting back and forth, like a boxer. Swearing his head off the whole time.

My own head hurt.

"Look," I said. "I —"

Charlotte interrupted. "Seb," she said. "I'd like you to do a drawing of Lex, after he was run over by the car. I need you to draw what he was thinking."

Seb swore.

"Please, Seb," said Mom, breaking her silence. Dad put a hand on her leg, and she flicked it off like it was an annoying beetle.

"LOOK," I said, more loudly. "THIS ISN'T FAIR."

"What, Tink?" said Charlotte. "Do you have a feeling that's relevant to Seb that you should share?"

"I don't care what is relevant to SEB!" I shouted. Then I really got going. I don't know where it all came from, to tell you the truth. "LEX is hurt! We should be visiting him in the hospital, not exploring Seb's feelings! SEB did something wrong! SEB did it, not AUTISM! I don't care what Seb's feelings are! I AM SO MAD AT SEB! Can't I be mad? I'm mad at Seb and at Mom and Dad and at you and everyone and Freddie Blue for abandoning me and Kai for not knowing what he's doing with me and I'm so mad at ME because no one ever asks me how *I* feel and I never tell anyone because no one asks and now I'm so mad! I'M SO MAD! I'm REALLY MAD!"

I looked around. Mom and Dad were just staring at me like I'd just woken them up from a deep sleep and was screaming, "THE HOUSE IS ON FIRE!" They both jumped to their feet, and then hesitated.

"Oh, Tink," said Mom.

And she hugged me. And then Dad hugged me. I don't even know what Seb was doing just then, and I didn't care.

For a few minutes, we stood there. I didn't want to move because I didn't want them to let go. For the first time in forever, I felt safe.

Then Seb started to pick up the encyclopedias, one by one. He threw them, one at a time, out the open window. The covers flapped open and the pages lifted in the wind. They fell like hugely awkward seagulls, crashing to the ground. I wanted to stop him, but also I didn't.

When they were all gone, Seb sat down and nodded once, like that was the thing he needed to take care of. Mom and Dad stepped away from me and sat too.

"Those books were dangerous," Seb said firmly. "People kept tripping."

"You can pick them up after," said Mom.

"I'll do it," said Dad.

"No," said Seb. "I'll get them."

"OK," said Mom.

Charlotte took a big breath and said, "OK, Seb, let's figure out what's going on with you."

I left the room. I suddenly felt like I had a call that I really, really, really had to make right then.

"Hey," I said when Freddie Blue answered. "Seb ran over Lex in the driveway."

"What?" she said. "OMG, Tink. Are you OK? Is Lex dead?"

"No!" I said. "I'm fine. I'm OK. He's got a broken leg. And ribs. Anyway, I just wanted to tell you. I know we're not, like, actual friends anymore."

"Oh, kiddo," she sighed.

Honestly, in that moment, I almost hung up. But I didn't. I hung on.

"Look," she said. "I think we'll always be friends. It's just that . . . like . . . um . . . I just want to see what it's like to be super pops for a while and be someone kind of shiny and pretty. And you're into boarding and Kai and Ruth, and I'm just . . . not."

"So you're into Stella?" I said. "That's malg, FB."

"She's actually OK," said FB. "She's nice. She's had a really crummy life and stuff, once you get to know her . . ."

"FB," I said. "I don't want to know her. She is my Worst Enemy Ever!"

"I know," said FB. "But I like her."

"Oh," I said. We stayed on the phone like that for a few minutes. I could hear her breathing. I lay back on my bed. "How was school?" I said.

"Ugh," she said. "So much homework. You missed a lot. You're never going to catch up, except you're so smart, you will."

"Um, thanks," I said.

"Brainiac," she said.

"You're a brainiac too," I said. "Gifted school, remember? They didn't let you in for having good hair."

"I know," she sighed. "Look, I have to go. I'm sorry about Lex. Give him a kiss for me, OK? I just . . . I have to go. I'm glad you called me."

"Bye," I said.

I don't know if I felt better or worse. I lay down on my bed to try to decide, and I accidentally fell asleep. I guess Mom was right, sometimes tragedy just makes you sleepy.

See also Autism; Ellery, Charlotte; Haywire; Respite Care; Tipping, Chair.

Tree of Unknown Species

A tree. My tree. Kai's tree.

Unknown because I don't know. I sort of don't want to know, to be honest. It's always been the Tree of Unknown Species. If I knew what it was, I'd have to think of it differently, like once you find out someone's name, they seem different than when they were just a stranger, like just the blue-haired boy.

I love the tree. The way it stands there and has stood there forever, seeing all this stuff that is tragic and also stuff that is stupid and stuff that is great and stuff that is funny and stuff that is exciting, and still just stands there, growing more leaves and getting bigger and more and more beautiful and turning colors and losing leaves and growing them back.

That might sound stupid. Probably I'll go back later and cross it out, but for now I'm going to leave it in because I really do love that tree.

If you promise not to tell, I'll admit that on my goal list, I have "sleeping for one night in the tree." I don't know if I'll ever do it. It probably wouldn't be safe. I just like the idea of it, and the secretness of that.

It's sometimes good to have secrets.

See also Aaron-Martin, Isadora (Tink).

U

Ukulele

This gentleman is single-handedly responsible for the bad reputation of ukuleles. He should look more ashamed than he does.

A musical instrument that looks like a tiny guitar and makes everyone who plays it look like they have freakishly large hands.

It is not a lie to say that anyone who plays a ukulele is automatically cooler than someone who does not play the ukulele. It's just the truth, squared.

Prince X just happens to play a ukulele. The tabloids say that this makes him the laughingstock of royalty. But he is not a laughingstock to me.

***See also** Aaron, Baxter (Dad); Prince X.*

Ulanova Academy, The

Named after the totally famous ballerina, Galina Ulanova, the Ulanova Academy is a ballet school that cranks out pretty dancers for companies across the nation. And ooooooh, boy, are they ever proud of that. Pictures of their successful grads are stuck on every wall that isn't a mirror.

And there are a lot of mirrors.

I took a deep breath and stepped into the studio. Right away, I was bowled over by the smell. It was like smelling a memory, or actually like smelling every memory I had of ballet. Ever. It was a lot.

A bunch of other kids were already there, stretching pretentiously at the barre while admiring their lovely posture in the mirror.

"Hey," I said to a couple of girls. One of them smiled and nodded. The other just looked down at her perfectly pointed feet. Everyone was so OMG-totally-serious, it made me want to do something ridiculous, make faces or start hip-hopping or something. Anything. It was just so . . . ugh.

I looked in the mirror. Now that I was embracing the Afro, I refused to glue it down in any semblance of a bun and it stuck out all over, grandly and proudly. So I saw this row of tall white girls with immaculate buns and straight backs. And me. Short. Slightly square-shaped. Not white. And with all these wild curls jumping out all over.

I smiled. It was sort of awesome.

I went over and picked up my bag and walked out of the room, undoing the ribbons on my shoes as I went and letting them drag behind me down the street. Then I ran, hair fluffy in the wind and my feet feeling every bump on the pavement.

I was never going back. Never.

I'd tell Mom later. Maybe not today, but soon. I mean, she had a lot to deal with, with Seb and everything.

I took the shoes off and threw them in the garbage. I probably shouldn't have done that; they were expensive. But letting go of them and watching them fall down into the mess of food wrappers and empty bottles felt like the best thing I'd ever done for myself.

I spent the rest of the hour at the beach, then went home, prepared to lie. But luckily, I didn't have to because Seb was haywire again.

And that took care of that.

You know, Galina Ulanova's mom was a ballerina too. AND she was Russian, so it's not like she had so many choices. I wonder how badly she wanted to rip her own pink slippers off and run away. I wonder if she'd be happy for me, for finally just saying "NO."

See also Afro; Ballet.

Umbrella

I won't bore you with a description of what an umbrella is, because I'm sure you know. I have no idea who invented the umbrella. Are you curious? Here, I will look it up for you in the real encyclopedia, which Seb did bring back inside, but dumped unceremoniously in the front hall. I moved them back to the living room, where they belong.

Well, so much for that. No one knows who invented it, although someone named Jonas Hanway seems to be taking credit. He hardly sounds like an ancient Egyptian, and the ancient Egyptians used umbrellas. Smells like a big fat fish of a lie to me.

Underall, Mrs.

The Spanish teacher at Cortez Junior.

Spanish teachers should have Spanish names, no? And NO teacher should have a name that is so easy to laugh about! Right? Right!

So the detention wasn't my fault.

On my first day back at school after the tragedy,[117] Freddie Blue plopped herself down right next to me in Spanish, which happened to be my first class of the day. "Tink!" she said. "I'm so glad to see you, kiddo!"

"Are you?" I said. I still hadn't worked out from that call if we were friends again or not, or BFFs or just acquaintances who were friendly or . . . what. "Why?" I glanced around to see if Kai was there yet. (He wasn't.)

"Because," she said. "BECAUSE. What do you mean, why? Duh. I was worried about you all weekend and stuff."

"Really?" I said. "Thanks."

"Shh," she says. "Mrs. Underpants is looking at us!"

Mrs. Underpants! And before I could stop it, a tidal wave of uncontrollable laughing burst from my mouth!

"Girls!" Mrs. Underall clapped her hands.

"Yes?" said Freddie Blue.

"No talking!" said Mrs. Underpants. I mean, Underall. "You haven't been listening to a word that I say! What is your name?"

"Freddie Blue," said Freddie Blue. "Tink here had a family tragedy. Her brother ran over her other brother in the car and I was comforting her because she was so sad."

"She's laughing," said Mrs. Underall.

I stopped laughing. I was pretty shocked that Freddie Blue just announced all that to the class. I felt myself blushing, like I should be the one who was embarrassed. Someone coughed. I looked around and noticed that Kai had come in sometime when I wasn't looking. My heart jumped. He gave me a look that either said, "Why didn't you tell me?" or "Wow, your family is weird!" Or really it could have meant anything. I had no idea.

---

117. I missed an entire week of school, in case you are keeping track of these things.

"Well, Freddie Blue," said the teacher. "You and your friend there will see me after school for detention, yes?"

Freddie Blue rolled her eyes at me and slumped down in her chair. I shot her a not-yet-patented Tink Aaron-Martin Stare of OMG, Did You Seriously Just Tell Everyone My Business? but she just grinned and winked. I didn't know what to feel. I snuck a look over at Stella, who was naturally right next to FB. She was wearing the ugliest brown sweater I'd ever seen. She glared at me as if I were a large tarantula climbing up the hairs on her leg, which were showing in her too-short pants. She really did take ugly clothes to a whole new level.

I glared back. Then I reverted to "devil-may-care" and gave her a cheeky grin. She half smiled back and then looked confused. Well, we're all confused. Why should she be any different?

Freddie Blue and I will be serving out our detention as Aardie the Aardvark at the weekend game against the Prescott Lion. She gets the first half, I get the second. As if I didn't have enough problems. I walked out without another word to her.

I'd really had enough of Freddie Blue Anderson.

See also *Aardvark; Anderson, Freddie Blue; BFF; Cortez Junior; Devil-May-Care Attitude; Spanish.*

Uvula

The little dangly bit at the back of your throat.

"Uvula" was Seb's first word. That is a piece of trivia that will come up in your life never again, so I am sure you will never forget it and it will take up useful room in your brain where you should be storing something like the square root of 144.[118]

See also *Aaron-Martin, Sebastian (Seb); Autism.*

---

118. It's 12, FYI.

V

Vertigo

Vertigo is the feeling that you get when you're afraid of heights.
It's like being dizzy, but not really. It's more like the feeling
that you're going to fall over. Sometimes I get vertigo when I'm
sitting on the Itchy Couch writing, and somewhere far away
in the house, Seb starts to go haywire. It's weird because I'm
already sitting. How can you fall when you're sitting down?
But when you have vertigo, it feels like you have to lie down flat
like a starfish to avoid spinning off into the sky.

See also Couch, Itchy; Haywire.

Virgo

I am a Virgo. People who are Virgos are born sometime around
now. Like, as in today. Yes, it is my birthday! I will stop writing
right now so you can stop reading and come running into the
room singing and carrying a cake! Unlike anyone else I know
in my real life!

No? That's OK. Don't feel bad. I still like you anyway.

Other Virgos I know include, but are not limited to:[119]
Freddie Blue Anderson.

Her birthday was yesterday. My birthday is today.

Our joint birthday party is on Saturday.

Which is only a problem because we haven't talked about
it. At all.

I sighed.

"What's up, Frecks Pecks?" said Lex, rolling awkwardly
into the living room, where I was sitting on the Itchy Couch.

---

119. Actually, she is the only other Virgo I know, but it doesn't sound as good to say it that way.

He knocked over Mom's poor lamp and a side table on his way. He may be a super-athlete, but he was really no good in a wheelchair.

"None of your business," I said.

"Come on," he said. "I'm trying to be nice. And I'm all strung out on painkillers! Whatever you tell me, I'll likely forget." He made an eye-rolling, baked face.

"Never mind," I said. "You wouldn't get it."

"Whatever." He shrugged and yawned. "Get off the couch, I want a nap. And I can't go upstairs."

"I'm going," I said. "Thanks for caring. Or for *almost* caring. You're a real champ."[120]

He grinned. "You're welcome."

I grabbed my board and went out.[121] It was windy and drizzling a bit. I shivered and dropped the board. Skating warmed me up. I didn't feel like Drop Mac, so I decided to lurk on my own. I went to the old pool first, but there were kids there I didn't know, so I just kept going. Finally, I ended up behind a preschool, where there was some playground equipment that was tiny and had ramps and bridges. I skated for a long time by myself. It was awesome. I did some tricks, but no one was with me, so I didn't know what they were called. I wished Kai was there.

I skated back home again all sweaty and I wanted to tell someone about the place, so I called Ruth Quayle. I wasn't used to it yet. Calling her. I had to look up her number again and everything.

---

120. When I was about ten, Dad went through a phase where he called all of us "champ" all the time, which honestly didn't bother me a bit. We still all call each other "champ" sometimes, as a non-funny family joke.

121. If any good came from the Tragedy at all, it was that my grounding seemed to be completely forgotten. So that was handy.

"Hi, Ruth," I said. "I lurked the coolest spot today."

"Hi, Tink," she said. "Where did you go?"

I described it. "Wow," she said. "It sounds wicked. But I have to tell you something, and I don't want you to take it the wrong way."

"What?" I said. I was nervous. It sounded bad, like she was about to say that we couldn't be friends. That's what I thought she was going to say. I was so sure of it, I almost hung up. "What?" I said again.

"It's just that I quit," she said. "Actually, I turned my deck into a totes awesome side table for my room!"

"What?" I said. "You turned your skateboard into a bedside table? How? Or WHY?"

"I decided to focus on making films with Jedgar![122] We're making the coolest one. You'll see it in drama, it's so wicked. Lots of blood and gore and whatnot!"

"Um," I said. "Wow."

"I still want to be friends!" she said. "I just am not skating anymore. You don't care, right? It's not like you were just using me for skateboarding, anyway. So what's the diff?"

"Right," I said. "I mean, of course. I mean. You know what? I have to go."

I hung up.

"I'm OK," I said out loud. "I can skate without Ruth. It can be my thing. I don't need someone else to do it too." I was totally lying to myself, of course, and I knew it. I really wanted

---

122. I had completely forgotten about Jedgar Johnston. I guess I sort of forgot that Ruth had a life that wasn't just skateboarding with me once in a while at Drop Mac or talking on the phone a few times. But Jedgar, in case you've forgotten, and I can't blame you if you did, is Ruth's BFF. He's cute-ish, but has a strange limp and sometimes is pretty weird. For a while, FB had him on her Crush List. I don't know if she still does. I haven't seen her list for ages. If you want to know, you should probably ask "Stell."

to have a friend to skateboard with! I didn't want one more thing to do alone!

Though what I really wanted to have was a friend to do dumb things with, like to rescue miniature pugapoos or sneak into films with. And Ruth already had that person, she had Jedgar. The skating thing was just a . . . thing.

"I am OK by myself," I said out loud. "I am enough just on my own. I don't need anyone." Then I pretended that was true.

Which was sort of like trying to pretend there isn't a huge, green parrot screeching swearwords from his perch on your head, when there actually is one.

What? It could happen.

See also Anderson, Freddie Blue; Boarding, Skate; Lurk; Quayle, Ruth.

Virgorama

The Party of the Year! The annual celebration of the birthdays of Tink Aaron-Martin and Freddie Blue Anderson, organized by Freddie Blue Anderson's mom.

It is the same. Every year. Except not exactly the same. When we were seven, there was a farm theme. When we were ten, it was mermaids. My favorite was the circus theme when we were eleven, even though there were elephants on the cake.

Let's assume that's not going to happen this year.

But actually, I didn't know what I could assume will happen this year.

Not knowing was like a knife through the tough muscly tissue of my heart. I didn't even know if we were going to do a party or if I should give Freddie Blue the really expensive ceramic technology curling iron I bought for her as a gift or if we just weren't *that* kind of friends anymore. I mean, what if she gave me a potted plant or a tube of toothpaste? Humiliation! What if I wasn't even *invited* to Virgorama?

I was so distracted by the stress of it all that I didn't even hear Kai rolling up behind me while I walked to school. I didn't skate to school because Seb still hadn't noticed that I'd "borrowed" his deck, and as he'd see me in the mornings because we left at the same time, I couldn't chance it.

"Isadora!" said Kai.

I jumped. "Argh!" I screamed.

"Sorry," he said. "Are you OK?"

"It's OK," I said. "I was just, um, startled."

He flipped the board up and caught it in his hand. "Can I, like, walk with you?" he said.

"Of course!" I said. I smiled. Mom told me a long time ago that if you smile a lot around someone, they'll think you're pretty. Mom was usually right.

"Um," he said. "So Freddie Blue sort of . . . invited me to your guys' birthday party on Saturday?"

"She did?" I said. "I mean, she said it was for both of us?"

"You didn't know?" he said. "I thought it might be something weird like that, because she was all . . . um. I hope I didn't wreck your surprise party. I'm such a jerk. I did, didn't I?"

I laughed. "No!" I said. "We have the party every year."

I felt lighter. Literally *lighter*. Like I was floating! Every year! This year would be no different! Obvi! Why was I so worried?

So I went to Freddie Blue's at noon on Saturday. She'd written me a note in Spanish that said, "Come over early and help me do my hair! *Besos!* FB." I knew it was a lie, because she'd never let me touch her hair, but still, it was sweet. For some reason, I was nervous and my armpits were wet, which was really wrecking my mood because these gross little wet moons were marking up my puffy yellow pirate shirt, which I wore as a joke that wasn't funny.[123] I went into her house without knocking because the door was mostly open. And I started singing "Happy Birthday" in Spanish because it's much more sophisto that way. Then I heard voices.

More than one voice.

Freddie Blue's voice. And Stella's voice.

I mean, I should have known. They were BFFs now. I was just the third wheel. You never want to be the third wheel. The fourth, sure. But not the third.

I followed the voices to FB's room.

"Tink!" squealed FB, and she jumped up and hugged me. I passed her her gift without saying anything. She opened it and said, "Wow, Tink! This is so so so so awesome! Thank you so much!" Then she whispered, "What I got you is sooooo much better than a gift, though! Just wait!"

And I'm like, "Um, OK." Then Stella started shrieking about my armpits because she does not have any manners, and next thing you know, Stella and FB were both doubled over laughing.

"It's cute!" laughed FB. "We're not laughing AT you. It's just that even your sweat stains are . . . cute! And adorable! It's because we love you that we laugh, right, Stell?"

"Right," laughed Stella. She grabbed her sides. "Cute!"

---

123. I had thought it was going to be funny but then I realized that it was kind of an inside joke and I was the only one on the inside now. FB loved the shirt. She wouldn't get it at all. And Ruth wasn't coming, not that she would get it either. And there really wasn't anyone else, so as it happened, I was just going to my own party in the World's Ugliest Shirt. Dumb. Please feel free to learn from my humiliating mistakes so you don't repeat them all in your own life, not that this one is repeatable unless you also own a puffy yellow pirate shirt. If you do, do yourself a favor and go throw it in the garbage right now. NEVER WEAR IT AGAIN!

"Shut up," I said. I grabbed the hair dryer and started drying the stains, which made them laugh even harder.

"Don't pee," I hissed at FB. She stopped laughing.

If you're thinking, "Oh, well, it will get better when everyone arrives!" you are dead wrong and should seriously consider just reading the book instead of trying to get ahead of where it's at.

So everyone arrived. I didn't know half the people. More and more kids piled in and started eating the food that FB's mom had put out. There was tons of it, popcorn and chips and veggies and dip. Everything was pink. Bright pink.

"What's the theme?" I whispered to FB.

"It's Barbie!" she whispered back. "It's supposed to be ironic because we're too old for Barbies. Isn't that hilair?"

"It doesn't make sense," I said in my normal voice. "That's not irony, it's just . . ."

"I totally love it sooooo much," she said. She laughed. "Didn't you wonder why I was wearing this?" She pointed at her outfit, which I hadn't really thought about because I was busy fixing my sweat stains. It was pink. And sparkly. And short. "I'm Barbie!" she laughed. "Do you get it?" She punched my shoulder.

I felt a bit sick to my stomach. Barbie? I hated Barbies. I have always hated them! FB knew that!

Nothing about this party was for me.

I whispered, "I'm not feeling that well, I think I might have to go home."

She squealed. "Oh, TINK, you're so funny! Remember how you used to not be funny? With the joke? Now you're hysterical! You're such a scream!"

"Why are you talking like that?" I said.

But she wasn't listening. She was busy hugging people. People I didn't even know. I closed my eyes and wished I was in my tree. Who were all those PEOPLE? And why would they care about my birthday?

Answer: They wouldn't! They cared about Freddie Blue's birthday, Miss Popular Barbie. I sat down on the stairs between the kitchen and the outside door. People passed me but mostly they ignored me. I ignored them back, fiercely, with my patented Tink Aaron-Martin Stare of Nonchalance.

There was something about being in a big crowd of kids my own age that made me feel like I wasn't even a kid my own age, like I was too different to belong. Like I was just pretending to be me.

It got old pretty quickly.

I was just about to pick my sweaty, puffy self up to go home when Freddie Blue stood up on the kitchen counter and started yelling, "Attention! Attention!"

"Oh, no," I said to myself. "What now?" I scanned the room again, but still no Kai. I guessed he wasn't coming.

Freddie Blue cleared her throat and giggled. "So we are, like, here for my birthday!" she shouted. At least seven parts of my insides died of embarrassment right then. She was so . . . loud. OTT (Over The Top)! Show-offy! Which would work if she was a rock star at a concert. But she was just a kid on a counter. I closed my eyes.

"But more important than that, we are here for TINK'S birthday!" I don't know why she was yelling. Everyone was listening. "Tink has been my best friend for, like, ever. She has been through SO much with me and I'm always getting her in trouble, but she's still always been so so so so so awesomely great to me. And I wanted to have this party for her because she deserves it! Because I love her. I really love you, Tink," she said. "You're like a sister to me. You really are."

I got choked up. I admit it. I think it was because she was shouting. It made it all seem real.

"We'll be friends forever and always, I pinkie swear promise. And I'll never tell anyone about how you used to have a crush on Wex!" She laughed.

And so did everyone else.

I gasped. Did she really say that out loud? "I DID NOT," I said.

"Don't freak out!" said FB. "I'm kidding. Anyway, that was last year."

"It was when we were eight!" I said.

"I knew you liked me," yelled Wex from the dining room. "Ooooh, Tink likes me." I couldn't see what he was doing, but I could guess from the laughter that it was something gross.

"I have to go," I said.

"Don't be so serious, Tink," said Freddie Blue. "I'm sorry. I mean it. I'm really sincerely totally sorry. I don't want you to feel bad. I want you to be happy! Which is why I got you . . . THIS!"

She pointed at a big box on the floor, which apparently I had to go open in front of everyone. I smiled, but my teeth were rubbing together like sandpaper.

I pulled back the paper, which was Barbie-themed and so pink I was nearly blinded. I was scared, but I opened the lid.

And inside the box, crouched down like a . . . well, like an idio, was Kai.

"What?" I said. I didn't get it.

"We planned it all during your photo-shoot thing!" Freddie

Blue laughed. "I wanted to get you something you couldn't ever get on your own!"

I was so confused at first, I didn't know what was happening, but I did know that if seven bits of me died when Freddie started talking, at least a thousand more died in that moment. Kai was smiling at me or maybe laughing at me and everyone was laughing. I felt a rush of tears sweep down my cheeks like Niagara Falls. Then Kai's face changed. I turned and started to leave the room.

But then something else happened.

Freddie Blue was still on the counter. And she was laughing. It was the phoniest, most awful laugh in the world, and the hardest. And she was just wearing that stupid, ugly sparkly dress, but it was tiny and way too short. She had nothing covering her up. Not really. And then there was this sound.

Like a huge splat.

Like someone had thrown a water balloon.

Only it wasn't a water balloon. I knew right away what had happened.

She'd peed her pants. On the counter. In front of everyone. *Everyone.*

After that, there was this horrible, awkward silence. Really awful. The worst silence I'd ever heard. So instead of staying mad, I just reached my hand up and grabbed hers and pulled her down and said really loudly, "Thanks so much, Freddie! You're the best!" I didn't care how fake it sounded, I just needed to fill up that silence with something. Anything. Then I hit the button on the stereo and turned the music up loud.

I pulled her all the way up to her bedroom. She was shaking like crazy. "Oh my god," she kept saying. "OMG OMG OMG."

"It's not that bad," I told her. "It's really not. No one will remember."

"I'll have to change schools!" she said. "I'm going to die. I can't live with it. No one will ever forget!"

I thought about saying how maybe no one would forget the totally not hilair Boyfriend-in-a-Box joke, but then I decided it just wasn't worth it. I bit my tongue, which hurt. I guess you aren't meant to do it literally.

I started rummaging through her drawers. "Don't you have anything else that's pink?" I said.

"No," she said. "I got this especially." She looked down at it. "I thought it would be funny, Tink. I thought at least you'd think it was funny."

"Which part?" I said.

"The Barbie stuff," she said. "Remember how you used to color them in and cut their hair?"

"Totally." I tried to laugh but it didn't come out right. "Do you want me to scribble on your face and cut your hair? 'Cause I will."

"No!" she said. "Don't!"

"I wouldn't really," I said. "I was joking."

"So was I, sort of," she said. Then she sighed.

I pulled a T-shirt and shorts out for her. "Go clean up and put your clothes on," I said. I lay back on her bed and waited while she showered.

She came out dressed, with wet hair and a brush. "Hey, Tink," she said. "Thank you."

"Forget it," I said. "I'm still mad at you. The boyfriend thing wasn't funny at all."

"Yes, it was!" She laughed.

"No," I said. "It wasn't."

She started to head downstairs. "You used to laugh more," she said. "Now you're all so serious."

"No, I'm not," I said. "I just don't want to be your punch line!" I kind of shouted the last bit down the hall. And of course, it was the silent second between songs. A bunch of people looked up at me. But then they just went back to their conversations or dancing or whatever. They didn't care that much.

Which was good. Because I didn't want them to.

Freddie Blue leaped back into the party room. I still admired her bravado. Did she really think they'd forget? But the truth was that she was pretty enough that people did forget things. They just looked at her and *fwooom*, their Etch A Sketch brains were wiped completely clean and blank.

And then I was invisible again, so I went outside and sat on the lawn. I tried to breathe in and out and remember to exhale all my troubles, as Charlotte Ellery once taught me to do. I liked the way the grass felt prickly under my bare legs, so I tried to concentrate on that. I picked daisies and wove them into a chain. It was late afternoon, but the sun was still nice and warm, even though the air felt cool and alive on my skin.

I hated Freddie Blue Anderson.

But I still sort of couldn't help but love her. We had been friends for so long! She was my Freddie Blue. She needed me. She needed me to tell me things like how she has to have a cup of hot milk before bed or she can't sleep. Or about how she asks questions to her alphabet soup and then scoops up a spoonful to find the answer. Or about that time that she called a psychic line and it cost over a hundred dollars and all she was asking was when she was going to get her period, and she got it the next day anyway, even though the psychic told her it would happen in November of next year. That's the kind of stuff you tell your sister.

And we were like sisters.

Who hated each other right now. I mean, that's OK. I hated Lex and Seb a lot of the time too, but they were still my brothers. I was OK with being her sister-who-couldn't-much-stand-her-right-now.

I guessed.

Stella was her BFF and I'd just have to get over it. I wouldn't want to be some mean girl you are trying to impress because you want to be popular. Or even "pops." Who cares about popular, anyway? Who decides? Freddie Blue wanted to be pops more than she cared about anything else, especially about me. And she wanted Andrew Young to be her boyfriend. And Andrew Young was pops. So if she was with him, she would also be pops. Ta-da! Popularity math.

I knew all this because I KNEW Freddie Blue Anderson. Better than Stella did, that's for sure.

And I knew it also because I read it on her phone notepad thing she keeps beside her bed. It's where she writes things that she wants to have come true. "Andrew Young, ask me out!" it said.

So it's not like I'm psychic or anything, but still, it was useful information. Maybe I could pay her back for being so horrible to me with the Boyfriend-in-a-Box. Somehow.

I made another daisy chain and tied it around my ankle. It was getting colder. I could hear the party going on inside, but I felt so separate from it. I was really done.

I stood up to go. My legs were covered with the weird pattern of the grass.

"Hey," said a voice.

I turned around. "Oh," I said. "It's you." I didn't know whether to smile or cry or what to do, so I didn't do anything. Kai walked over and stood in front of me. Right away my breathing got weird. I would have done anything for a paper bag, just about.

"She didn't say, like, that it was going to be, um . . ." he said. "I told her I was going to, like, see if you wanted to . . . anyway. I was going to ask . . . and she said that you would think this was funny. I feel really bad."

I shrugged. "Whatev," I said, like I didn't care, which was a lie because I totally did care. More than anything. I really, really cared.

"I'm such a jerk!" he burst out. "You should hate me. It just didn't, like, happen the way I thought it would. Freddie Blue said . . ."

"I just can't really imagine how you thought it would come across," I said. "What could be good about being in a box as a present for someone?"

"I don't know," he said miserably. "I'm so sorry, Is. I'm totally sorry."

I shrugged again.

He got down on his knees. "I'm like BEGGING you to for-give me," he said. "Please?"

I laughed because I was uncomfortable. "Get up," I said. "Come on."

"No," he said. "You sit down."

"No," I said.

"Please?" he said.

"Please is not a question," I said. But I sat.

He shot me a look that said, "You are weird but I still like you."

So I shot him one back that said, "I was really embarrassed, you jerk."

And he shot me one that maybe said, "I don't really know, but Freddie Blue made it sound like a good idea."

And I tried to shoot him one back that said, "I still like you, so please let's leave and go lurk or something and get away from these people I don't even know or like."

I mean, it was all silent, so our looks might not have actually said anything like that. That's just what I thought. He might have thought they meant, "Nice day, isn't it?" Or the like.

"Are you OK?" he said.

"Oh, yes," I said. And I was kind of surprised, but it was true.

"This is, um, a nice yard," he said. I looked around. There was a kids' swing set, a sandbox, and then some grass and a flower border. Most of the flowers were dead or dying. Freddie Blue and I hadn't used that swing set for at least a year.

"Um," I said.

We looked at each other and just start to laugh like crazy, clutching our sides and howling until we sobbed. It took ages for the laugh to die down. He had the best laugh. It was the kind of laugh that you wanted to reach out and hold on to, like a puppy, all soft and rolling.

We were already lying down, which was sort of a mistake because the grass was making me sneeze, but it didn't matter. I was happy. I was just happy to lie there and sneeze next to Kai and the dying flowers and the old rusty swing set.

Nothing else happened. So if you were expecting a big kiss scene or something, I'm sorry, there isn't going to be one in this entry. It was just a birthday party and that was it.

Kai pulled me closer so that my head was resting on his chest.[124] It was uncomfortable, but it was also the best feeling in the world. I couldn't have written it any better if it had been a play, except I would have not included the mosquitoes or the pain.

Kai: I'm glad we moved here.

Me: Me too.

Kai: I really like you.

Me: I really like you too.

Kai: I, um, like talking to you.

Me: I like talking to you too.

Then he did kiss me, actually. I lied before when I said he didn't. I wanted to make it extra amazing and have it catch you off guard, just like it did me.

Did it work? See? This isn't just an encyclopedia, it also contains FUN SURPRISES! It's like the Cracker Jack of books.

Best Virgorama Ever.

See also Anderson, Freddie Blue; BFF; Barbie Dolls; Bullies; Kai; Kissing.

---

124. This is something you see other people doing or you see on TV and it looks romantic and sweet and you think, *Awwwww, how adorable.* But in real life, when it happens to you, you realize that it kinks your neck horribly and causes cramps in your twisted shoulder. Not that it's bad! Just not as sweet as it looks.

W

WEE

Worst Enemy Ever. Yes, that's right, I DO mean Stella Wilson-Rawley. Still. Always. Forever.

Even though I guess we are friendly acquaintances now, through FB.

But I'm like an elephant, not in that I am a huge, hulking, scary gray mammal, but in that I do not forget things, ever, such as the meanness of SWR or that the Spanish verb "to annoy" is *molestar*.[125]

See also Elephants; Spanish.

Weekend

The two days — Saturday and Sunday — that happen at the end of the block of five solid days, MondayTuesdayWednesday ThursdayFriday. Most of the fun in your life will happen on a weekend. Unless you have a job where Monday and Tuesday are your days off, then the fun will be on Monday and Tuesday. Unless your job is incredibly fun and interesting, in which case you might just go ahead and have fun all the time! As I am planning to be a writer when I grow up, obviously weekends will have no meaning to me, as I will just write whenever I feel like it and stop when I don't, and all of it will be fun regardless. You may want to consider this as a career choice.

---

125. *Molestar* is my favorite Spanish verb. But my newest favorite Spanish noun is *monopatín*. Guess what it means? If you guess correctly, you will get ten bonus points and a shot at the big prize! If, in fact, there were points or prizes involved in reading this book, which there are not. In which case, I don't mind telling you the answer, which is "skateboard." Go ahead, use it and impress your friends!

Virgorama occurred on a weekend, as it happened. It was a Saturday.[126]

There were a lot of stars in the sky when Kai and I walked home.

Holding hands.[127]

We just needed a sound track and then we'd be an adorable teen movie!

But it was all real.

It was not a play that I made up.

It was not a dream.

Kai walked me all the way up to the porch, where he finally let go of my hand. My hand sighed with relief. I didn't exactly know what to say or do, so I fiddled with my hair a bit.

"Sorry about the eels," I said, wrinkling my nose. The smell was so much a part of the house now, I barely noticed it, but I knew he probably did. Most people did.

He shrugged. "Um," he said. "I had fun?"

"Me too," I said quickly. "It was good."

He grabbed me and pulled me over to him awkwardly. Well, awkwardly in that I nearly fell into an eel bucket. Then he gave me another kiss. I reached up to put my hands behind his head, like I'd seen in films when people were having a romantic kiss, and my hand got stuck in his hair.

---

126. Which proves what I was saying about how all fun occurs on weekends, regardless of the fact that a lot of the party was not fun. Possibly most of your life's most humiliating moments will also happen on weekends, making weekends a tossed salad of ups and downs that will likely exhaust you for the entire week, so my advice would be to choose a restful profession where naps are permitted. You know, if you're looking at the big picture.

127. I don't know how I feel about holding hands. Mostly my hand felt very self-conscious, but I couldn't find a way to let go and I didn't WANT to let go. But also I did. Holding hands was almost like a kiss that went on just long enough to get uncomfortable. Which I was. A little bit. Even though I really didn't want to be.

"Ouch!" he said.

"Sorry!" I said. "My hand is stuck!"

"Awkward!" we both said at the same time.

He kissed me again. This time, a bit harder, like he really, really meant it. So I kissed him back like I really, really meant it.[128] My knees immediately turned to ice cream and melted me into a puddle on the deck, where the eels would almost certainly have eaten me, given the option. And if they'd been actually alive.

"Bye," he said. "This was, like, so . . ."

"Yeah," I said. "For me too."

"OK," he said. "I'm gonna go. I don't really want to, though. Maybe I'll, like, sleep in the tree outside your window."

"That's my favorite tree!" I said.

"Yeah," he said. "When Mom and Dad bought the house, it was basically the best thing about it, I thought."

"Really?" I said.

He shrugged. "But I don't really climb trees much anymore anyway."

"Of course not," I quickly agreed. "That's, like, kid stuff."

"It's still OK," he said. "I mean, I might climb it now . . ."

"Ha ha," I said. I wasn't sure if he was kidding or not. Sometimes I'm not good at knowing what is a joke and what isn't. I nudged an eel bucket with my foot. The silence got bigger and the littlest bit awkward. "So," I said.

---

128. For my whole life, or at least for the last few weeks, I've been worrying a lot that I don't know how to kiss and what if I get kissed and don't know what to do? How do you know what to do? What do you do with your tongue, etc.? How do you breathe? So if you are worried about these things, I can help you. Here's the thing: IT JUST HAPPENS AUTOMATICALLY. The key to kissing — and I'm totally an expert now that I've done it at least ten times — is just shutting your brain up. Don't listen to it when it says, "Hey, what are you doing?" Just do it. And it will all work out. Promise.

"OK," he said. "Now I'm really going." He grabbed his board, which he'd left leaning up on the rail, and shifted it from hand to hand. "Bye," he said again.

"Bye," I said. "Go!"

"I'm going," he said, and he threw his board up in the air and then did the most awesome something-or-other I'd ever seen: He somehow landed on it mid-flight before it reached the ground and skipped the stairs altogether, grabbing it on the way down.

"Wow," I said. He was so talented, it was crazy.

I went inside. I was expecting to go straight up to write down everything that happened. I didn't want to forget any of the details. But Mom and Dad were sitting at the kitchen table, staring. Did they see the kiss? My entire body reddened with embarrassment.

"What's going on?" I said. I was trying to sound casual, but I was suddenly scared. "Did something happen?"

Dad cleared his throat. He looked really upset. *OMG*, I thought. Maybe Lex died from some mysterious complication! Maybe Seb did something crazy! It took only about ten seconds for one of them to talk, but in that ten seconds, I made about twenty-seven deals with fate that were like, "If Lex is not dead, I will drink eight glasses of water a day and feed the hungry and donate all my shoes to homeless people and sign up to give my kidney to science or whoever wants it or needs it, unless they just want it for creepy weird reasons, like they want to collect it in a jar on their shelf."

". . . Tink?" Mom said.

"Is it Lex?" I said. I could hardly squeak out the words. "Is he dead?"

"No! Dead? NO. He's asleep. Those painkillers will do

that, plus all the trauma he's been through," said Mom. "Poor kid." She sighed.

So then Dad said, "You may notice that it's really quiet around here."

"Yeah, where IS Seb?" I said. I cocked my head, like that would make me hear better. Nothing. No video games. No muttering. Nothing.

And Mom said, "Actually, Seb is going to stay in respite care on the weekends for a while."

"Oh," I said. "Oh." Then, "Wow."

Dad smiled, or tried to. "We're just trying it," he said. "See if it gives us a breather, OK?"

"OK," I said.

"It was a hard decision," said Mom. "But Charlotte says . . . And you were so adamant. And you were right about . . . Anyway, we just think it might be better for you. For all of us. For a while."

Mom and Dad stared at me, like they needed me to clap or yell or something, so I said, "Good call." It was all I could think of. They nodded. Mom reached across the table and held Dad's hand. I looked at their hands, lying there on the dark wood.

My ears felt funny and fuzzy, like there was a tiny trumpeter in one of them who was blowing a horn gently in a victory song, and in the other the sound of something breaking. It was so quiet that I wanted to bang the wall, just so Seb would yell at me, but he wouldn't, because he wasn't there.

I cleared my throat. "Respite care is a weird name. It sounds like something that happens when you're sick or quarantined or something. Like a TB clinic in the Alps."

"I know," Mom said. "It doesn't really fit, does it?"

"No," I said. I leaned against the wall and traced the pattern of the hole that Seb had made with his foot one day, thanks to karate. It was a long time ago. The hole felt fragile, like the wall itself was made of paper. "Seb's not sick," I said. "He's just kind of tiring sometimes."

"Yep," said Dad. "He's intense, that's for sure. But some of the greatest thinkers in history were like that, intense."

"I know, Dad," I said quickly, before he could get going on his favorite speech. "More human than the humans."

"Right!" said Dad. "You know, Tink. On one of these weekends, maybe we can go camping. You and me. You never get to go, usually. And we have all the equipment, even though Seb's not into it anymore. I thought maybe you . . ."

"Yes!" I said. "Sure. I mean, I'd like to."

Mom laughed. "You're your father's daughter," she said.

"Sure am," I said.

It was so quiet, I could hear the clock on the mantel ticking. I didn't even know it ticked. Mom and Dad were still staring at me.

"Mom?" I said. "I hate ballet. I quit. OK?"

She looked at me and blinked about three times. "OK," she said finally.

I turned around and went into my room. I opened the blind and then opened the window wide so all the cool, dark night air flowed in like water. I took a big breath of that, but I didn't hold it. I just let it right out again.

Then I started to write.

See also Autism; Eels; Kai; Kissing; Respite Care.

Woe

A feeling of slow sadness that sometimes overwhelms you and makes you feel out of control, like the sadness is a huge river rushing through your net, and in order to be happy again, you have to catch just one fish in your net, but the river is so wide and huge that catching the fish seems impossible.[129]

I don't feel like that right now. Right now I feel just happy. Straight up, simply happy. But sometimes I feel woe. Definitely.

The opposite of woe is joy. If I had two puppies, I would call them Woe and Joy and then I would write picture books about their adorable antics and mad misadventures. *Woe and Joy* is just a really good title, you have to admit. It's also fun to say out loud. Try it.

---

129. I saw this really neat documentary once about these guys who just dive into the river and grab fish. Like with their hands. They just snatch them out of the river. But the river is HUGE, like a ROARING OCEAN! And the fish are weird and toothy and EAT MEN! Sometimes I watch these things on TV and I sit on the Itchy Couch and I'm just so glad to be me, living here and having my own little, funny life.

X

X

As in "Ex," but better. Because it's shorter. So it's more text-friendly. Which makes it cooler. Think about it! It's hip to use short words when longer ones would do. So "X" is the new "Ex." You read it here first.

For example, "I am an X-dancer." That means I don't have to dance anymore. Ever.

Which is so exciting, I sort of feel like dancing.

See also Ballet; Irony.

X-ray

Pictures taken of your bones using radiation.

We currently have a series of four X-rays of Lex's leg taped to the kitchen window so Mom can frequently examine them and frown, and then nod. "Healing," she says, and reaches out her finger and traces the thick white lines that mark the places where the bones are knitting themselves back together. They look like cracks to me, but apparently they're patches. I guess it's sometimes hard to tell the difference.

See also Aaron-Martin, Sasha Alexei (Lex); Tragedy.

Xylophone

A musical instrument that looks like a kids' toy that involves bonking metal keys with a stick that has a ball at the end. The xylophone is to the keyboard what the ukulele is to a real guitar. I recently found out that people play these for real, and not just when they are two years old and do not yet have the finger control to play the piano. If I were going to play any instrument,

I think the xylophone would be the most fun, if only because people would be all, "What? Isn't that a kids' toy?" Then you could hammer out some Beethoven or Pearl Jam or something and knock them sideways with your brilliant musicality.

X is for "xylophone" is one of those things that I always think of with the letter X, because it was up on a poster on my bedroom wall when I was a little kid. X is a weird letter if you think about it, because it's only pronounced like an X sometimes and other times it might as well be a Z. Why not spell it "zylophone" if that's the way you're going to pronounce it? That's what I want to know. It's like X isn't really itself, it's just a different-looking thing that's pretending to be something it's not.

I am the girl equivalent of the letter X. Or I was. I mean, for a while I felt like I was X and Freddie Blue wanted me to be a Z, and so all I wanted to do was be Z. Because she was a Z, and what Zs cared about was being popular above all other things. And the truth is, I don't care if I'm popular or not. I'm just a skater kid with an Afro and I type better than I write.

Don't worry, I know what you're thinking, especially if what you're thinking is "What? The human equivalent of the letter X? You are as nutty as a Snickers bar, kiddo."[130] I feel the same way.

See also Afro; Boarding, Skate; Ukulele.

---

130. Even typing that makes me feel sad and weird because only Freddie Blue ever called me kiddo, and now I guess we are not friends anymore and no one will ever call me kiddo again, which is good, because I hated being called kiddo, but at the same time it's sad, because it's like time is passing and I'm not ready for all this stuff to change, even though it's not really a life change to suddenly not be called an insulting name.

Y

Yoga

The art of stretching your body around into strange shapes and trying to pretend that you aren't passing wind, when you are. Because it is impossible not to. Your body just can't twist like that without something having to give. It's physics!

It's new!

It's . . . family fun!

Except only Mom and Dad actually do it. Lex and I try. Sort of. I mean, we'll be in the room, but mostly we just look at each other and make faces. Which, in a way, maybe does more for us than yoga would. It's like rolling our eyes at yoga is now our thing. You know, a brother-sister thing. We are united in our hatred for yoga!

Seb, of course, refuses to even hear about it.

I don't blame him.

Like all the bizarre things this family does, the yoga was Charlotte Ellery's idea. It's meant to keep us calm and build up our chakras or whatever against the negative energy we might accumulate inside us if we feel conflicted about the respite care. When Charlotte Ellery starts talking about chakras, I wonder if she shouldn't have to call her university and give back her degree, because seriously, I don't know if autism counselors should spend that much time talking about something as flaky as a chakra. Especially when I don't know what a chakra really is.

A lot of movie stars do yoga to stay thin. I read about it in *Everybody* magazine, or rather, I used to read about it back when I read *Everybody*. Come to think of it, that's probably why Dad does it. I don't think it's doing much for family harmony, frankly, at least not as much as Charlotte Ellery was hoping.

See also Ellery, Charlotte; Everybody *Magazine.*

Yogurt

Curdled milk.

Mom makes homemade yogurt. This is the most disgusting thing in the world. Mom says it's amazing, miraculous health food that just may SAVE YOUR LIFE. When I feel like being really extra healthy, or even just ALIVE, I'll choke some down for breakfast, just because maybe she's right. Most of the time, I do anything to avoid it.

Young, Andrew

Andrew Young is Freddie Blue Anderson's new future boyfriend. He may or may not know this yet.

Andrew Young wears big black-rimmed glasses that would look geeky on anyone else, but he makes them look hip. I've noticed more and more boys are getting these glasses and most of them look pretty dorky, so I guess boys are just as susceptible as girls when it comes to trends.[131] He is new at Cortez this year. He says he came from New York. Everyone assumes this means that he is better than they are.

Andrew Young isn't my type. At all. Because my type is Kai. And no one else.

But then this happened.

It was three days away from the Zetroc Prom. This is

---

131. The death-on-a-stick-purple-puffy-shirt swept the school so immediately that a visitor to our planet — say an alien coming to inhabit our bodies after sucking our souls out our ears — would think that it was part of our uniform. I do not own one of those shirts and I am v. happy about that. NO ONE looks good in that shirt. Not even Freddie Blue, and she looks good in (almost) anything.

Cortez Junior's annual backward dance, where girls have to ask boys, and the prom happens in September instead of June.

"Gulp," I said, pointing at the Zetroc poster in the hall.

"What?" Ruth said. "You're not nervous about asking Kai, right? That's totes ridic, Tink! You know he'll say yes! I asked Jedgar." She sighed and rolled her eyes.

"Oh," I said. "I thought you were just really good friends or whatever."

"We ARE," she said. "I don't *like* him–like him, I just wanted someone to go with who wasn't gross. And he's cute-ish!"

"Sure," I said. "I guess." I did NOT think that Jedgar was cute, but maybe that's because I'd known him since I was two. It is hard to find someone cute when you knew them at a time when they still drank from a bottle with a nipple.

"But actually," Ruth said, "he's already going with someone else."

"He is?" I said. "WHO? I mean, that sucks."

"Yeah," she said. "I don't think I like him anymore. Not that I ever did! I totes didn't! We're just friends! AND I thought we could make a mock doc about the whole dumb thing. Anyway, I asked Brendan Carstairs and he said yes, but I don't want to go with him because I *like*-like Andrew Young now. He's dreamy. Don't you think he's dreamy?"

"Uh," I said. "I guess. Why does everyone like him? I don't get it. I like his glasses. Is it the glasses?"

"That's because you love Kai," she said. "So you don't notice anyone else."

"I don't LOVE him," I said, grinning. I tried to stop smiling, but I couldn't. The smile thing was getting annoying, even to me. But I couldn't stop!

Ruth stopped at her locker and started cramming books and papers onto the top shelf. Just then, I saw Freddie Blue and Stella. I waved halfheartedly. FB waved back, but Stella cut me dead with her laser-beam eyes. I pretended to die, but they weren't paying attention. They were busy giggling and talking really loudly for my benefit, and what they were saying is, "Jedgar Johnston is soooooo cute! OMG! When you asked him to Zetroc, I thought he was going to kiss you SMACK on the lips!" Giggle, giggle.

Ruth went pale. "He's going with FREDDIE BLUE ANDERSON?" she hissed. "That phony?"

"No!" I said. "I'm sure he's not." I marched up to FB. "Hey," I said.

"Tink!" she squealed and gave me a big hug.

"FB," I said, disentangling myself. "Are you going to Zetroc with Jedgar Johnston?"

"No!" she said. "Stella is."

Stella raised her right hand in a totally dumb, flat wave. "Hello," she said.

"I'm going to go with Andrew, of course," said Freddie. "Haven't asked him yet. Besides, why do you care about Jedgar? Aren't you going with Kai?"

"Do you LIKE Jedgar?" I said to Stella. She stared at the fluorescent light fixture and sighed. "STELLA," I said. "Do you?"

"Duh," she said. "No. It's a JOKE."

"How is that funny?" I said.

FB giggled. "You used to think stuff like this was funny," she said. "Now you're all, OH, I AM BETTER THAN EVERYONE AND NOTHING IS FUNNY TO ME."

"I am not!" I glanced over at Ruth, who was pretending not to listen. "Come on, Freddie Blue, why is it funny?"

"It's just part of a thing," she said. She flipped her hair. "It's a thing, you wouldn't get it."

"I don't get why it's funny to ask someone to Zetroc who you don't like," I said. I was getting mad. "How is it funny? Is it because you think you're so much cooler than him? Or do you LIKE him? What is the deal?"

"It just is," drawled Stella. "Mmmkay?"

"No!" I said. "Not MMMKAY."

"Also," she said. "It's none of your business."

I was trying to stay neutral, I really was. Like Switzerland, which — as I'm sure you know — doesn't participate in wars, and instead sits quietly in the middle of all the uproar, making chocolate and highly accurate watches.

"You're just mad because now that weird Ruth won't be able to go because she won't have anyone to go with," said FB. She lowered her voice to a stagey whisper. "She's so weird, Tink. Why do you care?"

I stared at her. "Freddie Blue," I said. "You just don't get it. You know what? YOU used to be nice. YOU used to be funny. Now I don't even know you at all. And I don't think I want to."

I was mad. Super mad. How dare they judge Ruth? Ruth was awesome! Even if she did overuse the word "totes"! And exclamation points! And it was a bit weird about the skateboard/side table.

But she was my friend.

So I marched right up to Andrew Young, who luckily walked by at that exact minute, and right in front of Freddie Blue, I go, "Will you go to Zetroc with me?"

He looked at me like, "Um, who are YOU?"

But then he said, "Uh, sure."

He was pretty cute. Behind the glasses, he had really intense dark eyes. I guess they were brown, but they looked black from where I was standing.

"So, like, what's your name?" he said.

"Isadora," I told him. I glanced over at FB. Her face said about a thousand things, like "WHAT JUST HAP-PENED?" and "I CAN'T BELIEVE YOU STOLE MY BOYFRIEND!" and "YOU WILL REGRET THIS!" plus some other stuff, I'm sure.

Then she stepped close and whispered, "Thanks, I like Kai better anyway."

Kai!

KAI!

What was I doing?

"Sorry, Andrew," I said. "I've got to go."

And then I ran past Freddie Blue and Stella and Andrew and Ruth and everyone to get to Kai. I found him with Wex, sticking something to the water fountain, which was probably chewed gum. Gross.

"Hey," he said.

Wex opened his mouth and paused, like he was thinking of something horrible to say.

"Shut up, Wex," I said.

Kai looked at me sideways. "Whoa," he said. "He hadn't even said anything."

"Not yet," I said. "But Wex always has something to say."

"No, I don't," said Wex, furrowing his brow. "Sometimes I don't."

"Whatever," I said. "Look, Kai, will you go to Zetroc with me? Please?"

Wex snickered. Kai punched him in the arm in a slightly less than friendly way.

"Ouch, man," said Wex. "Chill."

"Um, totally," said Kai to me. "For sure, I'll go with you."

I forgave him for saying "um" because he looked so cute, and I flashed back to how Andrew squinted at me through his glasses like I was a tiny grasshopper that he was forced to inspect for Bio class.

"I've got to go somewhere and do something," I said to Kai.

I ran back to Andrew, who was leaning against his locker looking cool in his awesome glasses. I was out of breath completely. I stood there for a minute looking at him, waiting to get enough oxygen to speak. Finally, when I could talk, I said, "Andrew."

"Hi," he said.

"Hi," I said. "Look, I made a mistake. I meant to ask you to the prom for Ruth. My friend, Ruth? Not for me. It was just a . . . I messed it up. Anyway."

"Oh," he said. He shrugged. "OK. I'll go with her. She's the babe with the short hair, right?"

"Er, right," I said. *Babe?* Who says *babe?*

"I'll write it down," he said. "Lots of girls are asking me. I've said yes to seven. How many can you have?"

"ANDREW," I said. "Are you serious? One. It's a prom. You take ONE person to a prom."

"Ohhh," he said. "At my old school, we _____."

I waited. He didn't finish. Just like Lex. I wanted to kick him in the leg, which is what I would have done to Lex, but instead I just walked away. He and Freddie Blue deserved each other.

"Sorry," I said to Ruth, when I explained later.

"It's OK." She grinned. "I'm going with Jedgar. Maybe I do *like*-like him, after all! I think he only said yes to Stella as a joke, you know. He said he was going to make a documentary about how annoying popular girls were. But then he changed his mind."

"OK," I said.

And I, Tink Aaron-Martin, am going to go to Zetroc, my first ever real dance, with Kai.

SQUEE!

See also Kai.

Z

Zebra

Is he black with white stripes? White with black stripes? STARE INTO HIS EYES. Are you slowly getting hypnotized? Are you feeling very sleeeeepy?

I have no new information about zebras. If you are looking for old information, I can tell you that they are horselike mammals that are either white with black stripes or black with white stripes. Which is true? You get to decide because no one knows the answer. Make one up. If you say something with enough authority, people will believe you, whether you know what you are talking about or not.

Zeppelin, Led

Mom and Dad's favorite band. You'd think that because my mom is a ballerina-dancing doctor that she'd like sophisticated music, such as Beethoven. But no, both Mom and Dad prefer to shriek along with Led Zeppelin, which is actually one of the few things I think they have in common that they agree on.

I like Led Zeppelin for that reason. Not their music, though. Their music hurts my ears.

Zetroc Prom, The

The backward prom that is held at Cortez Junior at the end of September, for the eighth graders.

Normally, I would hate something like the Zetroc Prom. But now I don't. Because I have a boyfriend! I won't stand in the corner, waiting for someone to ask me to dance and hoping they don't at the same time! I won't hyperventilate while hiding in the bathroom, wishing I could leave!

Even more amazing, Mom took me shopping for a dress. I don't remember ever shopping with Mom before. Usually, she's at work all week and she'd give me money and I'd go with Freddie Blue. It took a bit of getting used to, to be honest. Her taste in dresses was a little too ballet and a lot not edgy. I wanted something edgy. Something awesome. Something that would make me look pretty but still like ME.

We looked in ten different stores and all we could find was sea foam green and purple with lace. It was malg. Totally and completely malg. Then, just as we were about to give up, I remembered FB's mom's shop. I knew it would be a bit weird to go in there, considering . . . everything. But I somehow just knew what I was looking for would be there.

The store smelled dusty. FB's mom was on the phone, but she waved and smiled. I got the feeling that FB hadn't told her that we'd had a falling out. I waved back.

It took exactly two minutes for me to find it: my dress. The perfect dress. It was my dream prom dress. And it fit.

"Oh, Tink," Mom said when I put it on. "You look so . . . thirteen."

I grinned. "Mom?" I said. "I'm thinking of going by Isadora now. Or maybe just Is."

"OK," she said. "Is. You look all grown up."

I looked in the mirror and I couldn't help agreeing. The dress was silk. One side was black and the other was white. It had a square neck, with twisted straps. It wasn't floor length; it went to my knees. It was probably meant to be a mini, but I didn't care. It was just what I wanted. Sophisto. But not Barbie.

Just like me.

It was perfect.

When I got dressed the next night, even Lex said, "Whoa, Tink, you look _____." Then he paused and mumbled, "I mean, Isadora."

"Thanks," I said. Did he just compliment me? AND call me by my real name? Maybe the accident hurt his brain after all. Not that I minded. It was kind of . . . nice.

"Ready, kiddo?" Dad said.

"Yup," I said.

I snuck one last look in the mirror. My hair was getting long and I did it in a full Afro. Kai knocked on the door and I opened it.

"Oh, hi," I said. I felt really shy. He gave me a flower and I stuck it behind my ear.

"You look like a Caribbean queen," said Dad, grabbing his jacket and jangling his keys. I felt super exotic when he said that. I felt *interesting*. He gave me a huge hug. "I can't believe you're old enough to have a boyfriend," he added in a stage whisper.

"DAD," I said. I could be wrong, but I think Kai blushed.

The ride to school was kind of awkwardly silent. I stole a couple of looks at Kai. He was looking out the window. Luckily Dad had the music on loud enough that we didn't have to talk.

"You're growing up!" Dad sighed, looking at me in the mirror. Kai pretended not to hear. Dad looked a little choked up and then pretended he wasn't by bursting into a very, very exuberant version of one of his favorite songs.

"Thanks, Dad," I said as we got out of the car.

"Thanks, Mr. Aaron-Martin," said Kai.

"It's Bax," said Dad. He looked amused. "You're making me feel old. Oh, look, there's Freddie Blue. HEY, FREDDIE!" he yelled. I guess I sort of hadn't told him that we weren't BFFs anymore.

"You look really good," Kai whispered. He grabbed my hand. "You look, um, amazing."

"Thanks," I whispered back. Freddie Blue was marching toward us.

"Hi, Tink's dad," she said.

"You look nice, Freddie," he said. "Have fun! Do you have a boyfriend now too, suddenly? Where is he?"

Freddie's face dropped imperceptibly. I mean, no one else probably noticed it but me. "Nope!" she said, like she didn't care.

"Oh," he said. "Well, got to go! Have a good time!"

Freddie Blue stood smiling until the car pulled away, then the smile fell from her face. "Tink," she said. "I don't think I can ever forgive you." And she flounced off.

Really flounced.

Her dress was really amazingly . . . flouncy. Layers and layers of fluffy greenish blue sparkles. Truly, truly . . . awful.

"That looks like something a mermaid threw up," observed Kai.

I giggled. When we got inside, Freddie Blue was twirling around the dance floor, dragging Andrew Young behind her. A bunch of girls were shooting them evil looks, probably his twelve other dates.

I looked around for Ruth. I finally spotted her dancing with Jedgar. She had a video camera in her hand, and it looked like she was interviewing him while she danced. Her dress was too big and she had to keep hitching it up.

"Let's go talk to . . ." I started to say. But Kai put his finger up to my lips — JUST LIKE IN A MOVIE.

"Let's dance," he said. "I've been, like, practicing."

If you have never fallen in love, this will not make any sense to you, but I think that I did, right then, when he grabbed me and started doing some kind of weird slow dance to a really, really fast song. I didn't care. We just stood there and swayed.

I felt completely OK. For maybe the first time ever, I didn't feel nervous or anxious or upset or like I couldn't breathe. It was perfect.

I thought about how FB was always going on about how so-and-so "took her breath away." If we'd still been friends, I would have waited until the end of the song and excused myself from Kai, then I would have found her and I would have said, "No, FB. You're wrong. Love doesn't take your breath away. Love makes it so you CAN breathe. It gives your breath back."

Because that's what it was like, exactly. Like I finally could breathe without thinking about it.

We danced a lot. Mostly just like that, slow.

With kissing, when the teachers weren't looking. The kissing was the best part. I felt like a new person.

I was a new person.

I wasn't Tink anymore. Tink was a kid.

Now I was Isadora. Is.

Isadora is.

Isadora is happy.

See also *Kai; Kissing.*

Zoo

A place where animals are stored after being kidnapped uncer-emoniously from their regular lives on the savannah or in the jungle or even the Arctic Ocean.

I have never been to a zoo. There. That's all. That's all I have to say about zoos.

And the letter Z.

And myself.

Am I done?

Did I actually just write an entire encyclopedia about myself?

Seriously?

And you read it?

Seriously?

Wow.

Now for the quiz!

I'm joking.

There isn't any quiz.[132] I told you I wasn't much good at jokes. I'm only good at dark, gummy sarcasm.

But I'm not being sarcastic when I say I love you, I love you, I love you.[133] I really mean it. I can't believe you read the whole thing.

I never thought I'd be interesting enough that anyone would read a book about me. But then a lot of things you think will never happen DO end up happening, I guess.

Like you lose a BFF but gain a BF.

---

132. Real encyclopedias don't have quizzes either. They just stop at the end. After the last word. Which is almost always ZZ Top, which is this really awful rock band whose members all sport knee-length beards and sunglasses and which was very popular in the 1980s. That will almost certainly come up in a trivia game one day and maybe the fact that you know that will help you to win. Which makes this all worthwhile. So you're welcome.

133. That's how my favorite book of all times ends. Which you'd know if you'd followed my excellent advice back in the *Books* entry. But it's not the end of mine. At least, not quite.

Like you figure out who you are slowly, or it happens all at once, in a burst.

Like your family breaks and then, when it's put back together, it heals along the breaks and is stronger than it was before. That happens to bones, you know. The broken parts never break again in the same place. The repair that your body does makes it too strong.

Now all that's left to say is "THE END." Even though real encyclopedias don't do that either. But this isn't a real encyclopedia. It's better.

Just like I promised, remember?

THE END

ACKNOWLEDGEMENTS

This book took a very long time to write, during which time a number of people came and went from my life, both personally and professionally. In that way, this book feels like it spans a lifetime. I would be remiss if I did not thank the first people on the scene, the agents: Carolyn Swayze, who was first; Colleen Lindsay, who revitalized me with her amazing energy, and whose enthusiastic belief was contagious; and finally, Marissa Walsh, the last woman standing, who I hope will be with me for all the books to come.

To my editor, Cheryl Klein, who plucked this book out of the slush pile and breathed new life into my original idea, there are not enough words. "Thank you" feels inadequate, but . . . thank you. For the work, time, passion, insights, and consideration. I am still entirely astounded — flabbergasted, even— that I find myself on your roster, in the company of some of my most favorite of favorite authors. This experience was a dream — a dream that involved so much work, done with such passion, by such an amazing group of talented people. How did I get so lucky? Thank you, times a million, to all of you at Arthur A. Levine Books, both those I can identify and the ones whose names or faces I didn't see. I know you were there, and I appreciate it all.

I love social media. I once said it was a "blip" and I was wrong. I am thankful to all of you out there who ever made me smile, encouraged me, or were just there alongside me as I accumulated pages, procrastinated, and revised. The Internet is the watercooler that writers gather around, and it never stops providing exactly what I need to stay motivated, grounded, inspired, and laughing.

On a more personal note, I am so blessed by and intensely grateful for my beloved family, the Rivers, for their ongoing support, time, love, and (sometimes slightly crazy) belief in my abilities.

Thanks must also go to my other family, for the Saturdays. And especially to Malcolm and Clayton, who taught me what autism really means.

A huge, giant, massive hug to my kids, who are too young to read this . . . yet. Thank you for being so purely yourselves; for the way you make each other laugh when I'm swamped with work; for listening to my favorite song with me so often and so loudly that the speakers broke; for dancing like lunatics on the furniture; and for giving me every reason I could ever need to keep going and also, sometimes, to stop.

A shout-out to all of you who don't do olives and who know what that means. Every step of the way, you propped me up and kept me going and listened and gave me advice that I sometimes ignored but mostly followed. BFFs 4ever!

Finally, I am ever grateful for the financial support provided to me by the British Columbia Arts Council, whose grant program bought me the time early on to work on this novel and helped me to believe that it would really fly one day. Thank you.

This book was edited by Cheryl Klein and
designed by Christopher Stengel. The text was
set in Sabon, with display type set in Neutra.
This book was printed and bound by
R. R. Donnelley in Crawfordsville, Indiana.
The production was supervised by Cheryl
Weisman and Starr Baer. The manufacturing
was supervised by Adam Cruz.